GHOST HOLD

GHOST HOLD

The PSS Chronicles: Book Two

RIPLEY PATTON

Cover design by Scarlett Rugers of The Scarlett
Rugers Book Design Agency
Cover © 2013 by Ripley Patton
Edited by Lauren McKellar
Typesetting and Formatting by Simon Petrie

Library of Congress Control Number: 2013916425
ISBN 9780988491038

Publisher's website: www.ripleypatton.com

DEDICATION

For my Dad, both my Moms, and for Grandma Lucille.
Thanks to you the love of books is in my blood.

OTHER BOOKS
BY RIPLEY PATTON

The PSS Chronicles
Ghost Hand (Book One)

Novellas
Over The Rim (Young Adult Fantasy)

CONTENTS

1

ALMOST TO CIVILIZATION

I had never been so happy to see a barn in my life. Yes, it looked like it was about to fall over, which had me questioning the wisdom of storing all our worldly belongings in it, but the squat red building had a roof and four walls, luxuries I hadn't seen in over two weeks.

As our ATVs pulled up, their trailers rattling behind them, I moved my hand from Marcus's waist and yanked my bandana over my mouth to keep from inhaling the cloud of dust that billowed around us. I still hadn't gotten used to the constant grime of camp life, the way my clothes held a layer of dirt, like Pigpen from the *Peanuts* cartoon, or the grit I could always feel between my teeth no matter how many times I brushed them. They didn't show you that in the movies; that the life of a fugitive was filthy and sweaty, especially in the middle of an unseasonably hot Indiana October.

Marcus cut the engine of our wheeler and, one by one, Yale, Jason, Nose and Passion cut theirs too. We'd replaced Jason's stolen ATV fifty miles outside of Greenfield and gotten one for Passion while we were at it. I don't think I'd truly grasped the reality of Marcus's million-dollar trust fund until I'd seen him pay cash for those ATVs. But I hadn't missed the pained, quickly-masked look on his face as he handed it over. It was blood money, paid to him in a settlement for the untimely and accidental death of his parents, but it was money we desperately needed.

Marcus had offered to get me my own ATV as well, but I preferred to ride with him. I was a crap driver; that was the reason I'd given. But really there was just something about wrapping my legs around a thrumming motor while slipping my arms around Marcus's waist that made the hundreds of miles of dust and dirt-eating worth it. Even so, I was really glad to be back to civilization.

Marcus pulled off his helmet, and I lifted mine off too. He looked over his shoulder at me, and we smiled at one another, not needing to say anything. We were here. We'd made it to Indy without any apparent pursuit by Mike Palmer or the CAMFers.

Well, we'd almost made it. We still had about thirty miles to go, but this was where we'd trade in our wheelers for a comfy rental van. We'd lock away all our camping gear and dirt-stained clothes in the barn and disguise ourselves as wealthy suburban teenagers. This was where the mission to save Samantha James really began.

I slid off the vinyl seat, set my grimy helmet on it, and stretched my legs. My ass hurt, as usual, but I'd learned not to complain about it. It seemed there was nothing in the world teenage boys liked more than making sore ass jokes.

Marcus, still straddling the wheeler, dug in his pocket for the key that would unlock the padlock on the barn door. That was something else he'd picked up in the town where we'd bought the ATVs. The key, the use of the barn, the promise of a van waiting for us with certain forged documents and supplies inside of it—he'd arranged it all in the space of a couple hours.

But he hadn't found the key yet, and I could feel the mid-day sun beating down on me, so I strode forward and sank my ghost hand into the lock. It made a satisfying click as it popped open.

"Thanks," Marcus said, coming alongside me. "You're sure handy."

"Ha ha, very original," I said, poking him in the ribs with my elbow.

As Marcus and I pulled the heavy barn doors open, the others joined us, and we all entered the vaulted, slat-lit interior of the barn. It smelled musty inside, with a slight sweet undertone of rotting hay.

"You're sure our stuff will be safe here?" Jason asked.

"Pretty sure," Marcus said, "But if it isn't, we'll buy more. Anything personal you should bring in the van though, in case we don't make it back."

In case we don't make it back. There was a subtle message in that statement for all of us. We'd been outrunning danger for weeks, but now we were charging straight into the thick of it, and none of us knew exactly what that would look like, or what the ultimate outcome would be.

I looked around at their faces, these boys who had once been my rescuers. Was this how they'd felt when they'd been just outside of Greenfield preparing to come get me? This calculated fear? This tingle of excitement and anticipation?

My eyes fell on Passion, and she stared back at me, her pale face almost glowing in the darkness of the barn. Was she afraid or excited? I had no idea. She was a complete mystery to me, a mystery I'd spent weeks avoiding, despite the fact that we'd been living in the same camp.

It hadn't been that hard to keep my distance. She had her own tent and I'd shared Marcus's. She tended to keep to herself, just like I did, so we'd mostly encountered one another at meals or around a low fire on the nights Marcus had deemed it safe enough for one.

The first week after she'd joined camp, Nose had paid her a lot of attention, but she hadn't given him any encouragement, and eventually he'd backed off. She hadn't been mean or anything. And when he'd asked me if I thought it was his PSS Nose or the ski mask he always wore to cover it, I told him I doubted it. Passion wasn't like that. She was always nice to everyone. Too nice. Annoyingly nice.

So, if she was that nice, why did I have a problem with her? I had no good reason.

A couple of days ago, Marcus had taken me aside and said, "Don't you think it's time you two hashed this out?" But that had made me want to talk to her even less. Honestly, Passion had every right to dislike me, not the other way around. I was the one who'd yanked something out of her soul, used it for myself, and then handed it over to the bad guys. She probably thought I was a complete bitch.

And maybe she was right.

"Let's unload the stuff from the trailers into the barn," Marcus directed the guys. "But set aside the personal stuff for Olivia and Passion to pack into the van."

"Speaking of the van, where is it?" I asked.

"It should be out back," he said.

We all exited the barn, circled around to the back, and there it was gleaming in the sun like a golden chariot—an extra-long, brand new, white passenger van with bucket seats, tinted windows and a gray leather interior.

It was one of the most beautiful things I'd ever seen. My butt could already feel that padded seat. My face craved the cool, dustless breeze of the air conditioner.

Marcus opened the back doors of the van, and started passing out duffle bags for each of us containing a change of new clothes and our fake IDs. Mine said that I was Anne Clawson, seventeen, and Passion was playing the part of my cousin, Mirabelle Clawson, also seventeen, who'd come to live with us after her parents' recent and messy divorce. Anne was my middle name, and Mirabelle was Passion's. Marcus said it was always better to play close to the truth. It made the lies easier to remember.

I tried not to be disappointed that the clothes in the duffle weren't my style. Apparently, Anne Clawson, a rich girl with rich parents, didn't have my dark sensibilities. At least there was a new pair of black leather gloves to help hide my ghost hand.

But the clothes and the cousin thing weren't the worst of it. Not even close. The worst part was that Marcus would be playing the role of my older brother, Clayton Clawson, a twenty-one-year-old pre-med student. The story was that our parents were away celebrating their thirtieth wedding anniversary in the Mediterranean while Clayton orchestrated the family move to Indianapolis. Yeah, my boyfriend was going to pretend to be my brother. I was really looking forward to that.

As for Jason, Yale and Nose, they were a little too ethnically diverse to fit in to the Clawson family. So, they'd be hiding out in the house Marcus had rented for us, running security detail, and laying low. Still, they'd get new clothes and fake IDs casting them as three of Clayton's college buddies, just in case.

"We can get changed in the barn after we get everything loaded," Marcus said, handing the last duffle bag to Yale.

And then we got to work, like the well-oiled machine we'd become. The packing was easy compared to setting up and tearing down camp every day. Marcus had us store the guns and ammo deep under the back seat in case we got pulled over, though, according to Jason, Indiana had some of the most relaxed gun laws in the country, which was the argument he gave for refusing to put his away.

"Jason," Marcus said. "You're not going to need it in the next thirty miles."

"You don't know that," Jason said, gripping his gun more tightly. It was useless trying to talk Jason out of anything. We all knew it, so I wasn't surprised when Marcus let him keep the weapon.

After we all got changed, the last thing to go into the back of the van, carefully wrapped in a blanket, was my father's painting, *The Other Olivia*. Yes, it was singed around the edges, but it was all I had left of him. It was all I had left of anything, the sole belonging the CAMFers hadn't destroyed when they'd burned down my house and chased me from my home town.

As Marcus shut the back of the van Nose called out, "Shotgun!" and ran around to the passenger side door. Then he and Jason proceeded to fight over who should get to sit in the front. Jason's argument was that he was carrying a gun; therefore he should get the shotgun position by default without ever having to call it. Nose countered that Jason's gun was technically a hunting rifle, not a shotgun, therefore his argument was invalid and Nose should get the front seat. Marcus pointed out that neither a guy in a ski mask nor a country boy armed with a rifle were probably the best choice for most-visible front seat passenger, and I began to understand why he'd gotten a van with darkened back windows. In the end, he assigned Jason and Nose to sit all the way in the back. Yale and Passion sat in the middle, and Marcus drove with me riding shotgun.

I started nodding off almost as soon as we turned onto the highway. Under normal circumstances, I was a drowsy passenger. One of my dad's nicknames for me had been Sleepy Gonzales, because I'd always fallen asleep so fast in the car whenever we traveled. And these weren't normal circumstances. I'd slept like crap for weeks, and I hadn't sat in a comfy, cushioned, leather anything for way too long. It just felt so damn good. Camp life had definitely worn on me more than I'd realized.

I was just beginning to drool against the window when Marcus suddenly swerved off the interstate onto a dirt road.

"What the hell?" I asked, gripping the dash with my gloved hands and glancing frantically in the side view mirror, expecting to see a caravan of CAMFers in hot pursuit.

"Just a quick stop," Marcus said, avoiding my gaze.

When we passed an old wooden sign that read *Warren Gun Club*, I stared at him until he looked at me.

"We all need to know how to protect ourselves," he said, glancing back at the road. "Not just Jason."

I wanted to argue, but I really couldn't. I had always disliked guns, but I'd disliked seeing Marcus get shot in Greenfield while trying to save me even more. The CAMFers tended to come well-armed, and who knew what kind of opposition we were going to face in Indy?

Marcus pulled the van up to an old farm house, a long low building next to it stretching into the endless fields of rural Indiana. Just as he shut the ignition off, a large man in dirty coveralls came out of the long building, shotgun in hand, moving toward us.

"As soon as I close my door, lock the van," Marcus said, handing me the keys, "and get in the driver's seat. Don't get out, under any circumstances, unless I tell you to. And, if something goes wrong, drive away."

"Wait!" I said, but he was already out, slamming the door behind him.

He walked slowly around to the front of the van, arms out to show he had no weapon.

The guy with the shotgun was advancing on him, and two more guys had come out of the farmhouse, guns in hand.

What the hell was Marcus doing? Everything about these guys screamed CAMFers, but that made no sense. I had no idea what was going on.

"Fuck," I said, clicking the button on the key ring to lock the van. The little chirp it made was completely at odds with the adrenaline and fear surging through me. I looked back and saw the shock on the others' faces as they peered out the windows of the van. So, he hadn't told anyone about this little stop. Well, he wasn't the only one who could bark orders.

"Jason, I need you up here, right now, with your weapon," I said, sliding across to the driver's seat and putting the keys in the ignition. "Nose, can you reach the other guns?"

"I can try," Nose said, diving down to rummage for them.

Jason slid into the seat next to me, rifle in hand, and I tried not to show my surprise that he'd actually listened to me.

"Let them see it," I told him, "but don't point it at anyone. Yet."

Jason nodded and made his rifle as visible as possible.

Outside, Marcus had moved further away from the van, but he was still in front of it.

The three gun-toting country boys were nearly upon him, and I cracked my window just as the one in the front said, "You David?"

What the fuck? Why would Marcus give these guys his real name? He always went by Marcus, and he'd obviously gone to the trouble of getting us all fake IDs, including himself. Why not use his new identity? What was he thinking?

"I'm David," he confirmed, "and we've come unarmed, as specified."

"That one has a gun," Shotgun said, gesturing at Jason.

Marcus turned and looked at us, frowning. He turned back and said, "It's not loaded. I emptied it myself this morning."

I looked at Jason, and he looked at me. Then he yanked open the chamber of the gun and showed it to me. It was empty.

"Do you have any ammo on you?" I asked him.

"No," Jason shook his head, looking more pissed off than I'd seen him look in a long time: and he usually looked pissed.

"Nose, any luck with those guns?" I turned to the back of the van and Jason turned with me.

"I can't reach them," came Nose's muffled voice in response.

Shit. We were screwed. Jason and I both turned and looked back out at Marcus.

"How do we know you're who you say you are?" Shotgun asked, his buddies grunting in Neanderthal agreement behind him.

"Come and see," Marcus said, gesturing Shotgun forward.

At first, I didn't understand. I thought Shotgun was just getting a better look at Marcus's face or something. He walked up to him, his gun held up between them, and gestured at Marcus's chest with it.

Marcus reached down and began to unbutton his shirt.

Jason went stiff in the seat next to me. You could have heard a pin drop in that van. No, you could have heard a feather drop. This could not be happening. Marcus didn't reveal his PSS chest to anyone. He hadn't even told me about it until I'd seen him come back from the dead and, at that point, he'd pretty much had no choice.

I jammed the keys into the ignition of the van and turned it on. I thrust the stick into drive and, with one foot on the brake and one on the gas, I revved the engine.

Marcus paused in unbuttoning his shirt and glanced at me, looking annoyed. Then he turned back, resuming his little striptease.

Shotgun and his buddies were eyeing me, but they couldn't seem to keep their eyeballs from straying back to Marcus.

They were all right there in front of me. I could take them out like bowling pins. Yes, Marcus might get hurt in the process, but probably not fatally, and he could always reboot. The hillbilly brothers might get off a shot or two, but Marcus wasn't a complete idiot. I had noticed earlier the tiny little labels on the van's windows indicating they were not only tinted, but bulletproof.

I revved the engine again.

Marcus unfastened the last button of his shirt, and it fell open.

2

WELCOME TO THE WARREN GUN CLUB

Shotgun's eyes went wide, and he used the end of his gun to move the edge of Marcus's shirt aside. Then he gave a low whistle and a smile blossomed across his face. "I'll be damned," he said, his eyes gleaming like he'd just met his favorite celebrity. "It's true."

The other two good-old-boys stepped forward, also exclaiming and staring at Marcus's chest, and for a minute it looked a little like a close encounter in a gay bar. But the guns were all down and the smiles were up, so I took my foot off the gas and let the van's engine ease back to idle.

Jason looked at me, a question in his eyes.

"I guess they like his chest," I said, pulling the keys

from the ignition.

"Anne," Marcus called over his shoulder as he buttoned his shirt back up. "Get everyone out here."

Obviously, we were playing our new aliases starting now, even if he wasn't.

"Remember who you are," I said softly to the van in general. I nodded at Yale, and he opened the side door as Jason and I piled out of the front.

I marched over to Marcus, mightily resisting the urge to smack him in the back of the head.

"This is our group," Marcus said, introducing us to the country boys with a wave of his hand. "We all need to be trained and armed."

"You got it," Shotgun said, looking us over. His eyes stopped on Jason's hunting rifle and he said, "Nice Marlin. You know how to use it?"

"Yeah, I know how to use it," Jason said, jutting out his chin.

"Okay then," Shotgun said, "Let's get you all to the shooting range, and see what you can do." He turned, waving us toward the long building, and we began to follow.

Nose, Jason and Passion were ahead of me, traipsing behind Shotgun and his buddies, but when I looked behind me, Yale and Marcus were still back by the van, staring each other down.

I stopped, not sure if I should leave them alone or try to intervene.

"I'm not doing this," Yale hissed, glaring at Marcus, his face flushed with anger. I'd never seen Yale angry. He was a laid-back guy, but he also had a major thing against guns.

"I understand," Marcus said calmly. "You don't have to. You can wait out here. It's your choice."

Shotgun and the others had reached the door of the shooting range and were going inside. I saw Passion glance back at us and hesitate, but I waved her on.

"Damn right it is," Yale snapped, "and if you're seriously going to arm underage kids, you're a fucking idiot."

Kids? Yale was barely older than me. Yeah, he was eighteen, and I was still seventeen for another month, but I certainly wasn't a kid. At sixteen, Jason was the youngest of us and probably the least kiddish of anyone I'd ever met.

"You saw what happened in Greenfield," Marcus said to Yale. "Besides, we've been armed ever since we stole the hunting rifles. How is this any different?"

"We snagged those rifles so we wouldn't get shot leaving the game reserve," Yale argued. "And the same with Mike Palmer's gun. If Nose hadn't grabbed it after he shot you, Palmer would have shot us all. Those were defensive moves. But this—" he gestured at the farm and the gun club buildings. "This is completely offensive. You're gearing up your own little militia, and you know it."

"This is about self-defense," Marcus said. "No one is going to shoot anyone unless they try to shoot us first."

"Having guns automatically escalates it to that level," Yale said, throwing his hands up in frustration.

"It's already gone there," Marcus said, sounding just as frustrated. "The CAMFers took it there, not us. We have to be able to protect ourselves."

"Not like this," Yale said, his face tight and grim.

Marcus simply stared at him until Yale turned silently away and marched back to the van, his back a barrier between them. Yale climbed into the vehicle and slammed the sliding door shut with a bang.

Marcus turned and saw me standing there watching him.

"Are you going to give me a hard time about this too?" he asked, eyeing me warily.

"No." I shook my head. "But you could have warned me. I almost ran you over with the van."

"Thanks for not doing that," he said with a sigh, walking to me and putting his arm over my shoulder. "I didn't tell you, or anyone else, because I was afraid Yale wouldn't come with us to Indy if he found out."

"Will he come now?" I asked, glancing back at the van. "He seems pretty upset."

"I don't know," Marcus said, looking too. Then he turned back toward the gun club building. I could tell he was torn.

"Do you want me to go talk to him?" I asked.

"No," he said, propelling us both toward the gun club. "I need you to learn this. I wish I didn't, but I do."

"Who are these guys?" I asked, as we walked in tandem. "Are you sure we can trust them?"

"As sure as I can be," Marcus answered. "And who they are is complicated. They're basically the opposite of CAMFers."

I was about to ask what he meant by that, when the blast of gunfire filled the air. I instinctively flattened my body against the building, pulling Marcus with me. And then I felt like a complete idiot. We were at a gun club. Guns were going to be fired. When had I become as paranoid as Jason?

"You okay?" Marcus asked, putting his hands against the building on either side of my head and looking down at me. His body was pressed against mine like a shield, his eyes full of concern.

"Yeah." I nodded, the calmness of his presence seeping into me and wiping away the memory of him crumpling to the ground, a bullet through his chest. "It just startled me."

"You sure?" he asked.

"I'm good," I assured him, and he pulled away, taking my hand in his.

Together we entered the rickety old building to find Shotgun waiting for us with a toothy grin, holding two pairs of safety goggles and some earmuffs.

I'd never been to a firing range, so I really didn't know what to expect, but I was pretty sure the Warren Gun Club was not your typical establishment. There was a big red sign on one wall that read *Welcome to the Warren Gun Club* and a big yellow placard fixed underneath it titled *Gun Club Rules and Etiquette*. Someone had spray-painted the words "Don't be an Asshole" over the whole thing, obscuring the previous rules one through twelve.

The lobby, if one could call it that, was lit with dangling fluorescent panels, one flickering sickly in the back corner. On a table to Shotgun's right, there was an assortment of guns, arranged haphazardly next to a large army bag they had apparently been dumped from. And beyond that there were eight long well-lit aisles, partitioned off at the front, each with a man-shaped target dangling off in the distance at the back of the building. Nose and Jason were already set up in the lanes marked as seven and eight. Their targets were pulled forward and they were comparing the damage they'd inflicted on them with one of Shotgun's minions standing by. Passion was in lane three holding a little black handgun, the other guy looming at her back and helping her position her arms correctly.

I slapped on my earmuffs just before her little gun rang out five shots in quick succession.

"How did that feel?" Passion's gun-tutor asked her.

"Freakin' awesome," Passion said, grinning from ear to ear as he pulled her target forward.

"For you," Shotgun said, his voice muffled but audible, as he picked up a gun exactly like Passion's and held it out to me butt first. "It's not loaded yet, but always treat it like it is."

I put on my goggles to get them out of the way and took the gun, careful to keep the muzzle down. It seemed tiny and light, almost like a toy, but the spacing of the grip fit my gloved fingers perfectly.

"It's a Walther 9mm," Shotgun said, looking down at the gun in my hands. "And those will help," he said, eyeing my gloves. "The slide can tear up the web of your thumb sometimes, if you're not careful. But it's still the best purse gun out there."

"Purse gun?" I asked, looking at Marcus.

"It's just what they call them because they're small," he explained.

Shotgun reached down and picked up some sort of giant action hero weapon. "The AR15 semiautomatic," he said, handing it to Marcus.

Passion and I got purse guns and Marcus got an assault rifle? What the fuck?

I ended up next to Passion in lane four, with Shotgun helping me.

Marcus went over to lane six to join the guys and the real guns, one expert shared between them because, you know, they were guys and obviously genetically predisposed to be bad-asses. Passion and I, however, each needed our own personal gun instructor to learn how to wield a tiny hunk of metal because we had, unfortunately, been born with vaginas. God, it pissed me off. I barely heard Shotgun as he showed me how to load the gun, and hold it, and look down its dainty, feminine sights.

Still, I took aim at the target. It was more than an outline. It was some cartoonish fifties guy complete with slicked back hair, a bad sweater, and wrinkled pants. He also had a gun in his hand, and a shaded oval over his head, torso, and other various crucial spots, including the middle of his forehead and the center of his crotch.

I aimed for the crotch, pulled the trigger, and the gun tried to jump upward right out of my hand.

Something hit me on top of the head, and the spent shell went ricocheting off my noggin.

"You pulled up," Shotgun said, sounding annoyed. "Did you listen to anything I said? Don't pull the trigger, squeeze it. And hold the gun gently but firmly, like you'd hold a kitten that's trying to escape."

"A kitten?" I repeated, staring at him. "Is that what you tell the guys? Be sure to hold your assault rifle like a fucking kitten?"

"Hey. Calm your tits, Sweetheart. I'm trying to help you here."

Calm my tits, Sweetheart? Was this guy for real? No, he couldn't be. They must have cloned him from the sketch of Fifties Guy on the target. I glared at him, noticing the insignia on the front of his brown coveralls for the first time. It was a circle with the outline of two hands inside of it, clutched in some kind of arm-wrestling hold, and it looked kind of fifties era as well. I suddenly felt a sense of deja-vu, like I'd seen it before in a dream or something.

"You can't shoot angry," he said. "You won't hit anything."

Determined to prove him wrong, I took careful aim at the target's crotch again and let fly with four more bullets. I held the gun gently and firmly this time, but NOT like a kitten.

When I was done, Shotgun shrugged and pulled my target forward.

There was one hole in it, almost completely off target to the left.

"Shit," I said, reloading the gun with the ammo on the little shelf in front of me. Some part of my brain must have been paying attention earlier because I got that right.

Shotgun marked my one shot and sent the target back again.

Off in the distance, Fifties Guy taunted me with his outdated gender stereotypes.

"Here, stand like this," Shotgun said, moving behind me and knocking my feet farther apart with a nudge of his boot. "Put your arms like this." He reached his arms around my body, almost embracing me as he bent one of my arms a little and straightened the other. His chest was right up against my back and I did not like it. "Shake yourself loose," he said into my ear. "You're too stiff. Shooting is not a mechanical thing. It's organic. Like music or fu—painting." Was this guy coming on to me? Ew. Whatever he was doing, it wasn't working. The next five shots didn't even hit the target. I could see that before he pulled it back to us.

"Let's try something different," he said, pulling the paper target off its track and scrawling something on it with a black marker from his coverall pocket. When he hung it back up on its clip, Fifties Guy was sporting two very large black balls and a herculean dick.

"Um, gross," I said, staring at it.

"Women are 57 percent more accurate when male nudity is involved," he said, like he was quoting *The American Journal of Science*.

"And how much more accurate are men when female nudity is involved?"

"You don't want to know," he said, smirking. He sent the target back to the end of the lane, and he didn't touch me this time as I stared down the sites of my purse gun.

The first shot hit Fifties Guy square in chest, exactly where I'd been aiming. The next three didn't miss either. And the fifth shot straight to his crotch made all the men in the building audibly groan.

"See what I mean?" Shotgun said, giving me a friendly pat on the back.

After that, I didn't miss.

Shotgun switched out the guns so I got to try the

AR15, a shotgun, and a couple of rifles, but I had to admit that the Walther was my favorite. Passion liked it too, and she was as good with it as I was. We decided to have a target war, and Shotgun and the other guy left us to it, walking away shaking their heads and grinning.

"You can go first," I called to Passion from my lane, clicking my safety on and setting my gun on the weapon shelf.

"Thanks," she called back.

Her first shot was dead on the target's throat, a killer shot. The second was directly in his forehead. She was going to be hard to beat, unless she made a mistake soon. The third shot was accompanied by a cry of pain from Passion. It went wide, missing the target completely, and I heard her gun clatter to the floor.

"Hey, are you okay?" I bolted around the lane partition to find her clutching her right hand in her left, the gun at her feet.

"My hand got caught in the slide," she groaned, pain written across her face.

"Let me see," I said, reaching out.

"No." She turned away from me, still clutching her hand. "It's fine. It was just a pinch. I'm good."

"Everything all right?" Shotgun called from the other end of the lanes. "Anyone bleeding?"

"I'm fine," Passion called, but I could tell she wasn't.

"I've got a first aid kit around here somewhere, if you need it," he called back.

"No really. I'm good," Passion assured him, her eyes catching mine.

I could see fear in them, even though she was trying to hide it. For some reason, she didn't want anyone to see how hurt she was, and I suddenly thought of her cutting. She must be used to hiding it all the time. And for all I knew, she was still doing it. She still wore long sleeves around camp. Maybe she didn't want to explain the marks on her arms and wrists or see the look of dawning realization on someone's face when they saw them.

"There's a first aid kit in the glove box of the van," I said to her softly.

"Thanks," she whispered, nodding at me. Then she folded her thin body over her hands and quickly walked to the door, exiting into the sunshine.

I reached down, picked up the gun, and flicked the safety on. When I set it on the weapon shelf, the fingers of my glove came away slick with some dark substance—Passion's blood mixed with grease from the slide of the gun maybe.

"Hey," Marcus said, poking his head around the partition, AR15 in his hands. "Is Passion okay?"

"Yeah," I said, wiping my fingers on my jeans. "I think so."

"Good," he said, "because it's time to pay these guys, load up, and get out of here."

3

A STRANGE EXCHANGE

The illegal arms deal that preceded our departure was a fairly casual affair. At least at first. Marcus showed Shotgun his fake ID and a gun permit, though that seemed to be a mere formality. Money exchanged hands, a pretty significant wad of it, and then the two purse guns, several other hand guns, a Remington shotgun, and the AR15 were stuffed back into the army bag, along with a large and varied array of ammunition. Then Shotgun's men, Nose and Jason in tow, lugged the heavy bag out the door and headed to the van.

"And one more thing," Shotgun said, reaching into his coverall pocket and pulling out a minus meter.

I didn't even think about it. One second I was

standing next to Marcus, the next I was between him and the meter, my ghost hand extended through my glove and wound around Shotgun's neck like a boa constrictor.

"You turn that on and you die," I told him. A minus meter had killed Marcus's sister Danielle by draining her PSS. Marcus had been tortured with one in Greenfield. And I'd had a small taste of that agony myself when Dr. Fineman had turned his on me. I wasn't taking any chances with this one.

"Olivia," Marcus whispered in my ear, his arms reaching gently around me to take hold of the meter. "He's giving it to us. I bought it from him."

After Greenfield, we'd talked about trying to get our hands on one to see if we could figure out how it worked, maybe even find a way to defend against it. But dammit, Marcus could have told me we were getting one here. And what was Shotgun doing with a minus meter anyway?

The eyes of the man I was choking were fixed on my wrist, watching my PSS swirl and writhe. He didn't look angry, or afraid. If anything, his look was one of awe and admiration as he let go of the minus meter, releasing it to Marcus.

But I didn't let go of him. Didn't want to. I could sense something inside of him, and my hand wanted it. And Marcus wanted it too. I could feel him, pressed against my back, hoping, anticipating. I hadn't used my hand like that since the night I'd pulled the cube out of the Dr. Fineman. In fact, I hadn't used my ghost hand at all, except for little things like picking locks, because I could feel the ability lurking there, waiting for the chance to reach into someone.

Marcus had wanted me to experiment. He'd wanted me to pull something out of Nose, who had apparently volunteered out of the misguided notion that it would make up for tying me up in Mike Palmer's garage. And Marcus didn't seem to understand that I was terrified of what my hand could do, of the things it brought forth, of the way I could feel, even now, something inside this man calling to me, begging my hand to sink into him. But I would not do that again.

Slowly, I retracted my PSS, slipping it from around his neck and letting it coalesce back into my glove.

"Oh, you two are perfect for each other," Shotgun said, rubbing his neck and smirking at us. Then he made some sort of weird little salute and said, "Long live The Hold."

"It's not like that," Marcus snapped, pushing me to the side and right out of his arms.

"Does she know it's not like that?" Shotgun nodded at me, raising his eyebrows.

What the fuck were they talking about? Not like what? And what the hell was The Hold?

"We came here to do business. That's all," Marcus said, shoving the minus meter into his pocket and holding out his hand to Shotgun. "I paid you. We shake hands like business men. And then this transaction is over."

Shotgun stared down at Marcus's hand like it was an insult. Like it had just slapped him. Maybe in Indiana they didn't shake on business deals.

Marcus kept his hand out, waiting.

Finally, Shotgun reached for it, but at the last second he changed the position of his grip, forcing Marcus into an arm-wrestle hold very much like the insignia on his coveralls.

They stood for a moment locked in place, their faces close, their arms bulging as Marcus tried to pull away and Shotgun held him there. It was such a ridiculous display of testosterone, I didn't know whether to laugh or try to break it up, so instead I just stood there watching.

"I knew your mother," Shotgun said, staring intently at Marcus.

It was the last thing on earth I'd expected him to say, and Marcus looked as surprised as I was. He seemed torn between bolting, which he obviously couldn't do, and punching Shotgun in the face with his free hand, which was now balled into a fist.

"My mother is dead," Marcus practically spat, "thanks to The Hold."

"You don't know what you're talking about," Shotgun insisted.

"Neither do you, Fleshman," Marcus said.

I'd never heard the term spoken aloud before, but I'd read about it and I knew what it meant. Fleshman. Fleshy. Slang for someone without PSS. I had never thought of it as particularly insulting, but Marcus might as well have punched Shotgun in the face the way he dropped Marcus's hand and staggered back, eyeing him like a wounded animal.

"The Hold could use you," Shotgun said. "Both of you. That's all I was saying."

"We're not interested in being used," Marcus said,

turning and walking out of the gun club, leaving me there alone and gawking at Shotgun.

"That there is a very bitter young man," Shotgun said softly, staring after him.

"Wait. You knew his mother? How? When?" I couldn't resist asking.

Shotgun's face hardened. "That's none of your business," he said. "Now go on."

As I walked out, Shotgun's two henchmen were coming in, but they moved aside and let me pass.

I ran to catch up with Marcus, who was already halfway back to the van. "What the hell was that about?" I demanded, my shorter legs racing to keep up with him. "And thanks for leaving me back there with that guy in a room full of guns."

"Shit," he stopped, turning to me. "I'm sorry. He just—I didn't—I was going to hurt him, or at least try to, and that wasn't going to help anything."

I'd never seen Marcus like this. His whole body was shaking, and he didn't seem to know what to do with himself.

I took his hands in mine, trying to hold him together. "Do you think he really knew your mother? And why was he trying to arm wrestle you?"

"It's a long story," Marcus said, looking toward the van. "One I promise to tell you when we get to Indy. We got what we came for. That's the important thing."

"Okay," I nodded. Marcus had a dark past and a lot of secrets. I knew that. I also knew that whatever had just happened was not a topic for casual conversation in front of the others. Knowing Marcus, really knowing him, was not for the faint of heart.

I'd learned that the hard way. I'd also learned not to push him before he was ready. If we needed to be settled in and alone before he could tell me what this all meant, I could give him that.

"Thank you," he said, twining his fingers in mine as we resumed our walk to the van. "Thanks for trusting me."

When we got there, he opened the passenger side door for me and I climbed in.

"What took you guys so long?" Nose asked from the back.

"We got a minus meter," I said, glancing back and catching a glimpse of Passion's right hand heavily wrapped in gauze and medical tape. Had she hurt it that badly? She was sitting in the middle seat next to Yale, his face sullen but resigned. He and Marcus would work out their differences. They always did.

Marcus slid into the driver's seat, shut his door, and handed me the minus meter. "Put this in the glove box for now," he said. Then he started the van, slammed it into drive, and pulled a wide U-turn in the dirt, peeling out a little at the end just for emphasis.

I put the minus meter away, glad to see the Warren Gun Club receding in a cloud of dust behind us. But I also couldn't help noticing, as we whizzed past the sign, the painted insignia of a circle with two clasped hands inside it showing faintly under the club's name.

4

HOME SWEET HOME

"**O**livia, take these," Marcus said, and I opened my eyes to find him shoving a cardboard tray of drinks at me. The van was pulled up to a Wendy's drive-through, bags of warm, amazing-smelling fast food coming through the window like it was Christmas morning at fat camp.

Only half-awake, I passed things to the hungry mob in the back and heard the sound of wrappers being torn open and food being devoured. Finally, there were just two bags and a couple of drinks left in the front.

"Who ordered a *vanilla* Frosty?" I asked, gripping the abomination in my hand.

"That's mine," Marcus said. "Can you hold it for

me while I find a place to park?"

"Vanilla?" I said, appalled. "You do realize that the entire point of a Frosty is the chocolate, right?"

"I like vanilla," he said, driving away from the window and circling for an empty spot in the lot.

"I'm sorry then," I said. "I'm afraid it's over between us."

"Damn it," Nose moaned from the back. "I said no pickles. Anyone want these?"

"This is not a Coke. Who has my Coke?" Passion asked.

Marcus pulled into a parking space, turned off the van, and turned on the radio. As we all sat there munching down our fast food and joking with one another, it felt like we were just a bunch of normal friends hanging out. Or that might have been the fat and sugar hitting my blood stream. Either way, it felt really good.

Marcus inhaled his food, including the sacrilegious vanilla Frosty, and then we drove through the northern suburbs as the sun set over Indy. It was Saturday night so the traffic wasn't bad, and the further out we got, the bigger the houses became, the neighborhoods sporting fancier, more pretentious walls around them. Finally, we pulled up to a gated community with golden letters blazed across its defensive brick facade declaring it Hunterwood Estates.

"This is us," Marcus said, grabbing a remote from the glove box of the van and pointing it at the gates. They swung open slowly and closed automatically behind us after we'd driven through.

Along the winding little road, huge houses stood

far apart, with whole fields of well-maintained grass between them. There were no fences around the yards, and beyond the houses was a beautiful backdrop of native trees and plants with a bike path running along the edge of a small river. Marcus turned down one street, then another, navigating us through Hunterwood Estates to a huge house on the edge of the community, its back yard fading gently into the woods, the river, and the trail. He pulled into the driveway and turned off the van. "Home sweet home," Marcus said, grinning at me, probably because my eyes were bugging out of my head.

It was beautiful. A dream home. The kind of place you'd see featured in some magazine rich people read.

"Holy shit!" Nose said. "It's a McMansion."

"How many big screens does it have?" Jason asked, sounding unimpressed.

"Seven," Marcus answered.

"It has seven TVs?" I asked in disbelief. My mom had a thing against television. She thought it was a tool of mass psychological manipulation. And my dad had always argued that TV stifled creativity. We'd only had one small TV in our house, in the living room, and as a kid I hadn't been allowed to watch it much. Of course, that hadn't stopped me from watching tons of TV at Emma's house or on the Internet. But as much as I liked television, I couldn't fathom the need for seven big screen TVs in one house.

Marcus had the gate remote in his hand again, and he was punching in a code. A security panel on the side of the three-car garage blinked green, and the middle door slowly rose, revealing an empty slot for the van between a shiny red convertible and a black BMW. As Marcus pulled in, I couldn't help noticing the place was decked out with security cameras at every corner too. This place wasn't a McMansion; it was a McFortress.

"Is that a Porsche Boxster?" Yale asked, leaning forward and peering out the window at the convertible.

"Yep," Marcus said casually, a gleam in his eye. Oh yes, Yale would forgive him about the guns, probably immediately after he got his first turn behind the wheel of the Porsche. Marcus had planned this, just like he meticulously planned everything.

Marcus turned the van off, and everyone piled out as the garage door closed, sealing us into our new domicile. The guys admired the cars, and then we each grabbed our bag of personal stuff and headed into the house.

The interior door of the garage led straight into a beautiful, completely decked-out kitchen.

"It's fully stocked," Marcus said, opening the gleaming steal fridge to reveal that it was indeed full of food. Nose and Jason started rifling through the cupboards, which were also full, and each came away with a large bag of chips to scarf down, even though they'd eaten a full meal barely half an hour before.

"Nose, Yale, and Jason," Marcus said, "you have your own bathroom, stocked fridge, and food downstairs. Probably best if you're not upstairs during the day. At night though, we'll be doing security shifts, so stay rested. I'm taking the master bedroom upstairs, mainly because it's connected to the security suite where all the camera feeds are.

Passion and Olivia, there are two more bedrooms upstairs, but I'd like you to share the one on the north side of the house."

If Marcus noticed my surprise over that information, he didn't show it. He was still talking and giving orders. "We'll be setting up a security station in the other bedroom for whoever is on night watch," he explained. "It has the best upstairs vantage points for that sort of thing. Other than that, same rules as Piss Camp. No one goes out alone. Travel in pairs whenever you're outside the safety of the house. We keep our profile as low as possible, especially our PSS. Everyone understand?"

And everyone did. We all knew that despite the façade of a fancy house, the dangers were still the same. The CAMFers were after us, and you could never be sure who was working with them or for them. I'd learned that the hard way in Greenfield when the local Fire Chief, a man I'd known most of my life, had burned down my house with me in it. I wasn't going to make that mistake again.

"Let's go check out the new digs," Nose said through a mouthful of Doritos, leading Yale and Jason down the stairs to their new man cave.

"I've gotta use the restroom," Passion said.

"I think it's around the corner," Marcus said, pointing.

As soon as I heard the door close behind her, I turned to him.

"So, Passion and I are rooming together?" I asked, trying to keep the hurt out of my voice.

"Since you're pretending to be cousins," he said, "I thought it made sense."

"And you didn't think to ask me?"

"You and Passion have to be convincing," he said, shrugging. "And that's not going to happen if you won't even talk to each other. You have to come up with some family background and agree on what you're going to tell people. People ask a lot of questions when you're the new kid at school. You're both going to need answers to those questions, and those answers are going to have to match up."

"That's why I think it's stupid to send her in with me," I argued. "You did this on your own in Greenfield. Why can't I do it on my own here? Sending two people just makes it two times more likely we're going to get caught."

"We've talked about this," he said, pacing in frustration. "I don't want you going alone. Having someone with you gives you more credibility. It keeps you from being perceived as a loner, and that might help you convince Samantha to come with you. And if something goes wrong, if the CAMFers try to take you guys, it's much harder to grab two people."

"But I am a loner," I protested. "That's why I don't want anyone coming with me, or forcing me to be best friends with anyone."

"And that's exactly why you need to," Marcus said firmly. "No offense, but you're not exactly a social butterfly, and neither is Passion. Together the two of you might equal one normally outgoing girl. And that could be a problem because you're going to be in a completely new environment with very limited time, and you're going to have to make someone like you enough to believe something kind of hard to believe, and then convince them to come with you."

"You know when someone says, 'no offense,'" I pointed out to him, "the thing they say directly after that is *always* offensive." *Passion and I might equal one normal girl? Great. My boyfriend thought of me as a social freak.*

"What do you want me to do? Lie?" he asked, his voice growing heated too. "I'm worried about you, okay? I don't want you going at all. But we've looked at it from all angles, and this is the best scenario for getting Samantha out. If I could go in, I would, but the CAMFers know me too well, and we saw with you how hard it is for a guy to convince a girl. But if you can't work this out with Passion, if you can't prove to me by the end of the weekend that you're ready, I'll send her alone."

"Send *her* alone?" I blurted. It had never occurred to me that Marcus might nix me out of the equation. I was the one he'd been kissing and sharing a tent with for weeks, and he knew how much this meant to me, but he'd still just threatened to cut me out of the whole thing. "Are you crazy? She doesn't have PSS, or a power. She'd get eaten alive."

"She doesn't need any of that," Marcus said, his voice rising. "All she needs to do is make friends with someone the way she's been trying to make friends with you for two weeks. And if this Samantha has half a heart, that shouldn't be too hard."

"If she has half a heart?" I repeated, feeling my chest clench with pain. "Is that how you see me?

As a heartless bitch because I'm not best friends with Passion?"

And that was the moment Passion, who'd undoubtedly heard every word we'd said, opened the bathroom door and came out, looking anywhere but at us.

Great. Rooming with her wasn't going to be awkward at all now.

Marcus looked at her, then back at me. "I'll show you the rest of the house," he said.

Passion and I nodded, avoiding each other's gaze, and followed Marcus out of the kitchen into a vaulted living room filled with brown leather furniture and an entire wall covered in TV. I got a glimpse of several of the downstairs rooms, one containing a formal dining table and another sporting a baby grand piano. Then we traipsed up the stairs and past the amazing master bedroom. I only got a peek (but oh, that bed) before we were ushered down the hallway, which was also a balcony overlooking the great room, right to a bedroom door at the end of the hall.

Marcus put his hand on the doorknob, opened it, and moved aside, letting Passion and me enter.

We both stepped in and stopped, surveying the room before us.

It was large, easily twice the size of the room I'd had back in Greenfield, and that hadn't been small. But it wasn't the size that had me in awe; it was the way the room was decorated. It had been done up in black, deep blue and pink, three colors I never would have thought to put together, but they looked amazing. The walls had been painted in giant squares of the three colors, with half the room decorated predominantly in blue and black squares with pink as the dividing accent. The other half of the room was painted in mostly pink squares of varying shades, accented with the blue and black. The effect was a room divided into darkness and light, softness and power, strength and vulnerability: half-Olivia and half-Passion. Just the colors and the way they were rendered would have made it perfect.

But that wasn't all. The same attention to style and color had been given to the furnishings. Both sides of the room had a four-poster canopy bed, but where the pink one's canopy and curtains were soft, voluminous and sheer, the black one's were thick, rich and velvety. The arm chair on the black side was modern, curved and clean, where the one on the pink side was overstuffed and swallow-you-soft looking. Every detail of the room was mirrored like that, from the desks to the lamps to the rugs on the pale hardwood floor.

You know those decorator shows where the people leave home, and when they come back someone has replaced their funky old bedroom with a fancy new one, but instead of saying "Gee, thanks," they burst into tears and bawl hysterically? I never really understood that. I always felt like, "Come on, you're crying over curtains and a new bedspread. Your life must seriously suck."

What I never got, until that moment, was what it really meant to find a room like that, made especially for you. It wasn't about the furniture, or the colors, or even the design. It was the realization, hitting you like a Mack truck to the heart, that someone had truly thought about you. They'd thought about what you love, and what you don't, and what you want, and what sort of place you need, down to the minutest detail. And then they'd gone that one step further, as so few people ever do, and they'd actually made it a reality.

I turned to Marcus, and he had this nervous look on his face, like he thought he'd messed up because Passion and I weren't saying anything.

And that's when I burst into tears like those idiots on television.

Both Marcus and Passion stared at me, stunned.

"I'm sorry," I said, turning away in embarrassment. I do not cry. I am not a crier.

"Thank you for the room," I heard Passion say to Marcus. "It's perfect."

"It really is," I said, trying to pull it together.

"Yeah, okay, no problem," he said, looking at me worriedly. "I'll let you settle in and get comfortable. Oh, and the closet should be full of clothes."

I hadn't noticed a closet, and Marcus must have seen my confusion, because he stepped to one wall and pushed something. A panel slid aside, revealing the doorway to a huge walk-in closet, the fully mirrored wall at the end of it making it look twice as big. The hangers and shelves were full of designer labels: jeans, dresses, tops, bras and underwear. Shoes of every shape and style lined the racks underneath.

"I hope they fit," Marcus said. "I hired this fashion consultant online and told her I was surprising my sisters who weren't happy about the family move."

Passion and I looked at one another, eyes wide. The closet was jammed full of thousands of dollars' worth of clothing. I didn't know much about fashion, but I did know that much.

"Well, you probably want to get cleaned up," he said, crossing to the door and pulling it closed behind him, one last glance in my direction as he left.

As soon as he was gone, I knew I should have said more. I should have thrown my arms around him and planted a big, wet, wonderful kiss on those generous lips. Especially after the way I'd acted in the kitchen.

But there was some part of me that couldn't even fathom what he'd done. Why all this luxury and opulence? Why go to all this trouble to deck out a rental house that was essentially a stake out, just a temporary place for us to stay while we tried to get Samantha out of her high school and away from the CAMFers? Yes, it was part of our cover. I understood that. We were supposed to be rich kids, so we needed to act and dress the part. But how could he waste all this money on a dream bedroom and wardrobe for Passion and me? A dream bedroom and wardrobe we were going to have to leave behind in a matter of days anyway.

And that was going to royally suck, because we'd most likely go back to camping from the back of our wheelers, dressed in a coat of dust, on the way to wherever we had to go to find Kaylee Pasnova, the next girl on the CAMFers' list. It didn't make sense. Marcus was a smart guy. Why would he squander our resources like this?

But I knew the answer, even as I asked myself the question.

This bedroom wasn't only for Passion and me. It was for Danielle. This whole house was for her. And for him. And for us. His new family—his chosen family. This was the home he was carving out for us, no matter how briefly, in a world that had destroyed any family and home he'd ever known. Marcus was staking his claim to a new life, a real life. We all were. That's what we were fighting for, armed with the weapons of sheer will, hope, and even guns, if that's what it came to. That was why Passion and I had to get Samantha to join us.

She was a part of our family too.

She just didn't know it yet.

5

SLEEPING BEAUTY WAKES

I sat up, completely disoriented, wondering where I was and what had woken me. I was in a huge bed shrouded in curtains like something out of a fairy tale, a dim strip of light cutting between the gap in the material and falling across my face.

I pulled the curtains aside and looked around the dark room. *The Other Olivia*, tattered around the edges but as eternal as ever, was leaning against the nearest wall, staring back at me. Passion's gentle breathing whispered in and out, in and out, from within the billowy enclosure of her pink canopy bed.

That's right. It was our first night in the McMansion, and after everyone had settled in, cleaned up, and unpacked their stuff, it was as if the spell straight out of *Sleeping Beauty* had descended upon us. We had walked around yawning at 8:00 p.m., our eyes held open to bare slits. Yale had almost fallen down the stairs, and I'd run into a doorjamb with my face.

I reached up and felt the bruise on my cheekbone. At least the swelling had gone down.

Anyway, after the doorjamb incident, Marcus had suggested we all go to bed. There had been protests, of course, because we'd wanted to enjoy all the luxuries of the McMansion right then, tired or not. But Marcus had argued that we were experiencing physical exhaustion from all of the running and fighting and surviving we'd been doing, the side-effect of something he called sustained hyper-vigilance. In other words, there's only so long you can run, and then you have to crash. And now that we were surrounded by four walls, a roof, and a semblance of normalcy, that's exactly what our bodies were doing, like it or not.

So, we'd all shambled off to our beds. I hadn't even had enough energy to insist Marcus explain the whole incident at the gun club. It could wait until after my first night's sleep in a real bed since forever. And when Marcus offered to take the first security shift, it was proof of exactly how tired we'd been that none of us stopped to think he probably needed rest more than anyone. I'd been sustaining my hyper-vigilance for a little over three weeks. From what I'd gathered, Marcus had been sustaining it his whole life. But maybe it was something you got used to.

The clock on my nightstand said 3:36 a.m. Marcus's shift was long over, and one of the other guys would be staked out in the security room. They hadn't scheduled Passion and me for shifts, since we'd need to be alert and well-rested when we started school on Monday. But, despite the early hour, I was definitely awake. I might as well go see who was on duty. Maybe they'd want a snack or some company until I got sleepy again.

I slipped my legs out from under the plump down comforter and buried my feet in the plush rug next to the bed. It was warm, like it had just come out of the dryer. I slid my toes onto the wood floor, expecting it to be cool, but it was warm too. The floor was heated. Damn. A girl could get used to living like this.

Except this girl shouldn't. This wasn't really our house or our life. I had been happy living in a tent with Marcus, and I would be happy that way again.

I got up and pulled on some sweatpants, but I didn't bother putting anything over the tank top I'd slept in. The house was the perfect temperature, not too cold and not too hot. Maybe that was the radiant floor heat. Or maybe it was simply the feeling of home and safety and the indoors we'd all been missing. Another thing I'd been missing was a bathroom that wasn't a hole in the ground in the middle of the forest in the middle of the night. Oh God, I loved this place. I tiptoed to the door of the bedroom's adjoining bathroom and took a much needed pee.

When I came out, I crossed to the bedroom door, careful not to wake Passion, and slipped into the hallway. I had the glow of my hand, so I didn't bother with any lights as I made my way across the balcony hallway to the bedroom on the other side—not the master, but the one that was serving as the upstairs lookout.

The door was ajar and I pushed it open. The light was off and the curtains and blinds were pulled back from the large central window. The guys had removed the beds from the room, so no one would be tempted to sleep on duty, and there were two chairs positioned for optimum viewing of the street below, but no one was in them. No one was in the room at all.

I walked to the window and looked out, surveying the neighborhood from one end to the other. It was bathed in eerie bluish streetlight. And it was dead out there, all the suburbanites tucked away in their temperature-controlled fortresses, exactly like we were. Good thing too, because the wind was gusting, whipping the newly planted saplings that lined the street back and forth. As I watched, the neighbor's trash bin blew over, a loose, black, plastic bag escaping from it and skimming across the road and into our side yard like a runaway ghost. Now that I was more awake, I could hear the wind whistling over the top of the house. Perhaps that was what had woken me.

Anyway, it didn't really matter. But I was beginning to feel kind of freaked out that no one was on duty. Maybe they'd gone to the security suite to check something on the cameras.

I headed down the hall to the master bedroom, which I'd have to go through to get to the camera room. If Marcus was asleep, I wouldn't wake him, but at least I'd get to see him sleeping. Just thinking about it made my steps quicken and my heart race.

Those softened lips. That innocent boyish face. The way his forehead sometimes scrunched up as if, even in his dreams, he was hard at work strategizing how to save the world. My head was resigned to rooming with Passion, but my heart missed sleeping next to Marcus already.

The bedroom door was closed, and I pulled it open quietly. There was no one in the bed, and it was still made. Marcus hadn't slept yet? Was he trying to pull an all-night shift on his own? Idiot!

I crossed to the security suite, which had once been another huge walk-in closet, and slid the door open. Twenty display screens blinked back at me from the far wall, a built-in desk positioned below them, its chair empty. Where the hell was everyone?

Thankfully, I'd arrived at the best place to find out. I sat down in the chair and started scanning the screens. The array was easy enough to read. The top row of monitors showed the upstairs feeds, one in each bedroom, and one each in the hall and the entry to the stairs. That was the reason Marcus had gotten Passion and me canopy beds with curtains. That way we could still have some privacy even though there was a security camera in our room. Anyway, I'd just walked through the rooms upstairs, so I skipped those, going straight to the main floor monitors one row down.

Nothing and no one in the kitchen, dining room, piano room, or the garage, but the living room feed clearly showed Marcus completely zonked out on one of the leather couches. He must have finally succumbed to the sleeping spell, just like the rest of us.

But that also meant that no one was on security duty and probably hadn't been for hours. And that was bad.

My eyes dropped to the third row of screens, which covered the basement. The game room and home theatre were empty, but each bedroom had a dark sleeping form on its correlating bed. It was confirmed; I was the only one awake in the whole damn house, and suddenly I felt like I had been injected with a gallon of Red Bull. It was me; I was our security. Then again, nothing had happened since Marcus had fallen asleep, and it wasn't likely to happen now, simply because I was awake and watching for it. Besides, the cameras weren't our only protection. There was an alarm system on every door and window of the house. It didn't link to the police or anything though, because Marcus didn't trust the authorities.

I glanced down at the bottom row of monitors, which covered all four sides of the house and the various entry points. Something was weird about them. They were kind of blurry compared to the indoor feeds, like someone was shaking the cameras back and forth, and then I realized it must be the wind blowing them around. Camera sixteen, the one at the front of the house, started to cut out. It went black for a minute, then came back on, then went black again, probably a short caused by the gusts. Yale could take care of it when the wind died down in the morning. Still, I felt better when it popped back on again, restoring my view of the front approach.

I sat back in the chair, surveying the view in front of me like some savvy superhero, safe in her secret lair.

And that's when I saw it; a shadow, slipping across

the lower corner of camera seventeen. It was there, and then it was gone, something moving around the side of the house, making every effort to avoid detection. Or, it was my imagination. My overactive I'm-the-only-one-awake imagination trying to freak me the hell out. I fixed my eyes on that screen and watched for it to happen again, thinking it might be the wind, perhaps the shadow of a cloud or blown branch superimposing itself on the side of the house just under the camera.

And then, out of the corner of my eye, I caught motion in camera eighteen. This time the shadow was a little bigger, and I could make out its shape before it disappeared. It had been thick and bent, like an elbow.

Shit!

Someone was out there. Someone was pressing themselves up against the walls of the house, beneath the scope of the cameras, slowly making their way to the back of the McMansion. The easiest entry into the house was the French doors off the living room that led out onto the deck. And Marcus was down there, asleep.

I looked at camera nineteen and saw the shadow move across it, bigger and bolder this time. There was no longer any question; it was a person.

I glanced down at the control panel on the desk. There was a microphone and a house-wide radio intercom system for emergencies. The only problem was Yale hadn't finished wiring it yet. I pushed the downstairs intercom button, hoping maybe he'd done that one at least. "Guys," I said into the receiver. "This is Olivia. I'm in the security suite, and we have an intruder. Please respond if you can hear this."

I stared at the downstairs bedroom screens, willing the dark forms in the beds to move, but they didn't. They hadn't moved since I'd been in the suite. Did people sleep that soundly? What if they'd been gassed? What if we all had? I mean, we'd practically passed out earlier. Even the ever-vigilant Marcus had succumbed to it. What if everything, this whole house and our sudden drowsiness, had been rigged by the CAMFers, and I was the only one conscious enough to do anything about it? But, if that was true, why was I awake?

"Dammit, Yale," I said into the receiver. "Nose. Jason. Wake up, please. I really need you."

But they obviously couldn't hear me, so I switched my attention back to camera twenty, peering at the deck and the area around the French doors. The shadow hadn't made an appearance there yet. On the living room screen, Marcus was still asleep on the couch, his arm draping over its edge now. At least he'd moved. I had to get down there and warn him.

I scanned the room, hoping someone had left a gun or some kind of weapon, but no such luck. I wasn't even sure where my Walther was. I vaguely remembered someone saying that the guns had been brought into the house from the van, but I had no idea where they'd been put. Passion didn't have hers either, I was pretty sure of that. God, we were idiots. What good was an arsenal if no one knew where it was?

What the fuck was I supposed to do? Go out there and confront that shadow unarmed? What if somehow I'd missed it, and the intruder was already in the house? What if he was waiting out there in the darkness of the master bedroom for me? Or in the hallway? What if there was more than one of them, the shadow I'd seen only a single member of an entire assault team? *Shit, shit, shit. Pull it together, Olivia. It was just a shadow. No one can get in without setting off the alarm.*

Except alarms can be disabled.

Shit.

I looked back at screen twenty. The shadow was filling it, the head and torso of a man standing right in front of me, his arms reaching up to throw something over the camera.

The feed went dark, but not before I saw the face as clear as day, barely showing the faintest signs of the injury and abuse Jason had perpetuated upon it three weeks before.

It was Mike Palmer's face.

He was out there, trying to get in.

6

STEALTH R US

My eyes flew to the living room monitor. There was Marcus, still asleep. There were the French doors, but a light source in the living room was reflecting off the glass, obscuring my view to the outside.

Wait. There was movement out there. Something dark was moving across the deck. I could see the shape of rounded shoulders, like a man crouched at the door picking the lock or disarming the alarm.

I had to do something, and it had to be quick. I couldn't just hide and watch Mike Palmer break into our house. Marcus was down there.

With one last glance at the screen to assure myself the dark shape was still outside, I darted from the security suite into the master bedroom and looked for something, anything, to use as a weapon. Pillows. Bedding. Comfy, overstuffed chairs. None of it was any good. But the wrought iron curtain rods holding up the expensive drapes looked promising. Each one had an ornate, almost spear-like tip on its end.

I jumped up on one of the chairs and pulled a rod off its supports. Another quick yank in the middle and it came away in two pieces. I ran my hand along one piece, pushing the drapery material off, and the other end of the rod went with it, making a dull thunk as it hit the material now pooled on the floor. The piece left in my hand was solid, decently heavy, and about three feet long. It was better than nothing.

Curtain rod spear in hand, I slipped out into the dark hallway and pressed myself against the wall, sliding my way to the edge of the balcony that overlooked the living room. I peeked around the corner of the wall. From that angle, the back of the couch obscured my view of Marcus, but I could see the French doors and out onto the deck fairly well. There was no one out there.

Which meant he was inside.

I considered yelling to Marcus, but it would give away my presence and position, as well his. There was a chance that Palmer hadn't even realized Marcus was down there. I couldn't risk it. No, I was going to have to go downstairs and try to sneak up on Palmer before he set the house on fire, or whatever devious thing he was up to. The guy was a pyro, a bigot, and a coward, so it really could be anything. I certainly wouldn't mind sticking a curtain rod straight through him like a stick through a marshmallow. There was a time when I'd shown the man some mercy, but that time was over.

Mustering up every ounce of courage I had, I stepped to the opposite wall and got ready to round the corner to the stairwell.

I heard movement downstairs, footfalls scuffing against the Italian tile of the kitchen floor.

He was on the move.

Shit.

He was coming up the stairs. Fast.

I braced myself, stiffening my arm for the thrust, and lunged around the corner of the wall at the top of the stairs right before he crested them.

The curtain rod went through his shirt and his chest like a knife through butter. There was no resistance. None at all. And my hand followed right through the hole the rod had made, into Marcus's chest cavity, straight up to my elbow and out the other side.

His mouth and eyes held a question he never got to ask as the light and life faded from them and he began to fall backwards.

"No!" I screamed, bending my spear arm and throwing myself back against the stairs. Getting skewered wouldn't kill Marcus for good, but falling down the stairs might kill us both.

When he fell on me, he fell hard, my butt and back slamming against the unrelenting corners of the carpeted steps. And then we began to slide, bumping our way down each one. Thud. Thud. Thud, thud, thud, thud. I tried to keep my weapon arm ready, even with my boyfriend impaled on it and lying on top of me, even through the pain. Mike Palmer was still down there, and now that Marcus was down for the count, I was definitely on my own. Hopefully not for long though, because the racket we'd made would have woken the dead, and I was hoping it had woken Passion and the guys. Now. Like, right now. 'Cause I really needed them.

Marcus and I arrived at the bottom of the stairwell, and I struggled to push his body off my arm without letting go of the curtain rod, which didn't work at all. In a panic, I let the rod clatter to the floor, but even then, my elbow got stuck in the torn fabric of his t-shirt and I wrestled to extract it.

When Passion came hurtling down the stairs in her pajamas, her Walther in her bandaged hand, I had finally gotten my arm out of my boyfriend and picked up the rod again.

"Thank God you have your gun. Mike Palmer is in the house," I said, as she stared down at Marcus, horror in her eyes.

"Is he dead?" she asked, her eyes still glued on Marcus.

"Yeah. But he'll be fine. Passion," I said firmly, grabbing her arm and making her look at me. "You need to let the guys know we have an intruder. I'll stay here with Marcus."

"But how did he—"

Footsteps pounded up the stairs from the basement, and I heard the door slam open, Jason and Nose spilling out into the foyer, their guns trained in two different directions. Neither was wearing a shirt, and Jason's hair was a tousled mess, but he had the AR15 strapped across his back.

"Mike Palmer is in the house," I told them softly. "On this floor or the basement."

Jason eyed the makeshift spear in my hand, glanced at Passion, and then looked down at Marcus, dead on the floor.

"It was an accident," I said. "I thought he was Palmer. Where's Yale?"

"Still downstairs," Nose said, looking to Jason for instructions.

"You and Passion go and get him," Jason told Nose, "and search every crack and crevice down there. If you see anything or anyone, shoot it. If you don't, come back up and bring Yale with you."

"Got it," Nose said, grinning out of his ski mask. He wore it, even when he slept, because the glow of his PSS nose kept him awake otherwise.

"Okay," Passion said, crossing to the basement stairs and following Nose stealthily down them.

"Here, take this," Jason said, handing me his hunting rifle.

I set my curtain rod on the floor and took it as he pulled the assault rifle off his back.

"It's loaded and the safety is off," he said nodding at the gun in my hands. "How the fuck did Palmer get in?"

"He disarmed the alarm and came in the French doors."

"Okay, we search this floor together," Jason said, gesturing for me to head into the living room.

"We can't leave Marcus."

"No one's going to kill him while he's dead."

"No, but they could take him."

"Fine. Then I'll secure this floor by myself, and you stay with your boyfriend," Jason said snidely, skirting around the corner of the wall into the living room area, his gun out in front of him.

And then I felt silly and useless, standing there over Marcus. I could at least search the kitchen and check the garage while keeping him in my line of sight. I moved silently into the kitchen. It had an open floor plan and was obviously empty, but I still checked behind the butcher block and under the bar. Then I crossed to the garage door and slowly opened it, the rifle ready. I flipped on the lights, but that wasn't going to help me see behind the cars, especially the van. It was a huge garage, and there were a lot of places someone could hide. I'd have to wait for Jason or some downstairs backup.

"What the—" I heard Marcus moan. I turned to see him sitting up against the stairs, looking down at the hole in his shirt, and I gave an internal sigh of relief. It was one thing to know intellectually that he could reboot his PSS and come back to life. It was another thing entirely to have to count on that fact when you're the one who's accidentally killed him.

"Shhhh," I called softly as I headed back to him. "We have an intruder."

"What? Who?" he said, looking around in confusion, his eyes finding the curtain rod on the floor next to him. "You stabbed me," he said, bewilderment written all over his face.

"I know. Sorry. I thought you were Palmer. He broke into the house." I knelt at Marcus's side, wanting so badly to set down my gun and put my hands on him, to touch his chest, his face, his arms, and make sure he was really all back in one piece the way I needed him to be. But I couldn't do that until we were all safe and Palmer was captured or eliminated.

"What the hell is going on?" Marcus asked, staring at me.

"You fell asleep," I said gently, trying not to make it sound like an accusation. "No one was on duty for hours."

"Oh shit," he said, his face growing pale. "I thought it was only a few minutes." He would beat himself up over this. I knew he would. He was only human, but he didn't like to admit that, even to himself.

There was pounding on the stairs again, and Nose, Passion and Yale emerged from the basement.

"No one down there," Nose said, looking between Marcus and me, unsure who he was reporting to.

"And no one on this floor," Jason said, coming around the corner from the direction of the dining room. "It's all clear."

"I looked in the garage," I said, nodding toward it. "But I didn't search the whole thing."

Jason stared at me, and I stared back, and I knew we were both remembering the last time we'd had a discussion about searching a garage. Did he think this was a set-up? If I was a CAMFer spy, what better way to exact my revenge on Jason than to send him into an ambush in a garage, just the way he'd sent me? Marcus was convinced that Jason was a changed man, that he wasn't paranoid anymore because I'd pulled the bullet of fear from his soul and freed him. I wasn't so sure about that. Yes, Jason had stopped threatening me on a regular basis. He'd even begun to show me a small measure of respect, but I still seriously doubted he trusted me.

"Me and Nose will check it," he said, heading through the kitchen to the garage door, Nose following after him.

I was almost disappointed. I had come to think of Jason's treatment of me as the one steady, constant thing in my life. Something I could always count on. Plus, now Marcus had one more piece of proof that using my ghost hand to pull things out of people was a good idea.

"Where did Palmer come in? What was the entry point?" Marcus asked me.

"The French doors."

"Maybe that's what woke me up," he said, glancing at the doors in question. "I thought it was just the wind rattling them. And then I decided to go check the camera feeds to be sure."

"Where's your gun?" I asked. Marcus hadn't had his gun when I'd met him on the stairs. I was pretty thankful for that, or things could have turned out much worse than they had, but it was still odd.

"I had it when I sat down on the couch," he said, sounding confused, "but when I woke up, it wasn't there. I must have left it upstairs."

I hadn't seen Marcus's gun anywhere upstairs.

"The garage is clear," Jason said, emerging into the kitchen with Nose behind him. "No signs of a break-in or intruder."

"Okay," I said, looking around at the group. "Maybe he snuck out again. Marcus and I made a lot of noise coming down the stairs. It could have scared him off."

"Are you sure he didn't sneak past you upstairs?" Yale asked.

"No. I was watching him on the camera feed the whole time, except when I stopped to grab the curtain rod in the bedroom."

"How long did that take?" Marcus asked. "Because it doesn't take that long to sneak up one flight of stairs."

"I don't know. A couple of minutes. Shit. Yeah. He could have gotten past me."

"But I was up there asleep," Passion said, her eyes widening to giant pools of liquid fear.

"You're safe now," I said, touching her arm until she looked at me. "It's okay."

"He may still be up there," Marcus said, standing up and looking meaningfully at Jason.

"Here, take this," I said, handing the rifle to Marcus. "Passion, Yale and I will stay down here in case he tries to sneak past you and back out."

"You don't have a gun," Marcus pointed out.

"I know. But Passion is a better shot than me anyway. We'll be fine."

"No," he insisted. "Jason and I will go up and leave Nose with you."

"Okay." I grabbed the front of his torn t-shirt, pulling him toward me. "Be safe," I commanded.

"I will," he promised, those intense brown eyes looking down at me.

Then he stepped away, and I had to let go of his shirt.

Jason moved to the upstairs stairwell, gun out, and Marcus followed him. They both disappeared silently, step by step, up into the darkness where Palmer might be hiding, and I suddenly realized that I would never feel safe, no matter where I was, until that man was thoroughly and absolutely dead.

7

A MESS OR A MESSAGE?

There was no one upstairs. No sign of Mike Palmer in the entire house.

When Jason and Marcus came back down, they wanted to search outside, but Passion and I made them wait until we could get our shoes and put them on.

A few minutes later, we all stood at the French doors: Yale and Passion, Marcus and Jason, me and Nose.

"Don't turn on the deck lights," Jason instructed, "and let me go first."

As soon as Marcus opened the doors, the wind whipped in and Jason stepped out, gun ready, eyes trained on the perimeter of the deck and yard.

I was immediately hit by a whiff of gasoline so strong it made me gag, but the memories were even worse. Last time I'd encountered that smell, my house had just been burned to the ground around me.

Mike Palmer had been here. There was no question about that. From where I stood, I could now see the huge pool of slick liquid spilled across the deck, a large red gas can lying on its side, the nozzle still dripping.

Jason and Marcus exchanged a look.

"You, Nose, and I will go," Marcus said to him. "Don't step in or near the gas. The rest of you wait until we give the all clear."

So, Yale, Passion and I waited. I don't know how long it took, ten minutes maybe, until Nose came back and said that they'd scoured the entire perimeter of the grounds and it was safe to come out. But Jason still didn't want the outer lights on, as it might draw the attention of the neighbors.

As I moved out through the doors into the battering wind, I heard something flapping near my head and looked up to see a black plastic bag tangled over the deck camera.

Marcus came over, reached up, and pulled it off, letting the wind carry it away.

"He was here," I said, feeling myself begin to shake.

"But he didn't get in," Marcus said, wrapping his arms around me. "No thanks to me, but still, he didn't."

"Why didn't he light the gas?" I asked. "The way the wind is gusting, the deck and the house would have gone up like an inferno." As soon as I said it, I wished I hadn't. Then I caught a glimpse of a small dark square in the middle of the gas puddle. "What's that?" I asked, pointing it out to Marcus.

"I don't know." He guided me around the edge of the gas pool to the far side, near the gas can, where we could see it better. It was a matchbook, soaked and glistening. "I think he must have dropped it before he could light anything," Marcus said.

One matchbook? Mike Palmer knew a lot about fires. If he had meant to burn us out, he would have. No, this was a message. Some kind of warning. Palmer wanted us to know that he'd been here, and that he'd chosen not to set this fire. But why would he do that?

There was a huge gas grill in the corner of the deck, a pair of tongs hanging on it and clanging in the wind. I went over, grabbed them, and used them to extract the soggy matchbook from the gasoline.

Marcus and I looked down at it. On the front there was an American flag with the words "Freedom Lights the Way" under it, but on the back someone had written something in messy hurried handwriting.

"Don't go to Shades," I read it aloud and looked at Marcus. "What does that mean?"

"Shade is another word for ghost," Marcus speculated.

"But it says 'don't go there.' So, it's probably a place."

"Could be anything. A bar maybe, or a restaurant?"

"I can look it up on the internet," I offered. "See if it's someplace local."

"Good idea," he said. "Take it inside. We need to get this gas cleaned up before sunrise."

I looked up to see Nose wielding a hose, ready to spray down the deck right where we were standing.

I nodded at Marcus and took the matchbook into the house, wrapping it in paper towels from the kitchen and squeezing it dry.

Passion came and stood next to me, and we watched, silently, as the guys cleaned up the mess Mike Palmer had left us.

8

LET THE PARANOIA BEGIN

"Play it again," I said. "It has to be there."

"We've played it five times already," Yale said, looking over his shoulder at the others. "There's no one there."

"I saw him," I said, pushing Yale's hands aside and clicking the replay button of the feed for monitor twenty myself. "I clearly saw his face."

The shadowed deck and the outside of the French doors appeared on the screen once again, blurred but visible, as the wind shook the camera. At the edge of the frame, the dark hump of the gas grill loomed, the red boxy gas can sitting at its feet. Then a huge gust of wind kicked up, blacking the camera out for a minute. When it flicked back on, there was the gas can on its side, gas pouring from its spout and pooling across the deck. Two seconds later, something tiny flitted from the upper shelf of the grill like a butterfly, landing in the middle of the pool, right where we'd found the matchbook—because it *was* the matchbook. And then, as I watched for the fifth time, something dark swirled up the steps of the deck, rising on the wind to about shoulder level, then higher, and right as it hit the camera, it became obvious what it was: a black plastic bag. But there was no man this time. Or any of the other times. No arms, or torso, or face. No Mike Palmer.

Yale hit the button to stop the feed, and the silence behind us grew. We could play that recording a hundred more times and it was still not going to show what I knew I'd seen. I had seen Mike Palmer. I had not imagined that. Which meant someone had changed the camera feed in the hour since I'd seen it. Someone inside the house with access to the footage. Someone, one of us, was working with Mike Palmer and the CAMFers.

I looked at Yale. He had the technical know-how to do it, and he'd been in the security suite while the rest of us had been downstairs or cleaning the deck. Marcus had sent him up to work on wiring the intercom system, with additional instructions to hook up an alarm button so the entire house could be alerted next time we had a security breach. But I saw no evidence that Yale had done either of those things. Maybe he'd been too busy tampering with the feed.

"What about camera nineteen?" I said, hoping he hadn't had time to cover all his bases. "I saw him on that one too."

"Um, okay," Yale said, tapping a button and calling it up, then rewinding the footage to the timeframe we needed.

He pressed play, and there was the camera, shuddering in the wind, an angled shadow crossing beneath it.

"Stop right there. See, he's pressed up against the wall," I said, pointing at the corner of the screen. "That's his elbow."

Yale looked at me, something like pity in his eyes.

"What?" I asked, frustration rising in me.

"I think that's the shadow of a tree limb," he said, pushing the button and rewinding the feed more, "See, it shows up in this frame, and in this one much earlier." And there it was—the shadow I had interpreted as Mike Palmer's elbow—looking the same in all three frames. Could it really be the shadow of a branch that my mind had seen as something else? But why in the world would that anomaly be on Yale's radar? He had gone straight to the location of those other occurrences, as if he'd already known they were there. As if he had cross-checked the feed for those specific images earlier.

I looked back at the others. First Marcus, seeking his eyes for what I needed most. Belief. Trust. Unwavering support. But all I found was a guarded thoughtfulness, his brown eyes still glued to the camera feed, and my heart plummeted into the pit of my stomach. Passion appeared confused, but at least she had the decency to look me in the eye. Nose was staring at Marcus, probably waiting to see what he'd say. And Jason was staring at me, not with the suspicion I was expecting, but with a look of collusion that almost screamed, "Welcome to my world. I told you the CAMFers were everywhere."

"I saw him," I said, looking back at Marcus. "Think about what was out there on the deck. That was totally his MO. And what about the message on the matchbook?"

"The matchbook got blown off the grill," Yale argued. "Anyone could have jotted that note on it. This wasn't sabotage; it was the wind. We just saw that with our own eyes."

"Not with our own eyes," I corrected him. "We saw a recording, and recordings can be tampered with. But I know what I saw."

"It was the middle of the night, and you got freaked out," Nose offered. "You said so yourself."

"I didn't freak out until I saw Mike Palmer!" Why wasn't Marcus jumping to my defense? He was supposed to be on my side. And it was obvious this was a setup. Then again, he had been the one who'd conveniently fallen asleep on watch duty.

No, I would not think like that. I had to trust someone, or I'd go crazy. And maybe *this* was exactly what Mike Palmer had been trying to accomplish. Maybe all he'd intended to do was plant a tiny spark of distrust in our ranks and watch it ignite from the inside out. Paranoia was the wind that could burn Marcus's new household to the ground.

"We're all tired," Marcus said, finally glancing at me, but all I could read in his look was that he wanted me to drop it. There was something here, but he wanted me to let it go and look the fool, and that really hurt.

"None of this would have happened if I hadn't fallen asleep," he said, his words heavy with exhaustion and guilt. "And if nothing else, tonight was a good reminder that we can't let our guard down. Ever."

"Agreed," Yale said. "I'll take the next watch and work on getting the intercoms and alarm fully functioning."

Well, wasn't that convenient? If there was any evidence that Yale had tampered with the feeds, I was pretty sure it would be gone by morning.

"I'm wide awake," Jason added, looking at me and then at Yale. "I'll be your second and patrol downstairs." Jason wanting to keep an eye on Yale was suddenly very comforting to me.

"It's almost five now," Marcus said, "Wake Nose and me at eight, if we're still asleep, and we'll take a shift."

"Got it," Jason said, picking up his gun and leaving the suite.

In the awkward silence that followed, Nose and Passion both gave Marcus and me a glance and then left to go back to bed.

Yale was already crawling under the desk to work on the wiring, his ghostly plumber's crack peeking out from the top of his jeans. How could he possibly be a saboteur or a CAMFer spy? He was Yale, the guy with the PSS butt. He was my friend, and more importantly he was Marcus's best friend. I didn't want to believe he was anything else. But I also couldn't discount what I'd seen. I could not disbelieve my own perception of reality. If it was Yale or me, I would choose me.

I looked up to see that Marcus had slipped out of room. What the fuck? He hadn't even waited for me?

I charged out of the security suite into the master bedroom, but he wasn't there.

Then I heard water running in the bathroom, and I marched to the closed door, rapping it forcefully with my fist.

"Come in," he said, as if he'd been expecting me.

I opened the door, and found him standing next to the Jacuzzi tub, the faucet blasting hot water into its huge oblong basin. Steam was already beginning to roil up into the air.

"You're taking a bath?" I was unable to keep the utter astonishment out of my voice.

"Close the door," he said, sitting on the edge of the tub to take off his shoes and socks. "You're letting all the steam out."

I closed the door behind me, suddenly aware that I was in a huge, steamy, luxurious bathroom with Marcus. Too bad I was so pissed at him.

"Do you really think, after everything that just happened, that the best course of action is to take a bath?" I asked him.

"Absolutely," he said, getting up and crossing the bathroom to stand directly in front of me. "Whether you saw Mike Palmer or not, nothing has changed. We've always known the CAMFers were coming here next, and that we'd be in danger from them. I don't see how this really makes a difference."

"It makes a difference to me. Just tell me, do you believe I saw him, or not?"

"I believe you," he said, reaching out for me, but I

stepped away.

"Then what the hell was that back there?" I demanded. "If you believed me, why didn't you call Yale out for the traitor he is?"

"Call Yale out? What are you talking about?"

"Oh, come on, he obviously tampered with the camera footage."

"What makes you think that?" Marcus asked, sounding surprised.

"Well, what other explanation is there? I saw Palmer on that feed, and now he's gone, and Yale was the only one up there in the security suite."

"I guess him changing it is one explanation," Marcus said grudgingly.

"Do you have a better one?" I demanded. Maybe he just didn't want to see it.

"Several actually," Marcus said, crossing behind me to the door and turning on the overhead fan. Then he crossed back to the faucet of the now-full tub and turned it off. He bent over and turned on the jets. They kicked up a lot more steam and a lot more noise. I was starting to melt inside my clothes, and he must have been too. When he turned back to me he was slipping his torn t-shirt over his head.

"What are you doing?" I asked, my voice coming out a little strangled.

"You and I need to talk," he said, letting the shirt drop to the floor. "About what happened tonight. About what happened at the gun club. I promised to tell you, remember?"

"Yes," I said, trying not to gawk at his chest and the way the steam swirled into it, his PSS shining back and coloring the mist a soft blue hue. "But can't we do that with our clothes on?"

"We could," he said, giving me that cocky grin of his. "But where's the fun in that?" His hand went to his waist, undoing the snap on his jeans. "Plus, I'm pretty sure no one will interrupt us in here." The zipper was next. He had red tartan boxers on. "And it has been way too long since I've had a bath." He slid the jeans down his legs, kicking them away. Then he turned, slipped off the boxers, and stepped into the tub, sinking down into it with an audible moan.

I stood there, stunned. I had just seen Marcus naked. He'd stripped to his beautiful bare ass right in front of me, as if it were nothing. Yes, we'd been sleeping in a tent together for weeks, and making out, but when one of us changed clothes, the other looked away. Marcus and I had not gotten naked together, mainly because I always held back. I couldn't even bring myself to reach my hands inside his shirt. What if my flesh hand accidentally went into his chest and disrupted his PSS while we were getting intimate? Even worse, what if my ghost hand reached into him and pulled something horrible out? So, yeah, Marcus and I were not at the level of strip-naked-together. Not even close.

"God, this feels amazing," Marcus said, almost a purr, laying his head back on the edge of the tub and closing his eyes.

I looked away, down at the tile floor, completely flustered. Did he have any idea how breathtaking he was?

"Olivia," he said softly, and I looked up to find his

eyes boring into me, dewy drops captured on those thick dark lashes. "Come here."

I crossed obediently to the side of the bath, both relieved and a bit disappointed to find that the burbling of the jets obscured most of what was in it. Except his PSS chest. It glowed and pulsed like some half-submerged, cerulean, underwater treasure.

Marcus put his hand out for mine. The invitation was obvious.

This was crazy. There was no way we were going to be able to talk, coherently, in a bathtub together.

"It's a big tub," he said, nodding toward the other end, "and I promise to be good."

Yeah, but it wasn't just him I was worried about. If I got in the tub with Marcus, *I* would be in the tub with Marcus. "But I—" I looked down at myself. I had on my sleeping tank with no bra underneath, my sweatpants, and underwear.

"You have no idea how relaxing this is," he said, slipping his hand back into the water and closing his eyes. Either he was taunting me, or giving me a chance to undress without him watching. Probably both.

"You bastard," I muttered under my breath. I slipped off my shoes and sweatpants and padded barefoot to the far end of the tub. I wasn't going in completely naked. I wasn't that much of a fool. I kept my tank and underwear on and stepped into the hot swirling water. As I slid down into it, the jets pulsed against my butt and back. The wet heat rose up, swallowing all my aches and pains in its pure liquid magic. I couldn't keep the moan from escaping my lips either.

And I didn't miss the effect that sound had on Marcus.

One of his lean, muscular legs brushed mine, trembling. His eyes widened. And his breath came a little faster across the water, far less relaxed than it had been only a moment before.

9

EXPLANATIONS IN A BATHTUB

"If Yale didn't tamper with the camera footage, then who did?" I asked, trying to stay focused. God, the bath felt amazing. And Marcus looked hot. And it was hard to even remember how frustrated I'd been in the security suite only ten minutes before, but I still needed answers.

"I don't know," he said, looking at me through dreamy, half-closed, bedroom-eyes. "Yale is one possibility, I guess. But it could have been any of us, including me or you."

"Me?" I said, sitting up with a splash. "Why would I say I saw Mike Palmer and then change the camera feeds so he wasn't there?"

"To cause confusion and suspicion. To turn me

against Yale. To make us all turn against each other."

"But I didn't—I would never—"

"Olivia," Marcus said softly, pinning my legs between his and stopping me in my defense. "I don't think you did it. It's just one of the many possibilities."

"Then tell me what you do think happened," I insisted. It wasn't easy channeling rational thoughts with his legs against mine like that.

"I'm not sure," he answered, relaxing his legs, but still boxing mine in gently. "For Palmer to find us this quickly, it probably means he's been following us the whole way. Or he knew where we were headed to begin with. It's possible the house was compromised before we even got here."

"If that's true, what are we still doing here?" I asked, leaning forward.

"I never consider myself safe anywhere," Marcus answered, shrugging his glistening shoulders. "The truth is I don't know what happened tonight, but I believe you saw Palmer, and that means the CAMFers know we're here. In this house. Which means we have to be more careful than ever."

"I'm glad you believe me," I said, leaning back again. "But you could have backed me up out there."

"I know," he said, his eyes drifting down below my neck, a small smile playing across his lips.

I followed his gaze to find that the front of my tank was now soaked, the thin gray fabric adhering to my skin and making my nipples very present.

Oh, he was so pleased with himself.

And he was kind of starting to piss me off again.

I crossed my arms over my chest and glared at him.

His eyes rose to my face, the smile quickly turning to a frown. "And you're right. I should have backed you up, but I didn't want to freak anyone out more than they already were. Honestly, I'm not even sure we should go forward with this anymore. I mean, if the CAMFers already know we're here, maybe we should scrap the whole plan and get out while we still can."

"And leave Samantha for them?" I asked, appalled. I had never heard Marcus question his own mission or doubt himself like this. Was it because of me, and what was developing between us? Was he trying to protect me? "We can't do that," I insisted. "I can't do that."

"Not even if you knew it was highly unlikely they'd be able to take her?"

"What is that supposed to mean? Why wouldn't they be able to?"

"Because," Marcus said, exhaling heavily and looking away, avoiding my gaze, "Samantha James is a member of a very powerful cult called The Hold. A cult her father presides over as head Priest. And, because of that, she has a posse of followers and bodyguards watching her pretty much twenty-four seven."

"Wait a minute, The Hold? The thing that guy at the gun club kept mentioning?"

"Yes, that thing," Marcus said, rolling "thing" off his tongue like it was a drop of poison.

"And he knew your mom because—"

"He's a member of The Hold, and so was she," Marcus finished for me. He was looking down at his hands in the water, as he continued. "It's a long story. A long complicated story, but the whole thing kind of started with my grandparents. They were both full-blooded Tenino People; that's a Native American tribe back in Oregon. They were shamans—Spiritwalkers, they called themselves. And they both came to this belief that humanity would evolve into pure spirit beings, that we would lose our husks of flesh and become creatures of light and energy, not in the next world, but in this one. Their teachings began to spread, mostly within the Tenino and a few other tribes, but that was way before I was born when my mom was a kid. I don't think they really meant to start a religion. They were just listening to the spirits of their ancestors. But when babies started being born with PSS, things got out of hand."

"Your grandparents started a cult?" I didn't know what else to say, which bizarre fact to latch onto; there were so many of them in that one explanation. I hadn't known Marcus was Native American, though now his luscious skin color and dark features made more sense.

"They didn't mean to," Marcus said defensively. "But people will exploit anything, especially when it comes to my people."

"So, you're Tenino?" I asked, realizing how little I really knew about him. The way he'd said "my people" had felt so possessive. They were his people, and I was not, as though somehow we'd suddenly been thrown back to the time when my ancestors had oppressed his ancestors. And who was I kidding? That oppression had never really stopped.

"Only half," Marcus said. "My father wasn't from the tribe. Why? Does it matter?"

"If it's important to you, it matters," I said, pulling my legs up to my chest and resting my chin on my knees.

"Sorry," he said, shaking his head and catching my eyes again. "I'm too sensitive about it. I didn't grow up in the tribe. My mom left the reservation to go to college, and that's where she met my dad. But she was very close to my grandparents, and she tried to help them when The Hold was first starting to latch onto their beliefs and twist them. She was pregnant with me then, and I was born on the reservation. And that's when things got really bad. The Hold believes that anyone born with PSS belongs to them, so they recruited my mom like crazy, and she got sucked into it. She even left my dad, because he was a scientist and he thought the whole thing was ridiculous."

I'd never asked Marcus much about his parents, because they were dead, and gone, and I could see it was a deep wound he avoided as much as possible.

"Then my grandparents died," he continued, "and my mom felt obligated to stay in The Hold to represent their wishes, to help keep it from becoming what they feared it would. But it was a losing battle. And then Danielle was born," he continued, "and she was marked too, and there was no way they were going to let us out after that."

"And by 'marked' you mean she had PSS?"

"Yes." He nodded. "The Hold considers it a divine sign. The Marked are the first proof of the spirit evolution."

"What the hell is a spirit evolution?"

"They believe, eventually, that everyone will have PSS. Not just partially," he added, "but wholly. Humanity will become whole beings of pure energy without bodies."

"Well, that's different," I said. "But what about your mom and dad? Did they get back together?" They'd both been in the car-train collision that had left Marcus and his sister orphans. I knew that much. "Did he join The Hold?"

"No." Marcus shook his head. "The deeper she went, the worse it got. The Hold has certain policies it presses on its members. At first they're suggestions, but eventually, they become mandates."

That didn't sound good. What had they asked her to do?

"They wanted her to marry someone within The Hold," Marcus explained before I could ask. "But she was still in love with my dad. And they were still married. So, she got word to him, and he snuck us all out. But The Hold wasn't far behind," Marcus said, and I could feel the water ripple as his body tensed. "There was a car chase." I knew what was coming next. Why Marcus had told Shotgun that his mother was dead thanks to The Hold. "My dad was driving, and he must have thought he could get across the train tracks in time and lose them for good."

Marcus's parents had died running for their lives, or at least for their love.

I looked across the tub at him, the water lapping between us. He was so brave and good and gorgeous in his vulnerability that it overwhelmed me. It made me feel like just knowing him was a gift I didn't deserve and could never earn. Of all the girls in the world, why would he pick me to trust, to confide in, to sit in a bathtub with pouring out his heart?

"Are you pissed that I didn't tell you about The Hold earlier?" he asked, completely misreading my silence.

"No." I shook my head, feeling the wet tips of my hair brush against my knees. At least he was telling me now, before I went in there and found Samantha all wrapped up in a cult.

"I know what you're thinking," he said, his face dark and serious. "My life is totally fucked up."

"That wasn't what I was thinking," I objected, reaching out my ghost hand and touching his leg. "Everyone's life is fucked up. That's not your fault. It's just life."

He leaned forward and caught my hand in his. "Thank you," he said, his eyes warming me despite the fact that the bath was growing cold and we were both turning into human-sized prunes.

"What about after the accident?" I asked. "Didn't The Hold try to take you?"

"I honestly don't know," Marcus said. "I mean I was dead. And Danielle hid. Maybe they thought we were all dead, and they didn't want to have to explain to the police why they'd chased a family of four into an oncoming train. All I know is they never bothered us again. By the time I got out of the hospital, The Hold had moved its headquarters out of Oregon and gone underground. That was eleven years ago, and we've had nothing to do with each other since."

"Until now," I clarified, certain things finally

falling into place. "Until we came for Samantha and you needed guns."

"I figured they at least owed me that," Marcus said, bitterness creeping into his voice. "The guys at the gun club are way down on the totem pole. All I had to do was tell them I was marked and that I needed supplies. I didn't expect any of them to realize who I was."

"And now The Hold knows you're here in Indianapolis, their new headquarters."

"Not necessarily," he said. "If anything, they probably think I was arming myself against the CAMFers, and I've gone back to Oregon. They would never expect me to move against them."

"But taking Samantha is moving against them." What had Marcus gotten us into this time? "And you just told me that she's heavily guarded. How did you expect me and Passion to get her out? And why? You said it yourself earlier. If she's guarded like that, then she's perfectly safe from the CAMFers."

"Just because something is kept, doesn't mean it's safe," Marcus said, staring at me. "Ask my mom."

And there we had it. This wasn't only about saving Samantha from the CAMFers. It was about saving her from The Hold. Saving a young woman trapped in a cult, just like his mother had been. Except this time, we didn't even know if she wanted to be saved.

"You think Samantha is in danger from The Hold?" It wasn't really a question.

"I know she is," he said. "And from the CAMFers, if they figure out a way to get her out before we do."

"And you really think Passion and I can do this?" I asked, more unsure than I'd ever been before. "That we can get Samantha away from not just one group of crazies, but two?"

"Yes," he said, confidence in me shining from his eyes.

10

OUT OF THE BATHTUB
AND INTO THE FIRE

"**A**ren't you cold?" I asked, my teeth chattering a little. I cast a longing glance across the room to the white fluffy towels hanging on a heated chrome towel rack.

"You're the one with clothes on," Marcus said, smirking. "Get out and get us some towels."

"But it will be colder out there," I argued, "and you're the man. What ever happened to chivalry?"

"You just want to see my bare ass again," he teased. "Admit it."

"No, never. I'll even close my eyes."

"Really?" he said, sounding disappointed.

"Yes, really," I said, squeezing my eyes shut.

There was a moment of silence, perhaps the sound

of Marcus nursing his bruised ego, followed by a splash and a slosh of the water in my direction as he climbed out of the tub.

I stole a glance just in time to see his gorgeous ass stroll across the bathroom and grab a towel. He wrapped it around his waist and turned toward me.

"Hey, you peeked," he accused, acting appalled as he brought a towel over and held it out for me.

"Only a little," I admitted, standing up in the tub and feeling like a drowned rat. I stepped out, my basically see-through tank top clinging to me, cold water cascading down my legs and making a puddle on the floor around me like I'd peed myself. Yeah, sexy!

But Marcus must have felt differently, because when he wrapped me in the warm white towel, he pulled me into his arms, wrapping himself around me as well.

I looked up, and found his mouth descending toward mine. It was a gentle kiss at first, but there was heat behind it. I could feel it building in both of us.

His hands slipped inside my towel, trailing warmth across my damp skin right through my clothes. I kissed him back, running my hands over his shoulders and around his neck.

"We—should probably—stop," he panted, the third or fourth time we came up for air.

"I know," I groaned, resting my head on his shoulder. My towel was on the floor, and for one mad moment I wanted to yank his off too. This is what I wanted. My whole body was screaming for it. And so was his.

"Olivia Anne Black," he said, whispering my name

against my wet hair, almost like a prayer. "You are a beautiful and amazing creature."

My face was pressed against his chest, inches from his PSS, the blue beauty of it swirling in my peripheral vision. I wanted to touch it. I didn't want to be afraid anymore, holding back. I wanted to know I was safe with him no matter what.

"Hey, I'm up here," he said, touching my chin and tilting my head up towards his. He was smirking a little.

"This is you too," I said, placing my ghost hand on his ribs, reveling in his quick intake of breath.

"Yes, it is," he said, glancing down at my hand, his breath coming even faster.

"Why do you think we have PSS?" I asked, trailing my fingers inward, marveling at the incredible beauty of his ice-like ribs, his heart and lungs pulsing in blue tranquility. You might think it would be grotesque staring into someone's chest cavity. But there was nothing gross about Marcus with his shirt off, PSS or not. Maybe it was because it was all blue, and glowy, and intricate. "It's beautiful," I sighed, "but you have to admit, it's kind of weird."

"No weirder than human cells," he said, his voice gone suddenly husky, "or hair made of dead protein, or the fact that we have two legs instead of three. It's simply a product of evolution."

"Spiritual evolution, like your grandparents believed? Are you and I becoming pure spiritual beings?"

"Um, no," he said, his eyes transfixed on my touch, his body swaying toward mine. "It isn't religion. It's biology and science. We definitely aren't pure."

His hands were stroking my back. It was like we were having two very different conversations, one with our brains and mouths about PSS, and one with our bodies that was definitely not.

"But what about the powers?" I argued. "Being able to reboot or reach into someone, that's not normal."

"I don't know," he said. "PSS is a part of our body, and all parts of the human body work very hard to keep it alive. Why should it seem unusual that our PSS would develop that too?"

"I never thought of it that way, I guess. I mean yours keeps you alive."

"And your hand kept you alive back in Greenfield," he insisted.

"So what about Jason, or Nose or Yale? How has their PSS ever helped them?"

"Maybe it hasn't. Yet. But maybe like you and me and Danielle, when they have the need, their PSS will develop a power to save them."

It was a theory Marcus and I had talked about before. That maybe the CAMFers had put us all on their list because we had a power or the potential for one. But whenever I tried to imagine what power Nose or Yale's PSS might develop, it just gave me the giggles.

"But that's only a theory," I said, my fingers roaming again and pausing just at the edge of his PSS.

"Yes, it is," he said, looking into my eyes, almost daring me. "And it could be wrong."

"I don't think it's wrong," I said, staring back at him.

"Neither do I," his breath huffed against my face.

What were we talking about? His theory?

Me touching him? Both?

"Olivia," he said. A hope. A plea. More than a name or a word.

"I'm afraid of what will happen," I whispered, looking down at my hand there, so close.

"Nothing bad," he promised, leaning into me and pressing his lips against my forehead.

Isn't this what I'd wanted? To lose my fear of this. Of him. Of us.

Slowly, I slid my ghost fingers over his PSS, skimming the surface like water, feeling silky pleasure leaking out of me and into me through my fingertips. My hand felt electrified, like all the cells or energy or whatever had been zapped at once and every tiny particle of me was racing around telling all the other particles how good it was, how good he was, how much I should touch him like that more and more and more.

And then as I watched, drowning in that sensation, the most amazing thing happened—the PSS of my ghost hand began to swirl and form patterns. At first it looked like random streaks and curves, but quickly the designs took on more clarity, forming thin lines of veins and arteries, the crystal outlines of joints and bones, the minute detail of each carpal and metacarpal coming into clear focus.

"Whoa," I said, yanking my fingers from Marcus's PSS, but breaking contact didn't change anything. My ghost hand still had ethereal bones and blood. I looked up at Marcus, and he was staring down at my hand too, a small sad smile settling across his lips.

"That used to happen to Danielle when she was

healing me," he said, putting his hand gently under mine and raising it to his mouth. "I wondered if it would work with you." He kissed the end of my ghost fingertips, one at a time, as we both watched the PSS bones and blood vessels slowly fade until my ghost hand was simply an ethereal outline again.

"That's amazing," I said, touching his lips, feeling them curve into a happier smile. "But how does it work? What does it do?"

"She had this idea that it meant we could transfer our PSS," he said, frowning against my fingertips. "Like I was giving her some of mine while she was giving me some of hers. Some sort of energy exchange. But the effect never lasts."

"What did you feel when I touched you?" I asked, letting my hand fall away from his mouth. "Because I felt—something."

"What I always feel when you touch me," he said, his eyes blazing into mine.

Suddenly, I was crushed against him, my hand smashed between us. His lips were on mine, one hand tangled in my hair, the other yanking my hips against him. The next thing I knew I had my legs wrapped around his waist and his face was buried in my neck, his breath hot and panting, his lips trembling against my skin, maybe saying my name. It was hard to tell. We were teetering on the edge of something very specific, and we both knew it. And there were words tumbling toward my lips too. Words I'd never said to a guy. Three words I'd only ever said to my mom, and my dad, and Emma.

"I want you," I said, stroking the back of his neck.

Not the exact words I'd been thinking of, but close enough.

"I want you too," he said, pulling back and looking at me, his arms squeezing me so tightly I could barely breathe. "But not in a bathroom." I felt his hands on my hips, his strong arms lifting me gently out and away, my feet finding the floor again.

About the time I realized he didn't have his towel on anymore, he was quickly bending down and picking it back up to tie it around his hips. But it didn't lay flat in the front. Not by a long shot.

"And not in a room full of cameras with Yale, Nose and Jason watching," he added.

"Oh my God," I said, frantically looking around the bathroom.

"There aren't any in here," he assured me. "But there is one out there." He nodded toward the door to the master bedroom. "And in pretty much every room in this house."

"That sort of kills the mood, doesn't it?" I said, turning and crossing to the tub to retrieve my sweatpants and pull them on.

"Hey, I thought you wanted me," he teased, trying to grab my hand and pull me back to him.

"I do," I said, handing him his boxers and his jeans. "But not with the whole world watching. I want you all to myself."

"Well, then we should probably wait until we have our own tent again," he said, smiling wickedly.

"Then let's hurry up and get this mission over with."

"Agreed," he said, pulling me to him and kissing me again. "Do you want me to walk you to your room?"

"No, I'll be fine," I said, pulling away from him reluctantly. "I'll see you in the morning. Good night."

"Olivia," he said, a catch in his voice.

I turned to look at him, and I saw it in his eyes. For a moment I thought he was going to say it. Those three words. The three words I'd almost said moments before but had changed at the last second.

"I'm sorry I let you down," he said, running his hand through his damp hair. "I promise that Palmer will never get near you again."

"You didn't let me down." I crossed to him and touched his face. He looked so tired. "Now get some sleep," I said, kissing him one more time before I headed back to my own bedroom.

11

DOG TAGS

I woke in my curtained bed, my hair still damp, my body relaxed, and I couldn't help the smile that crept across my face as I remembered my early morning bath with Marcus.

I stretched and rolled over. The clock next to the bed said it was 11:30 a.m. It had been a long time since I'd slept in on a Sunday, and not even the reeking matchbook next to the Walther on my nightstand was going to ruin that.

I threw back the duvet, and got dressed in some sweats and a t-shirt. I wasn't ready to wear Anne Clawson's expensive clothes, wasn't willing to become her just yet. I had one more day to be Olivia.

After brushing my teeth and running a brush

through my hair, I made my way downstairs to see what everyone else was up to.

Passion was sitting at the kitchen table, nursing a cup of orange juice, looking like she hadn't woken up much before I had. She glanced at me and gave me a shy smile. "Nose made fried potatoes and eggs," she said, gesturing toward a huge skillet on the stove with her bandaged hand. All she had on it was a gauzy wrap around her palm and the web of her thumb. "It's pretty good heated up in the microwave," she added.

"A microwave," I moaned, reveling in the promise of instantly hot food.

I went to the pan, filled up a plate, and nuked it for a minute. Nose always added cool stuff to his scrambled eggs, and this version had diced pepperoni, feta cheese, crispy potatoes and onions in it.

As soon as I pulled my plate out of the microwave, I started shoveling it in my mouth, not even waiting until I got to the table. It was amazing.

When I sat down next to Passion, she leaned toward me and said, "I believe you about last night. I believe you saw Mike Palmer."

"Thanks," I mumbled between bites. I was about to ask her why she believed me and what she thought had happened to the camera footage, when Marcus came into the kitchen from downstairs.

Just seeing him made all the heat of the night before come rushing back, and I could see it in his eyes too—a flash of desire quickly masked.

"Good morning," he said, smiling at Passion and me, his laptop in his hands.

"Good morning," Passion said.

I let that stand for both of us. First, because I hated mornings and he knew it. Second, because I was pretty sure anything I said to Marcus would sound like "I want you. Right now. Right here on this kitchen table," no matter what words I actually used. And that would be embarrassing.

"I was hoping you were both finally awake," he said, setting his laptop on the table and sitting down next to Passion. "We need to go over the Samantha James stuff and make sure you know as much as you can." He flipped open his computer and turned it on.

Marcus had a whole file on Samantha James, including a bunch of pictures that looked like they'd been snagged off the Internet. She was pretty in an unusual sort way, willowy and tall like one of those high fashion models. She dressed like one too.

"She has a PSS ear," he said, pointing to a close-up of her face, her long brown hair tucked behind a glowing ethereal left ear. "She's a senior, an only child, and the daughter of one of the richest families in Indianapolis. Her father, Alexander James, is a philanthropist and art collector." Marcus showed us a picture of a dark guy in a dark suit with dark glasses. It was hard to tell what he looked like, other than that. "Her mother, Chloe, owns and manages rental vacation properties in exotic locations, so she travels a lot." The picture of Samantha's mother looked like a picture of a movie star. She was descending the stairs of a private plane. And she was beautiful, tall, and willowy, just like her daughter.

"Samantha is a musical prodigy," Marcus went on. "She's a pianist and composer, and has won international awards for the music she writes. Some people believe it's because of her special ear for music, her PSS ear."

Yippee for Samantha! Of course, a beautiful, modelesque, rich girl would get a socially acceptable ability like a musical ear, while the universe saddled me with a hand that yanked weird stuff out of people.

"Because of her social status and the risk of being kidnapped," Marcus continued, "Samantha has an entourage of security people around her most of the time. But at school she doesn't, other than your usual high school security staff, and that's where you two come in. The goal is for you to get inside her inner circle of friends as quickly as possible. You're going to have to earn her trust," Marcus said, looking at me, "and the fastest way to do that is going to be to show her your PSS."

Passion looked from Marcus to me, then down at her own hands, and she quickly tucked them under the table. Was she actually self-conscious about *not* having PSS?

"So what?" I asked. "You want me to go in there, say 'Hi, nice to meet you,' and pull off my glove?"

"No." Marcus shook his head. "It's going to need to be more subtle than that. We have to assume the CAMFers have an agent in place like they did in Greenfield. It will be someone close to her, probably an adult in a position of authority, which means it could be a teacher. The reveal should only come when you're alone with her. Your cover for wearing gloves is that you have severe eczema and have to wear them to protect your skin. I even put that in your school medical records."

"Okay," I said, wondering if Marcus was going to get around to mentioning the cult thing. He hated to talk about his personal life, and The Hold was so enmeshed with his family and his loss, I knew it would be hard. Still, shouldn't Passion know everything I did?

"So, after Olivia reveals her hand, do we tell Samantha about the CAMFers?" Passion asked.

"No," Marcus said. "She'd just run to her father with that. You need to convince her to come back here with you. And I'll take it from there."

I caught Marcus's eyes and nodded toward Passion, hoping he'd get my signal.

He looked at her, but I could tell he had no idea what I wanted. "Passion, how's your hand?" He took a stab in the dark. "Is it healing up okay?"

"It's fine," she said. "But I should probably go put some more antibiotic stuff on it. Don't want it to get infected." She got up from the table. "I mean, if we're done talking about the mission."

"Yeah, we're done," Marcus said, sliding into Passion's vacated seat as she headed upstairs.

"Don't you think we should tell her about The Hold?" I asked when I was sure she was out of earshot.

"Why?" Marcus asked, looking genuinely surprised.

"Because she's part of the mission. Because we trust her. Because why not?"

"You are way too trusting," he said. "Think about Greenfield, Olivia. People you were sure you could trust ended up trying to kill you. I told her there'd be extra security on Samantha outside of school. That's all she really needs to know."

"You think Passion is a CAMFer spy?" I whispered, appalled.

"I'm not saying that," he said, "but I still don't understand why she decided to come with us. She seems uncomfortable around PSS. She doesn't strike me as a fighter. It doesn't add up. And that's one more reason I want you to get to know her better."

I'd thought Marcus wanted me to get to know Passion because we were going to work as partners and pretend to be cousins. And because she was so sweet and vulnerable. But I should have known better; this was Marcus we were talking about. And now that I thought about it, I wasn't exactly sure where Passion had been after the Palmer thing. At first, she'd been in the kitchen with me, but then she'd gone upstairs. What if she was the one who'd tampered with the camera footage? Mike Palmer had been a regular attendee of her dad's church back in Greenfield. I think he'd even been a deacon or something.

"If you suspect her," I said, feeling panicked, "why use her for this mission? She could sabotage the whole thing, and throw us all to the CAMFers."

"Because you have to keep your friends close," Marcus said, "and your enemies closer."

"Wait. Was that whole thing yesterday about sending her in without me complete bullshit?" I asked, glaring at him.

"That whole thing yesterday," he said, reaching out and touching my face, "was about me being terrified of losing you."

"You're not going to lose me," I said, my anger vanishing.

"You can't promise that," he said. I could see it in his eyes. He was thinking of Danielle. And of his mom and dad. He'd lost a lot of people he'd loved. Not that I qualified for that category. At least, not yet.

"I promise I'll do everything I can to stay safe," I said, turning my face and kissing his palm.

"Everything?" he asked, a desperate gleam in his eye.

"Yes."

"Good," he nodded, dropping his hand, reaching into his pocket, and pulling something out. "I was hoping you'd say that because I want you to wear these."

I stared at the dog tags dangling from the chain in his hands. There were two of them, small, and oblong, yet rounded on the corners, the metal looking like it had been pounded to a thin wafer. Each one was engraved with my fake name, Anne Clawson, plus all her fake stats (birthday, blood type, and religion).

"Dog tags?" I said, staring at him. "You think I'm going to need dog tags?"

"They're not just any dog tags," he said, jingling them in his hand. "Yale made these out of our razor blade. As long as you have them on, the CAMFers won't be able to trace you or detect your PSS. We already tested them with the minus meter, and they work like a charm."

I stared at the things dangling from his hand. Since the moment we'd left Greenfield, I'd let Marcus handle the items I'd pulled out of people. The bullet from Jason didn't work anymore anyway, since it was inside Dr. Fineman's cube. And there was no way I was going to use that cube and risk whisking us forward in time again. As for the blades, whenever I touched them I could feel where Passion was. And I was pretty sure she could feel me back. Which was another reason I'd avoided handling the bullet-cube; if Dr. Fineman (or Julian, or whatever his real name was) ever woke up from his coma, that last thing I wanted was for him to feel me on the other end of it.

"I'm not wearing those," I said to Marcus.

"They won't zap you," he assured me. "Yale and I tested that too and it seems to have worn off. Maybe because it's only one blade and doesn't have the others to resonate with. Anyway, there's still a sensation, but it's more like a tingle than a shock."

"I'm still not wearing them," I said.

"You promised," Marcus said, holding out the tags, his eyes challenging me.

"You tricked me into promising," I objected, knowing I'd lost already.

"But it was still a promise," he said gently.

"Fine." I turned and presented the back of my neck to him. "Put them on me."

First, his arms came over my head, the cold chain brushing against my skin. Then his warm fingers fumbled at the clasp. He finally hooked it, and the dog tags slid down my chest, nestling there.

"They look great," Marcus said, looming over my shoulder and looking down at them.

"Hey." I elbowed him in the ribs and pulled the tags to rest on the outside of my t-shirt.

He sat back down next to me, smirking, as my fingers explored the feel of my new necklace.

"Can you feel where Passion is right now?" he asked, his face serious again.

I turned and stared at him. Oh, he was a clever bastard. Marcus never, ever did anything for only the obvious reason. Yes, the dog tags would hide me from the CAMFers, but they would also help me keep tabs on Passion.

"Try it," he said, nodding at me.

I wrapped my ghost hand around the tags, squeezing them inside my PSS, and instantly knew that Passion was upstairs, not in the bathroom tending to her hand, but in our bedroom, standing at the window. I wasn't surprised, and I didn't doubt the perception; it was that clear.

"It's never been this strong before," I said to Marcus. "I don't like it." I dropped the tags, and the sense of Passion faded, though I could still feel her upstairs, a faint presence haunting the back of my awareness.

"I know," he said, taking my ghost hand in his, "but wear them. For me."

12

UNDERSTANDING PASSION

The rest of the day was weird in its Sunday normalcy. The guys that weren't on security duty played video games, and Passion and I joined in, diligently referring to one another as Anne and Mirabelle to try to get used to it. Marcus found his gun under the couch, and the other guys gave him a hard time about it. I tried to sooth the inner voice that kept reminding me that I'd seen Mike Palmer, and I went on the Internet and looked up the word Shades, but there were way too many hits to narrow it down to a relevant clue. We all did our laundry in the huge washer and dryer, and one of my camp shirts literally fell apart in my hands afterwards. For dinner we ordered cheap pizza and gorged ourselves, then filled in the cracks with giant root beer floats. No one mentioned Palmer, or the CAMFers, or our looming mission to rescue Samantha, and I kept my dog tags tucked inside my shirt, slowly adjusting to the fact that I always knew where Passion was, even when I couldn't see her. I wasn't sure if she felt it too, though I did catch her glancing at me more than usual.

At ten, Marcus and Yale went on security detail, and Jason and Nose decided to watch some horror movie on the big screen in the living room. Since Passion and I had to get up for our first day at Samantha's school, Edgemont High, in the morning, we decided to head to bed.

As soon as we got to our room, I crawled into my curtained cocoon, but I could hear Passion moving around, going in and out of the closet as she tried to pick out the perfect outfit for the next day. She was nervous, and so was I, but her restlessness wasn't going to help anything. It was just going to drive me crazy and keep both of us up all night.

I pulled my curtain open and found her trying on yet another long-sleeved top.

"It looks great," I offered. "So did the last one. They all look great on you."

She turned to me, an annoyed expression on her face. "Aren't you nervous, or terrified, or anything?"

"Yes," I answered honestly. "I'm nervous and terrified, but what I wear tomorrow isn't going to change that."

"Really?" She glanced down at my t-shirt, and I followed her gaze to see the dog tags dangling there, completely out in the open.

I leaned back, but I didn't tuck them out of sight. If the shit was going to hit the fan about Passion's blades, it was long overdue. Maybe Marcus didn't trust her, but I needed to if we were going to do this Samantha James thing together. And she needed to trust me.

"Can you feel them?" I asked, touching the tags. It was a stupid question. Of course she could. She'd known the tags were her blade, even though it looked completely different now. Just the way Jason had known his bullet was in Dr. Fineman's box.

"Only when you have them," she said, looking away.

"Can you tell where I am?" I asked, and she looked back at me, surprise flickering in her eyes.

"Yes," she said. "Can you feel me too?"

I nodded.

"Like twins," she said, crossing and sitting in a chair next to my bed, her long legs folded under her. "Twins are supposed to be able to tell where the other one is. But it isn't true."

"It's not?" I asked, wondering how she could be so sure.

"No." She shook her head. "I'm a twin, but my sister drowned when we were twelve. I could never feel where she was. I still can't."

I didn't know what to say. This was the longest conversation Passion and I had ever had, and she'd just told me about her dead twin sister. Nothing about that had ever circulated through the Greenfield rumor mill. I don't think anyone in Greenfield even knew.

Then again, Passion's family hadn't moved to town until her freshman year of high school. And maybe that's why they'd moved. To start over after the death of her sister. Maybe that was why—

"Is that why you cut?" I blurted, my tongue flapping before my brain could think to stop it.

"No," she said. If she was put off by my bluntness, she didn't show it. "Maybe. I don't know. There are so many reasons to cut."

"I don't get it," I said. "Does it make you feel better?"

"Feel better?" she asked, pondering that. "Maybe. But mostly it makes you feel something."

"Yeah, but there are tons of other ways to feel something without doing that."

Passion looked down at my ghost hand, glowing against the bed sheet. "What if cutting was the only way to find out something important about yourself?"

"You really believe that?" I looked down at her hands. The injured one only sported a small Band-Aid now, but her skin was so pale I could see the blue web of her veins crisscrossing just beneath the surface.

"Sometimes," Passion said, looking up at me. "But it doesn't matter. I don't cut anymore. You cured me, I guess."

My head snapped up, my eyes boring into her.

"I haven't done it since you pulled them out of me." Her eyes flashed down to the dog tags, then back up to my face. "I haven't even wanted to." She sounded almost sad, like she was grieving the loss of a friend or something.

"But what about at the hospital? I saw you with your wrists all bandaged? And you had fresh cuts that night down in Palmer's basement."

"They weren't fresh," she said. "They were from before, and they were already healing. My parents made me wear those bandages to the hospital. They were pretty freaked out that day. They'd never seen my scars, and to find out like that, in the nurse's office—it completely humiliated them, and all they wanted to do was cover it up. Even when they listened to your mom's advice that night and took me to the hospital, they didn't want anyone to see. They didn't realize that all those bandages just made it worse." She smiled wryly. "The receptionist in the emergency room totally thought I'd tried to kill myself. But it did get us a room faster."

"Wait, your parents didn't know you were cutting until *that day*? But you were seeing my mom. How could they not know?"

"Um, because they didn't want to," Passion said. "And I wasn't seeing your mom for my cutting. I mean, we talked about it, but that wasn't the reason my parents sent me to her."

"Then why did they send you?"

Passion looked away from me, and I followed her gaze. She was staring at *The Other Olivia*, some wistful, deeply pained look in her eyes.

"You don't have to tell me if you don't want to," I said. "It's none of my business."

"No, it's okay." She looked back at me. "My parents sent me to your mom because I like girls."

"Like girls?" I repeated. "You mean *like* like girls?" Well, that certainly explained why she'd rebuffed Nose's advances.

"I'm pretty sure," Passion nodded. "I mean, I've

never been attracted to a guy in my life. And when my parents finally figured that out, they kind of freaked. They didn't want me to change in the girl's locker room anymore, or wear shorts, like that was what had caused it or something."

"Oh my God, that's terrible," I blurted.

"Yeah." She shrugged. "But it made other things easier to hide. And eventually they sent me to your mom, which ended up being a good thing. It helped just to have someone to talk to."

It was weird how you could know someone on the surface and think you understood who they were, or why they did things and then, when you really got to know them, you discovered this hidden underworld of hurt and pain and confusion. Did everyone have that? Were we all just broken people wandering around pretending we were fine? I had always thought of my life as kind of tragic, because I'd lost my dad, but that was nothing compared to what both Marcus and Passion had lived through.

"Listen," I said, taking a deep breath. "I owe you an apology. I've been a total asshole to you ever since we left Greenfield."

"Before we left, actually," she corrected me.

"That—is fairly accurate." I agreed. "And I don't have an excuse. Sometimes I'm an ass. My only redeeming quality is that, occasionally, I am capable of realizing it and doing better. That's the most I can promise you. I never meant to take anything from you, and then I was afraid to talk to you about it because I had no idea what to say. But these are yours," I said, grabbing the dog tags and pulling them over my head. "I can have Yale change the name on them." I held them out to her. "And if you don't trust me after the way I've treated you, I totally understand."

"I accept your apology," she said, staring at the dog tags in my hand, "but I don't want those back. And I actually do trust you," she continued, looking me in the eye, "because even when you're being a complete bitch, at least you're not fake."

"Why, thank you. I think."

There was silence between us as I put the dog tags back on, but it was good silence, not the uncomfortable wall that had been hanging between us for weeks.

Suddenly, my cell phone started ringing, muffled but persistent.

"Crap, what time is it?" I asked, scrambling for my duffle bag, but I already knew. It was 10:30 on Sunday night. The exact time I'd set up for Emma to call me this week and let me know what was up with my mom, and Dr. Fineman, and everyone else in Greenfield. And I'd completely forgotten.

I found the phone in a side-pocket and pulled it out. "Hello?" I said, hoping it hadn't already bumped the call to messages.

"Olivia?" Emma's voice sounded in my ear.

"Hey you," I answered. We'd only talked two other times since I'd left Greenfield. Nose had put some kind of scrambler in the phone but he'd still advised me not to use it too often, or for too long.

"I was afraid you weren't going to pick up," Emma said. There was an undertone to her voice. She had something to tell me. Something bad.

"Yeah, sorry. Just a minute." I gestured to Passion,

letting her know I was going to take the call into the bathroom for some privacy. As I pulled the door shut, I saw her returning to the closet to try on yet another shirt.

I sat down on the toilet seat in the dark and braced myself for the news that the evil doctor had woken from his coma. Maybe this would light a fire under people's butts to realize I really had seen Mike Palmer. "Okay, go ahead. What's up?" I asked, trying to sound casual even while my insides wound themselves into a knot.

"It's your mom, Liv. She left Greenfield yesterday. We don't know where she went. She wouldn't even tell my mom. But she was in bad shape. I can tell my parents are really worried, even though they're trying not to show it."

"She left?" I asked. "What about her practice and her clients? What about her comatose boyfriend?"

"He's still in a coma. And she closed her practice."

"She closed her practice?" Fuck. That was bad. My mom hadn't even closed her practice when my dad was dying. "Are you sure she doesn't know where I am?" I drilled Emma.

"Well, I didn't tell her," Emma said defensively. "I don't even know where you are."

"I know. Sorry. This just doesn't sound like my mom."

"She's changed, Liv, since you left. She's been through a lot."

"And I haven't?" I asked, my hackles up instantly. If my mother was some kind of changed, broken woman, was that my fault? Yes, I'd left, but I hadn't really had a choice, and if she would have believed me at all or been willing to help me, things might have been different. She'd made her decisions. And I'd made mine.

"I didn't mean it like that," Emma said. "You've been through a lot too. We're just worried. Do you have any idea where she might have gone?"

"I don't know. My grandma's, maybe? She lives in Orlando near Disney World. They don't get along, but we went there once when I was a kid and stayed for a while." My mom and I had stayed with my grandma for about a month when I was four, after my parents had a very big fight. I had not enjoyed that trip at all. My grandma was a cranky, bitter old widow who had bad-mouthed my dad, called me chubby, and treated my mother like a child. The only good part about the trip had been the frequent visits to Disney World.

Eventually, my mother had a much bigger fight with my grandma than she'd ever had with my dad, and we returned to Greenfield. And it was after that trip that my mom went back to school and got her PHD in psychology, probably because she'd finally realized my grandma was crazy and she needed to figure out why. We hadn't visited Grandma since, but it was one of the few places my mom might go.

The other possibility was my Uncle Bert, who was an architect and lived in New York—the state, not the city. They'd been close as kids, but since he'd moved to the East Coast they'd drifted apart.

"Do you know your grandma's number?" Emma asked. "I could have my mom try to call, or you could."

"No, I don't have her number. I'm sure my mom will be fine. She probably just needed to get away."

"Okay," Emma said, sounding unsure, like she was more worried about my mother than I was. And I *was* worried about her. But I had a lot of other shit to worry about, and there was nothing I could do about her leaving. Besides, at least she'd left that CAMFer psycho's bedside, and wouldn't be in Greenfield if any more of them showed up.

"What about Passion's family?" I asked Emma. "Are they looking for her?"

"No. They're still sticking to that story about her being at some Christian rehab camp."

Unbelievable. No wonder Passion had needed therapy. She was missing and her parents didn't give a rat's ass.

"And there's been no sign of Mike Palmer," Emma added, "but the rumor going around is he retired and went to live on some ranch in New Mexico."

No, Mike Palmer wasn't in New Mexico. I was sure of that.

"Everything else is the same old boring Greenfield," Emma grumbled. "There's been no sign of the CAMFers. I almost wish I'd gone with you guys."

"I wish you had too," I said, missing her. Missing home, and my dad, and even my mom so hard for a minute that it lodged in my throat and hurt my chest.

"Well, I know you can't tell me much. But you're okay, right?"

"Yeah, I'm good. We're getting a break from the tents for a few days and staying in a real house."

"Oh, good," Emma said.

I could tell she wanted to ask more, and I wished I could tell her about the mansion, and Indy, and The Hold, but I couldn't.

"How are you and Marcus?" she asked. It was a loaded question. One I wanted to spend hours answering. But Nose had warned me about talking too long. The longer Emma and I spoke the more easily the call could be traced, and having that in the back of your mind didn't exactly make for chatty conversations.

"We're fine. Yeah, good. But I should probably go. Thanks for calling, Em, and for telling me about my mom."

"Sure, okay." I could hear the worry in her voice. "I'll send you a text setting up the next call. Be safe, Liv."

"I will. I love you, Emma."

"I love you too."

I hung up the phone and I sat in the dark bathroom. Emma and Greenfield and my mom—it didn't feel like that world even existed anymore. It was fiction, like a bunch of characters in a story I'd read once.

I'd barely even thought about my dad in the last few weeks. In Greenfield, everything had reminded me of him, every day, a thousand times a day. But since I'd left, everything had been new, without any mark of him on it, except for *The Other Olivia*. Thank God I had that, but still, the further I traveled away from home and the more I experienced, the harder it was to remember him. And if I lost those memories, what did I have left? A singed painting. Even as I sat there, I tried to call up his face in my mind, and I couldn't. I couldn't see my dad's face.

"Olivia," Passion's voice came through the door. "I really need to pee."

"Sorry," I said, getting up and opening the door.

Passion and I went to bed late that night, but I was awake even later, thinking of my dad, trying to call forth his face. And then it came to me, right before I drifted off to sleep.

But it finally came.

13

FIRST DAY AT EDGEMONT HIGH

Edgemont High was not only one of the wealthiest public high schools in Indianapolis; it was one of the wealthiest in the country. It had two different campuses, one for lower classmen, and one for upper classmen. The "New Student Welcome Packet" Marcus had handed me that morning had a double-sided, multi-folded map of the Senior Campus.

Passion and I had come from a high school of 116 students. Edgemont High had a larger population than the entire town of Greenfield. Add to that the fact that we'd been camping and hiding in the woods for a couple of weeks, and it probably wasn't a huge surprise that as soon as Passion and I stepped into the

Edgemont High School Senior Complex, we freaked.

We clung to each other just inside the door as bodies rushed past us, bumping us, invading our personal space, oblivious to us.

Someone slammed into me from behind, crushing my designer back pack into my shoulder blades, and almost knocking me to the floor.

"Stop blocking the fucking doorway," a stocky, dark-haired girl said, and then she was gone, swallowed by the masses.

When I straightened up, I could feel the coolness of the dog tags brush against my skin under my shirt. They might keep me safe from CAMFers, but they wouldn't do anything to protect Passion and me from an entire campus of hostile rich kids. At least we could be fairly confident none of them were armed. Every public school over a certain size was required to have weapons scanners built into all its entry points. We'd probably been scanned as soon as we stepped through the door, which was precisely why we'd left our guns at home.

Someone else almost ran into Passion, so we shuffled to one side, arm in arm, trying to skirt the edges of the mob—but that put us in front of the lockers.

"Get out of the way."

"Hey, I need in there."

"What's your problem?" a tall hipster guy asked, staring at my gloved hands. "You do know that Michael Jackson is dead, right?"

We moved again, out into the center of the hallway, and were quickly swept along.

A bell rang right over our heads and the frantic mayhem, if possible, increased.

I'd had enough. I planted my feet firmly on the floor, held onto Passion with one hand, and grabbed at the arm of a passing student with the other.

"Where are we?" I asked the tall geeky-looking guy I'd pulled out of the stream of teenage humanity flowing past us.

He looked down at the school map I was holding, jabbed at it with his finger, and said, "Right here." And then he was gone, pulled back into the torrent rushing down the hallway.

"Great," I growled under my breath, turning to Passion. Marcus had supposedly dropped us off at the school entrance nearest the office, but it had only taken five minutes for us to get hopelessly and completely lost. According to Geek Guy, we weren't even in the right hallway.

"Let's wait for the second bell," Passion said. "It's our first day. We can be late."

"Good idea," I said, noticing a small alcove with drinking fountains not too far from where we stood. I nodded toward it. "Let's see if we can make it over there."

With Passion in the lead, we pushed our way through the moving crowd, looks of momentary annoyance flashing past us like the fast-forward of a first-day-of-school nightmare.

We made it to the drinking fountains, and I took a drink. Who knew when we might find water again in this labyrinth someone had disguised as a high school.

Passion took a drink too, as I watched the students

rush by, marveling at their diversity, and yet their oneness. Every one of them knew where they were going, and why, and seemed to belong. Except for us. We dressed the part, but we were pretty poor imposters.

The bell rang again, its trill echoing around us. Suddenly the flow of students in the hallway drained away, leaving behind only a few stragglers rushing madly past, a couple of dropped flyers for some upcoming event swirling in their wake.

I looked up and down the hall and saw the last classroom doors slam shut.

"All clear," I said to Passion, looking at the map of the school again. "I think if we take a right up here, and then a left, we'll be heading in the direction of the office."

"Lead the way," Passion said.

We passed several classrooms and a large double doorway marked Auxiliary Gym Two. Holy shit. This school was so big they had two extra gyms?

Just as we rounded the first corner, we began to hear a strange sound, like motorized bees, buzzing down the hallway toward us.

I stopped, looking at Passion, and she looked at me.

A herd of teenagers on Segways came barreling around the corner and we stood, immobilized with surprise.

We didn't even have time to move aside before the leader of the pack was on us. Samantha James, tall, willowy, beautiful and with a presence that commanded your attention, pulled her Segway up right in front of us and stepped off of it.

"You must be the new girls," she said, tucking her hair behind her PSS ear and staring at Passion while completely ignoring me. "Welcome to Edgemont High."

Passion and I had rehearsed this first encounter, but we'd never expected it to come so soon. What were the chances that in a high school as big as Edgemont we'd run into Samantha in the first ten minutes? They were slim to none. Which probably meant Marcus had been completely wrong and The Hold had been expecting us.

Anyway, even if that was true, I had to play it cool. I had to act like I didn't know they knew. And hopefully Passion would remember what we'd talked about concerning Samantha's PSS.

"Wow, your ear, it's beautiful," Passion said, exactly like we'd practiced. "Is that PSS? I've never seen it before."

"Yes," Samantha said, looking Passion up and down, a puzzled but intent expression on her face.

The students behind Samantha, two guys and three girls, dismounted their Segways, but they didn't come forward, or smile, or even really look at us. They just stood there watching Samantha stare at Passion, as if waiting for some cue. What was this? The Edgemont welcome committee? If so, they definitely needed to brush up on their hospitality.

"I'm Mirabelle," Passion said, holding up the conversational end of our plan much better than I was. "And this is my cousin, Anne. And yeah, it's our first day. We were trying to find the office to get our schedules."

Samantha didn't even glance my way or indicate

she'd heard the introduction. She was still staring at Passion, her eyes traveling up and down the poor girl's body, practically undressing her. There was a look of such intensity on Samantha's face, I felt myself blush just being a witness to it. And that look certainly wasn't lost on Passion who began to turn several distinct shades of pink as well.

"So, it's this way, right?" I said, gesturing down the hall, limp map in my hand, trying to break the spell of that look.

Finally, Samantha James glanced at me with a quick flick of her eyes, a two second evaluation followed by immediate, unmitigated dismissal.

"I can take you to the office," she said, directing her words at Passion. "I'm Samantha, by the way. Samantha James."

Ouch. I mean I was used to being overlooked by the male half of the population. Adding the other half to that equation wasn't too big of a blow to my ego. But still, acknowledging my existence would have been nice.

"These are my friends," Samantha said, waving at the group behind her. "This is Renzo," she said, indicating the tall, dark, handsome guy wearing a black leather jacket and sunglasses who'd stepped up next to her. "And this is Dimitri," she said, gesturing at a thick-necked, blond jock-type. "And this is Eva, Lily, and Juliana," she said, introducing the three girls, all gorgeous, but with smiles that never quite reached their eyes.

The whole gang stepped forward and said hi to us both, but I thought I saw a flash of jealousy on both

Dimitri's and Lily's faces as they appraised Passion. What had we stepped into? I wasn't sure it served our purpose to have Passion intrude on what seemed to already be a rather complicated love triangle. Then again, it might be exactly the thing we needed to break Samantha away from it all. Or I could be completely off base. My social radar was notoriously awful.

"Hi, everyone," Passion said, shyly. "What's with the Segways?"

"Dimitri is the president of the Physics Club," Samantha explained, "and we have the science fair coming up. We're trying to get the turning-radius perfectly calibrated for the obstacle course."

So, he was a jock-type with brains. "You're racing Segways for the science fair?" I choked out, thinking of the three failed volcanoes I'd entered in the Greenfield science fair three years in a row.

"Technically, the obstacle course is just to raise funds," Dimitri said proudly. "The parents love to bet on it. But the real project is the Segways themselves. We build them from scratch."

I didn't even know what to say to that.

The classroom door nearest us swung open, and a guy came out holding a pass in his hand, probably on his way to the bathroom.

"Hey," Samantha said, grabbing him by the arm and propelling him onto her Segway. "Take this back to the physics lab," she ordered. "Follow Dimitri. He'll show you what to do. The rest of you head back, and I'll meet you in the practice room next period. I'm going to help Mirabelle and her cousin get to the office."

"No, really," Passion said. "Just point the way. We'll be fine."

What was she doing? We were supposed to be making friends with Samantha, not blowing her off.

"It's no problem," Samantha said, turning to Passion with a radiant smile. Her friends and the bathroom boy were already mounting their Segways and rolling away.

"Well, thanks," Passion said, looking at me, a question in her eyes as we both followed Samantha down the hallway.

Even as we walked, it was clear I was the third wheel, and it was starting to kind of freak me out. Every angle of Samantha's body was turned toward Passion, tuned to Passion, focused on Passion, as she chatted away, telling her about the school, the teachers, the classrooms we were passing, and how much she would love Edgemont.

Passion didn't say much. She didn't really have to. But I might as well have not existed, except, I think, if I hadn't been there, Samantha might have grabbed Passion's hand and tried to run out of the school with her much like Marcus had tried to do with me. It was one of the most awkward walks down a school hallway I'd ever made, and I'd made some awkward ones.

When we got to the office, Samantha sweet-talked the sour-faced secretary immediately.

"Karen, these are all wrong," she said, looking over our class schedules. "Both of them should be in morning physics lab, second period music symposium, and they should have fourth period lunch hour with me. I'll take them around to all the right classes today, but make sure this gets changed in the system before tomorrow." She handed the paperwork back to Karen as if the woman was her personal secretary.

I expected Karen to object. I expected her to say, "Who the hell do you think you are, little missy?" but she didn't even bat an eye. And that's when I knew that Passion and I were in deep trouble. No school secretary I'd met in my life would take orders from a student like that. Samantha had just rearranged our entire class schedule—probably to match hers perfectly—something Marcus had avoided doing when enrolling us because it would have looked way too suspicious.

At that moment, I knew what it must feel like when the predator turns around and suddenly discovers that it has become the prey. One thing still made absolutely no sense, though. If The Hold had known we were coming, if Shotgun had warned them to watch for a boy with a PSS chest and a girl with a ghost hand, why was Samantha James focused on Passion Wainwright and completely ignoring me? Maybe her attraction to Passion was overriding her orders and their plan. Whatever the case, we could probably make it work for us. But I still didn't like the way Samantha had taken charge, like we were just two more tiny cogs in her giant high school machine.

"Come on," Samantha said, ushering Passion and me out of the office. "I want to show you the music wing."

14

A MUSIC FOR PASSION

The entrance to the James Memorial Music Wing was up several flights of stairs and down I-don't-know-how-many non-descript hallways. The plaque on the wall outside the Samantha James Music Hall pretty much explained why the secretary had been so agreeable to Samantha's demands. Money talks. And throwing that money around shuts everyone else up.

Samantha had continued to ignore me and chat up Passion all the way there. And Passion, shy as she was, had done a pretty good job of holding up her end of the conversation by asking Samantha the occasional question about herself and her music. I had given up trying to do anything but be invisible.

Samantha proudly gave us a tour of the music wing, showing us the red velvet seats of the performance hall, the various instrument rooms, and the trophy cases filled with musical awards and trophies, mostly with her name on them. Everywhere we went there were students, lots of them, casting admiring glances at Samantha and envious glances at Passion.

I followed the two of them, biding my time until the three of us were alone so I could show Samantha my ghost hand. But I got the feeling she wasn't going to be that impressed. And maybe it didn't matter anymore. Marcus had wanted us to find an in with Samantha, and it looked like Passion had done that just by being Passion.

"And these are the practice rooms," Samantha said, leading us down a long carpeted hallway with white doors on either side. "They're soundproof and very private." She stopped in front of a door with her name on it and pushed it open.

Inside was a large room with a white baby grand piano in one corner, a couple of armchairs, and a clock on one wall.

"I hope you don't mind," Samantha said almost shyly to Passion, "but I'd really like to play you something."

"Oh, that would be wonderful," Passion said, "but don't we need to get to class?"

"Second period starts in five minutes," Samantha said, glancing at the clock. "And I signed you up for Music Symposium, so this is your next class."

"Well then, sure," Passion said, smiling. "I'd love to hear you play."

"Good," Samantha said, looking at me and nodding

at the door. "You want to give us some privacy?"

It took me a minute to realize she was talking to me, because she hadn't. Ever.

"Excuse me?" I said, staring at her.

"Oh, no." Passion jumped in. "Anne loves music. She'd love to hear you play too."

"Yes, I love music," I said, grinding the words past clenched teeth. No way was I leaving Passion alone in a sound proof room with this narcissistic, woman-eating bitch.

"But it's a special piece. Just for you," Samantha said, looking at Passion.

Like the theme to *Psycho*? This girl was getting seriously creepy.

"I—wow—that's so nice," Passion said. "But I want Anne to hear it. We're really close. We share everything."

Samantha stared at me, appraising, weighing my worth, and I could tell she wasn't impressed.

I held her gaze, barely resisting the urge to flip her off.

"Okay," Samantha said, looking back at Passion. "If you're close, it should be fine." She strode to the piano and sat on the bench. "Pull the chairs up to the piano," she directed us, and Passion and I moved them to the right of the bench, with Passion closest to Samantha.

"Now, don't be afraid," Samantha said to Passion, which seemed like a really odd thing to say right before you serenade someone. Then, she put her long, thin, fingers on the keys and began playing the most haunting, mournful, beautiful piece of music I had ever heard.

Contrary to what Passion had claimed, I was not a huge music fan, especially when it came to classical piano. My tastes ran more in the vein of punk and grunge, with their hard sounds and harsher vocals. But the melody that poured from Samantha's fingers was something else, something beyond music, something that transported me out of that room into the vivid recesses of my own mind.

It carried me away, spinning visions of Passion in my head. I saw Passion the first day I'd met her at Greenfield High. Passion, alone and forlorn, on the bleachers as she sat out of gym class. Passion at her church in her dad's play the time Emma and I had decided to go. Passion in my Calculus class, her pale arms scarred and cut. Passion in the hospital, her mother praying at her bedside. Passion drugged and loopy in Mike Palmer's basement. Passion, every significant moment I'd ever seen or known her, dancing as notes and chords and symphonic progressions in my head and in my heart. It was incredible, and amazing, and terrifying.

The music stopped, and I opened my eyes. I hadn't even realized I'd closed them. I glanced to my side, wondering if Passion had seen and felt the same things I had.

She was staring at Samantha, who had turned on the piano bench. Their eyes were locked, and tears were streaming down Passion's face.

"I know what you've been through," Samantha said softly, reaching out and clasping Passion's left wrist.

I didn't have time to stop her, even when I realized what she was about to do.

Samantha James slid Passion's sleeve up to her elbow, and all three of us looked down at the nasty pattern of pain and punishment mapped out on her pale arm.

Now I could see the tears swimming in Samantha's eyes as she said, "What have you done to yourself?"

"I—it—I was trying to understand," Passion said, her lips trembling.

"Dimitri," Samantha said, "bring me your knife."

And that's when I realized we were no longer alone in the practice room.

Sometime during the private recital for Passion, while we were lost in the magic of Samantha's playing, Dimitri and Renzo had slipped into the room behind us.

They both stepped forward, and Dimitri pulled out a small milky-colored pocket knife.

Samantha took it from him and snapped it open, the sharp blade as strangely colored as the handle.

The entire thing was made of bone, I realized, to escape detection from a weapons scan.

"Hey, what the hell?" I said, rising from my seat, ready to disarm Samantha any way I could.

Arms clamped around me, holding me back, and Renzo's smooth deep voice said softly in my ear, "Take it easy. No one's going to get hurt."

"I have a special ear," Samantha said, still holding the knife out, as she turned her head and showed Passion the ear she was talking about. "Most people think I have a special ear for music, and that is certainly true. But what they don't know or understand is that I can hear PSS."

What the fuck?

"PSS energy is made up of both particles and waves," Samantha went on. "I hear the wave aspect as music. To me, each person's PSS is a unique composition, a distinct symphonic melody."

Holy shit.

"And it doesn't matter how small or deep or secreted away that PSS is," Samantha said, turning the knife slowly in her fingers as Passion watched it, transfixed. "I can still hear it."

Okay, I had no idea what the fuck was going on. If Samantha could hear PSS, why hadn't she called me out on my ghost hand the moment we'd met? Why hadn't she recruited me, instead of ignoring me and fixating on Passion? And what was all this crazy talk about hearing PSS no matter how deep or hidden it was? You either had PSS, or you didn't. And why threaten Passion, a cutter, with a freakin' bone knife?

"Put the knife away," I said, struggling against Renzo's hold. "You're scaring her." When that didn't work, I tried my relax-and-throw-a-reverse-head-butt-move on him, but he was too tall for me to clip his chin, and it only made him grab me more firmly, his arm pressing around my neck, making my dog tags dig into my skin.

"Take her out," Samantha said, nodding at me.

"No!" Passion cried. "Let her stay."

"Does she know?" Samantha asked.

"No," Passion said, shaking her head, "But I trust her."

Did I know what? Fuck. What was going on?

"Fine." Samantha turned the knife in her hands

and presented the handle to Passion. "Show us."

In the entire dossier on Samantha James, Marcus had apparently managed to miss the one crucial piece of information that she was bat shit crazy.

Passion took the knife in her shaking right hand, her thumb still sporting a small Band-Aid from the gun accident.

"You don't have to do this," I pleaded with Passion. "I don't know what you heard in that music, but you don't have to do this." Maybe Samantha had brainwashed her. Maybe that's what her music did—how they got new recruits for The Hold. Shit. I was going to have to use my hand.

Passion must have sensed what I was thinking, because she looked up at me and said, "It's okay, Anne," just as she stabbed the knife into her left thumb, gouging a hole smack in the middle of it.

"Hey!" I yelled, bucking against Renzo.

Passion pulled the knife away, the sharp tip wet and red.

Blood oozed out of the wound.

And so did something else.

Something blue, and glowing, and incandescent, slowly welling from the wound and separating itself from the blood across the curved plane of her thumb like oil from water.

Dimitri leaned over Passion's shoulder and peered down at it. "Looks like her red blood cells are normal," he explained calmly, "but her white cells and plasma are definitely PSS."

15

SURPRISE, MY ASS

I stared at Passion's thumb. I watched blood and PSS well out of her. Liquid PSS. At least that's what Dimitri said it was, and I certainly didn't have a better explanation. Normal people, regular people, did not have blood like that. Even as we stood there, it continued to separate, red blood pooling in one spot, glowing blue pooling in another. Either Passion was an alien, or Samantha had heard PSS pulsing in her veins and this was the proof.

Shit. That was why Passion hadn't wanted me to see her hand when she'd injured it at the gun club. That's what had been smeared on the gun. Her PSS.

"Here, put some pressure on it," Samantha said, pulling a tissue from her pocket and wrapping it around Passion's thumb. "And thank you for showing us," she said, gently taking the knife from Passion's other hand and giving it back to Dimitri.

"I'll go test it in the chemistry lab," he said, producing a plastic baggy from his pocket, slipping the knife into it, and putting them both back in his pocket as he headed out the door.

"Wait—you—I—" I said, looking from Samantha to Passion and back again. Renzo had relaxed his grip, but he was still holding onto me as if he wasn't sure what I'd do.

"Anne," Passion said, locking eyes with me. "I know this is a surprise. I'm sorry I didn't tell you."

Surprise, My Ass. Passion had PSS. She had always had PSS. And she hadn't told me, or Marcus, or any of us. Why would she tell me about her cutting but not about this? What had she said the other night? *What if cutting was the only way to find out something important about yourself?*

"Are you sure it's PSS?" Passion asked Samantha anxiously. "I've never heard of PSS blood. I know people have it on the outside, like your ear, but not blood, not something inside them. And it looks different than yours."

Passion had seen Marcus's PSS, and it was certainly inside of him. But she was right; this was different. Maybe it wasn't PSS.

"I'm sure," Samantha said. "Dimitri needs his little lab test, but I don't. I've been listening to your PSS sing since the moment you walked into the school. The first time I hear someone is always a bit overwhelming: It drowns out everything until I can process it and play it. The music I just played—that's what yours sounds like. It's very strong and complex. I've never heard anything quite like it."

So, Shotgun hadn't ratted us out, and The Hold hadn't been expecting us. Samantha had simply honed in on us because of Passion's loud PSS blood. But what about my hand? Hadn't Samantha heard it too, or had Passion's PSS overwhelmed it and drowned me out?

"But how did you know it was my blood?" Passion asked.

"I wasn't positive at first," Samantha said, "but when I play the music, I know things—where it is, what the person has been through, especially any experiences that have to do with their PSS."

"And you can hear anyone's?" Passion asked, casting a side-long glance at me, her eyes darting, only for a moment, to my gloved right hand.

"Yes, anyone's," Samantha said, following Passion's gaze, but her eyes slid right over me, bored. "Which makes fle—" she stopped herself mid-word and looked back at Passion, "which makes people without PSS relatively uninteresting to me."

Samantha James had almost called me a fleshman. Samantha James, who could supposedly hear the music of everyone's PSS, didn't have a clue that I was standing right in front of her with a PSS hand.

"Let her go," she said to Renzo with a flick of her hand.

As Renzo pulled his arms from around me, the band of his expensive gold watch momentarily snagged the material of my shirt, pulling it askew.

Passion's eyes darted to my neck, and I knew what she was looking at—the chain of my dog tags, now exposed. Dog tags made from a razor blade that could block minus meters. And what did those minus meters read? The waves of energy or sound or whatever it was PSS put off.

Samantha James was a human minus meter.

And she couldn't detect my PSS because I was wearing the tags.

"Have you ever met anyone else with PSS blood?" Passion asked Samantha.

"Not with PSS blood, no," Samantha answered. "And please don't cut yourself anymore. You're very special. You have to understand that."

"I thought there was something wrong with me," Passion said, her voice breaking a little. "I was afraid to tell my parents or my therapist, and then my doctor said—" Passion stopped, looking at me. Did she mean Dr. Fineman? What had he told her about her blood while she'd been under his care? Was all this just an act, a way to get more sympathy from Samantha, or had Passion really been this clueless about her PSS?

"What did your doctor say?" Samantha asked, leaning forward, as drawn into the story as I was. "Did he take a sample of your blood? Did he send it to a lab?"

"Yes, he took my blood." Passion nodded. "But he didn't send it to a lab. He did some tests right there." Right there in Mike Palmer's basement.

"And what did he tell you?" Samantha asked, sounding concerned.

"He said I had a rare blood disease. He said we'd have to do more tests."

"Then he was an idiot," Samantha scoffed, putting her arm around Passion's shoulders.

Had Dr. Fineman said that? And had Passion actually believed it? Is that why she hadn't revealed her secret to anyone in Piss Camp? Had she come with us because she believed she was dying or because she'd known she had PSS all along? My mind was reeling. Marcus didn't fully trust Passion. He'd questioned her motives for coming with us. But what better way to discover more about PSS than to join a band of people with it?

"It's a good thing he didn't send it to a lab," Samantha continued to comfort Passion, "because most doctors and scientists don't know the first thing about PSS. You don't have a disease. You have a gift. And people without PSS," she cast her glance my direction, "will never understand that unless we show them the way."

Why did that sound like a veiled religious threat? Probably because it was. I could see Passion looking at me, glancing at my hand. This was probably as alone as we were going to get with Samantha.

I looked at Renzo. He certainly didn't strike me as a CAMFer spy. Well, he did have the annoying habit of wearing sunglasses indoors.

His lips quirked into a smile, and he raised his hand to the dark glasses, lifting them up so I could see his eyes. One brown eye and one glowing pale blue eye stared back at me. He winked at me with the PSS eye and slid the glasses back in place.

It looked like Samantha was collecting people with

PSS just like Marcus was. Dimitri certainly hadn't seemed surprised by Passion's blood, and Samantha had made it clear she found people without PSS barely tolerable. That probably meant the other girls who'd been on the Segways had it too. And all I had to do to be welcomed into their happy little clique was whip off my glove and reveal my hand.

But then I would have to explain why Samantha hadn't heard me. And that would involve revealing the ability of the dog tags which would lead directly to things I did not want to divulge about my hand. Besides, Passion had already accomplished what we'd set out to do. Plus, suddenly, more than anything, I could not bring myself to show Samantha James my ghost hand just so she would like me and consider me worthy of her attention. If she couldn't respect me as a human being, PSS or not, screw her.

The door to the practice room swung open and Dimitri came back in, the sound of a bell echoing behind him. "That's the bell for third period," he said. "Oh, and this is for you." He crossed to Passion, handing her a Band-Aid for her thumb.

"Thanks," she said, removing the tissue and putting the bandage on.

"I've got a school yearbook meeting," Dimitri said, looking to Samantha. "Unless you need me."

"No, we're fine." She twined her arm around Passion's. "You and Renzo go ahead," she dismissed them, and both guys headed out the door. "Our third period is Calculus," Samantha said, getting up and pulling Passion with her.

"Calculus?" Passion squawked, glancing at me in

alarm. The last time Passion and I had been in a calculus class together things had not exactly gone well.

"We could skip out," Samantha added quickly, "if you don't think you're up to it."

"That would be great," Passion said eagerly, raising a questioning eyebrow in my direction.

I looked back at her and shrugged. She was in the driver's seat now. I was just along for the ride.

"Cool," Samantha said. "My house is really close." She took out her cell phone and tapped a text into it. "And don't worry about the office marking you absent. I can take care of that."

"Sure, okay," Passion said. "And maybe later you can come to our place. I'd love for you to meet my cousin and his college friends."

And we were back to Marcus's plan. True, we hadn't exactly gotten there the way he'd mapped it out, and it looked like we were going to make an extra stop along the way, but the important thing was, we'd get there.

That's what I told myself anyway, as Samantha, Passion and I snuck out a back door of Edgemont High. Nothing like ditching school on your first day.

"And where are you ladies going?" I heard a deep authoritative voice ask, and I looked up to see a black, dark-windowed car pulled up in front of us, blocking our escape, a large beefy man frowning at us out the driver side window.

Passion and I both froze like startled rabbits. I glanced at her and I could see the same thought spinning behind her eyes that was spinning behind mine. *CAMFers.*

"We're going home, Leo," Samantha said, pulling open the car door and jumping into the leather back seat. "I told you that in my text when I called the car around."

"And why, may I ask," the man said dryly, "am I driving you home in the middle of the school day?"

"Feminine issues. And my friends here are coming with me for moral support. Do you want the gory details?"

"No, please, spare me," Leo said, looking in the rear view mirror.

I followed his gaze and saw another dark-windowed car pulling up behind his, peopled by men in dark suits. These weren't CAMFers. This was Samantha's security detail.

"Well, come on," Samantha called to Passion and me. "Get in the car."

And so we did. Passion climbed in to sit in the middle next to Samantha, and I climbed in after her. It was a big back seat. We weren't scrunched. But Samantha managed to sit as close to Passion as possible.

"Sorry about the goonish entourage," Samantha said, looking slightly embarrassed. "My dad is crazy protective. I hope you don't mind or think he's psycho or anything." She looked at me as well this time, instead of only addressing Passion. Apparently, the one thing in the world that made Samantha James insecure was her security.

"No, it's cool," Passion said. "It kind of feels like we're movie stars or something."

Then Leo drove us exactly four blocks to the gated entrance of a wooded estate straight out of *Lifestyles of the Rich and Famous.* The other car followed close behind, but when the gate opened, it parked outside, letting us make our own way up the long, tree-lined lane to Samantha's house, which looked like the front of some art museum in Europe.

Passion was sitting next to me with her mouth hanging open, and I wondered if I looked that awestruck.

"Come on," Samantha said, stepping out of the car. "We can grab something to eat, and don't worry; once we're inside, security will leave us alone."

16

ART HISTORY AND RELIGION 101

Ditching school is never as exciting as it sounds. Somehow, you imagine you'll do something daring and different with the time you've stolen. But the truth is you're usually at home feeling bored to death while everyone else is where they're supposed to be. And despite the opulent surroundings of Samantha's house that seemed likely to hold true.

We were met at the door by two huge, white, shaggy dogs, who inspected us exuberantly with their long curious noses.

"This is Claude and Pablo," Samantha said, introducing them as she rubbed each one on the head. "They're Afghan hounds."

Passion gave each one an enthusiastic back scratch,

but I only managed a tentative pat. My mom was allergic to dogs and cats, so the only pet we'd ever had was a zebra finch. I had heard of Afghans though. Picasso had owned one.

After the dog greeting, Samantha led us through the three-story high foyer past a grand staircase to a kitchen straight out of a cooking show. She snagged some chips and soda for us and we all sat down at the table. The dogs positioned themselves on either side of Samantha's chair, like sentinels, waiting for the smallest crumb to drop from her lips.

Samantha and Passion chatted away, and Passion got to use almost all the lies we'd made up about our fake life; how we'd moved from Chicago because my dad, her uncle, had gotten a great job in Indy. How she lived with us because of her parents recent and nasty divorce. How my parents were on a trip for their anniversary, and we had the house to ourselves, and it would be totally cool if Samantha came over and met the guys.

I didn't listen to most of it. I hated small talk, even when it was true. Plus, Samantha didn't care if I participated or not. I was a non-entity, and not only because she thought I was a fleshy. It was pretty obvious by now that she was into Passion in more ways than one. The tucking of her hair behind her PSS ear seemed to be one of her flirting tells.

As for Passion, she didn't seem to mind at all. In fact, she was doing an amazing job of playing the shy, coy flirt right back, teasing Samantha with just enough information about herself to keep her interested. Or maybe Passion wasn't playing, and she was truly into Samantha James. I had no idea.

While they were talking, fixated on each other, I glanced around the kitchen. It was clean and spotless, almost freakishly so. There weren't even any family pictures on the gleaming stainless steel fridge, but there was a brochure fixed to it with a magnet, the front boldly marked with the arm-wrestle icon of The Hold. I shifted in my chair, trying to see what it said, but it was folded up too tightly. Still, maybe I could snag it when no one was looking.

"So, Samantha, do you go to church?" I asked, interrupting their conversation.

They both turned and stared at me like I'd sprouted a unicorn horn.

"Because, I mean, Passion is religious and you might have that in common or something," I added lamely. Like I said, I don't do small talk.

"Passion is a family nickname," Passion rushed to explain, answering the confused look on Samantha's face.

Crap. I'd called her Passion, not Mirabelle. I'd just blown our cover, but Passion had smoothed over my mistake, thankfully.

"Passion suits you better," Samantha said. "Do you mind if I call you that?"

"No, that's fine," Passion said, blushing.

"And as for Anne's question," Samantha said, sounding cautious. "I am a spiritual person. I believe in the divine, and that humanity needs saving, and that we were put on this planet for a purpose, but I don't go to a traditional church, no."

Did she mean "we" as in humans, or "we" as in

people with PSS? I had a feeling it was the latter.

"I believe in those things too," Passion said, following my lead, but I could tell she had no idea why. "I'm a Christian. My dad's even a pastor. But I never feel God in church the way other people seem to. Sometimes I think I feel him when I see a good movie, or look at a beautiful painting, or hear some amazing music."

"Me too!" Samantha said, beaming. "That's exactly how I feel. All art is a form of worship. But I've never met anyone who expressed it so well."

I stared at Samantha, warming to her a little. My dad had always said that anyone who appreciated art couldn't be all bad.

"I have something to show you," Samantha said excitedly, getting up from her chair and pulling Passion by the hand. "Anne can come too. I think she'll like it." Wow. Samantha had included me by name and actually considered what I might like? I guess I'd earned worthiness points for bringing up the religion question.

Excited dogs in tow, Samantha led us through the grand foyer, up the stairs, down several hallways to a metal door that looked like a cross between a space ship lock and a bank vault. There was a security panel to the right of the door, a camera above it, and a monitor to the left that displayed readings for temperature and humidity.

As soon as we arrived, the dogs both lay down in the carpeted hallway and rested their heads sadly between their outstretched front legs. They obviously knew they would not be invited into that room.

"Like I told you, my dad is an art collector," Samantha explained. "And this is where he keeps his most valuable collection. I'm not really supposed to show people, but I know you'll be able to appreciate it," she said, squeezing Passion's hand.

"I don't want to get you in trouble," Passion protested.

"No, you won't," Samantha assured her. "He's a big softy when it comes right down to it."

"Okay, if you're sure, I'd love to see," Passion said.

"Good." Samantha punched a code into the panel, turning the huge metal handle and ushering us in, the door closing with a hiss behind us.

The room we found ourselves in was huge and set up like an art gallery, with long white walls for the larger pieces and carefully lit alcoves for the smaller, more intimate works. The air held a hint of hush and magic, and a unique silence settled over us as we entered, the silence of humans in the presence of things beyond our banal existence. This was a very special place. And if I hadn't been a good little agnostic like my father, I might have believed, for a moment, it really was a place that God might dwell.

"Just don't touch anything because it's all alarmed," Samantha said, leading Passion into the room and up to the first painting.

My father had raised me to know my art. You don't grow up in a painter's house without learning to distinguish your Rousseau from your Dali and your Monet from your Renoir. I'd been visiting galleries and museums since before I could walk. And I knew, even from a distance, that the first painting

Samantha was leading us to was a Grimshaw. I had always loved John Atkinson Grimshaw's work, but this was a Grimshaw I had never seen before. It was a moody moonlit landscape with a lone shadowy human form, as he often painted—but the figure receding down the rural road, obviously a woman, was not completely dark. One of her arms was glowing, blue and radiant, the faint hint of the landscape beyond showing through it.

"That's not a Grimshaw," I said, stepping closer and looked at the signature in the lower right-hand corner of the painting. It said Marion Grimshaw Bennet.

"Do you know his work?" Samantha asked, sounding surprised.

"A little," I said, shrugging. I was supposed to be Anne Clawson and her dad was not a dead painter. "I remember him from freshman art class."

"This painting is by his grand-daughter," Samantha explained. "It is a very early piece of hers, painted eighteen years before the first occurrence of PSS."

"It's beautiful," Passion sighed.

"Yes, it is," Samantha said, "and it's prophetic."

"What do you mean 'prophetic?'" I asked. "You mean like she was predicting PSS or something?"

"Well, what does it look like to you?" Samantha asked.

"Like she was painting a ghost. Ghostly figures are one of the most common symbols used in classic and modern art to represent mortality, death, the ethereal nature of human existence—" I stopped because both Passion and Samantha were staring at me.

"True," Samantha said, her eyes meeting mine for the first time since we'd met. She wasn't just looking at me—she was finally seeing me. "But then why only paint the arm that way? Why not the whole body?"

"I don't know. Maybe because she was only feeling her mortality a tiny bit on the day she painted it. It doesn't mean she was predicting PSS. It's only one painting. Besides, people can't predict the future."

"Can't they?" Samantha asked smugly, like she'd somehow won the argument. "Why don't we look at the next painting?"

As we approached it, I recognized the next painting as a Vermeer. It was a portrait of a servant girl wearing a blue head scarf, caught giving a pensive glance over her shoulder. But as we got closer I realized that the girl, dressed in circa 1600s domestic Dutch attire, had been painted with one very unusual feature: she had a PSS ear.

"Oh!" Passion exclaimed, turning to Samantha. "It looks like you."

"It does a little," Samantha agreed, smirking in my direction. "But it was painted by a descendant of Johannes Vermeer fifty years before I was born."

"You've got to be kidding me," I protested. "It's a complete knock-off of *The Girl with the Pearl Earring*."

"This 'knock-off', as you call it," Samantha said sternly, "is worth two hundred thousand dollars."

"What? Why? Because it's by a descendant of Vermeer?"

"No." Samantha shook her head. "Because of its place in this collection." She gestured around the room. "This is the largest body of proof in the world that humanity knew its ultimate destiny long before the first baby was ever born with PSS."

I looked around the room, at the various paintings and sculptures. Every one of the pieces within my view had a glowing, blue, ethereal element. Samantha's father didn't merely collect art; he collected a very specific kind—art that he thought depicted PSS. And under normal circumstances, I might have found that both cool and thrilling, but not when someone was trying to use it to ram their crazy PSS-worshiping cult down my throat.

Passion was also looking around the room, and I could see the wonder on her face, the look of pure adoration she gave to Samantha when she turned back to her.

"This is incredible," Passion said. "But what do you mean about humanity knowing its destiny?"

Here we go, I thought. Now we're going to get the full regalia of cultish proselytizing, and Passion will learn all about The Hold, and she'll probably want to join it. No, this was not going according to plan.

But, much to my surprise, Samantha didn't launch into a sermon. Instead, she said, "Follow me. I want to show you the most valuable piece in the collection." She took off toward the end of the room, pulling Passion by the hand.

I followed reluctantly, dragging my feet and trying to figure out how best to use this whole art angle to our advantage. We needed to get Samantha out of this guarded fortress of a house so Marcus could talk some sense into her. And obviously Passion could be bait, but I doubted that Marcus realized the work he had cut out for him. This was going to be way more difficult than getting me out of Greenfield, and that hadn't exactly been a walk in the park.

Ahead of me, Passion and Samantha disappeared around a walled partition into one of the smaller alcoves.

"Oh!" I heard Passion gasp in awe.

God, I hoped she was only pretending to be this easily impressed.

"This piece is worth 1.5 million dollars," I heard Samantha boast as I stepped around the corner into the gently lit area, but all I could see was Passion's back. "It is the pinnacle of the collection because it symbolizes the fulfillment of that destiny I mentioned earlier. You see, humans weren't meant to be flesh forever." Here came the sermon. Her voice was trembling with conviction and emotion. "We weren't meant to have PSS in part, a piece here or a limb there, or hidden away like yours. That's only a step in the process of our evolution as men and women of the new spiritual era. The goal is pure ethereal existence. And, just like those other paintings predicted what was going to come, this one does too. It shows us our future."

Passion turned toward me, the strangest look on her face, and I looked past her, finally able to see what amazing piece of "prophetic" art had Samantha's religious undies in such a bundle.

The painting hanging in front of me was *The Other Olivia*.

17

THE OTHER OTHER OLIVIA

Sometimes there is a darkness you can hear, a swallowing of your senses that blots out everything going on in the world around you, leaving only the chaos colliding and exploding in your own head.

I knew that Passion was talking to me, but I couldn't hear what she was saying.

Probably because I wasn't even in that special locked-down art gallery in Samantha's house anymore.

Instead, I was four, sitting at my father's desk, my legs dangling off the chair in his study where my parents had sent me while they fought. Again. We'd just gotten back from Grandma's in Orlando, and I'd so hoped the fighting would be done.

I hadn't seen my father for over a month, and he'd greeted me at the door and hugged my guts out, and then my mother had said, "I'm sorry, Stephen. I never should have pressed you to destroy it."

And he'd said, "No, I'm sorry. I've had a long time to think about it, and I never should have painted it without asking you. But it's taken care of now. While you were gone, I got rid of it."

"What do you mean 'You got rid of it?'" my mother asked, the blood draining from her face.

"I sold it," he said.

That's when my mother had stuffed a box of crayons in my four-year-old hands and sent me to my father's study to color with the door closed while the grown-ups talked.

There wasn't any paper in Daddy's scrap box to color on. There wasn't any blank paper anywhere, but there were papers on his desk, important papers with important writing on them that I knew I wasn't supposed to mark up.

But I did it anyway. I grabbed the nearest paper, and I colored all over it, scribbled on it until my crayon broke, and then I scribbled some more and more, until every crayon but my favorite, the black one, was broken and Daddy's papers were a mess.

Then I saw one more paper, trapped under the rest, and I pulled it out. In the middle, it had lots of grown-up writing in tiny print like the others, and at the bottom it had my daddy's name on a line, his signature in beautiful swirls and loops the way he wrote it at the bottom of his paintings. But, at the top of the paper was a picture of two hands, clasped together, with a circle around them. And I took my black crayon and I traced the pattern of that symbol. I traced it over and over again with my black crayon until Daddy opened the door to the study and found me doing it.

"Hey, Peanut." He caught me up in his arms, squeezing me to his chest. "I love you so much. I'm so happy you're back."

"Where's the other Olivia?" I asked, because she hadn't been hanging in the foyer when Mommy and I had come into the house.

"Well." His voice sounded funny. "She went away on a little trip, just like you did, but she's going to come back soon. I promise."

"She didn't go to Grandma's, did she?" I frowned. "Because she won't like it there."

"No." He smiled. "She didn't go to Grandma's."

And a month later, *The Other Olivia* was hanging in our entryway again, looking as fresh and new as if she'd just been painted.

Because she had been.

"Anne," someone said, and I realized that Passion was touching my arm, a look of concern on her face. "Are you all right?"

"Yeah," I said, looking past her to my father's painting on Samantha's father's wall. "I, uh—it's a powerful piece." I looked at Samantha. "Who's the artist?"

"A relatively unknown American painter named Stephen Black," she answered, happy to regale us with her knowledge of my father. "This is one of his first works, and it's the only one of its kind. There hasn't been a duplicate or print of it made, ever. And that makes it very valuable."

"It's not the only one," I said.

"What?" Samantha asked, staring at me, and Passion squeezed my arm in alarm.

"You're telling me that this painting has never been photographed, or reproduced on the Internet, or printed out by some bimbo at Kinkos? How can you know that?"

"It was a part of the purchase contract," Samantha said. "Total exclusivity. And it isn't on the Internet anywhere. You can look it up."

I didn't need to. I knew it wasn't. But it was in my room back at the McMansion. My dad had broken his contract, but then maybe it had become null and void after I'd scribbled the crap out of it.

"That still wouldn't make a painting by an obscure painter worth that much money," I argued. "You're exaggerating its worth."

"You think I'm lying?" she laughed. "Why would I lie about that? But you're right: its value comes only partly from its uniqueness. The rest comes from its place in this collection and the fact that the artist died a few years ago at the height of his career. All of that makes this painting extremely rare and valuable."

"Well, isn't that great for you?" I said, unable to keep the snark out of my voice. My dad had died, and that had made Samantha and her dad richer and happier. Hurray for them.

"We're not happy he died." She frowned at me. "He was a great painter, and he might have produced many more great works in his lifetime."

Passion had let go of my arm, but she was glancing

back and forth between Samantha and me as if she were watching a car wreck, helpless to look away.

I glanced at *The Other Other Olivia*, the original, a piece my dad had created just for me so I wouldn't be a lonely only child. It belonged to me. This painting was mine. Never mind that is was locked away in this room and guarded like Fort Knox. Here she was, my ghostly counterpart, sealed behind locked doors, watched by cameras, and shrouded in the perfect climate. She was in pristine condition, framed in gleaming, ornate, burnished wood, with a lovely gold title plate mounted on the wall underneath her.

My eyes froze, locked onto the title engraved on that plate.

Passion followed my gaze, her eyes lighting on it too.

It did not say *The Other Olivia*.

Someone had given this painting a completely different name than my father had given it.

Passion glanced at me, a question in her eyes. She had never seen David's list. Marcus and I had never been specific with her about the mysterious last name on it, the girl who, as far as we could tell, simply didn't exist.

Kaylee Pasnova.

But the title plate we were both staring at under my father's painting read *Kaylee Pas Nova*.

"Who's Kaylee Pas Nova?" I asked Samantha, trying to sound casual.

"She is our sister, our mother, our future," Samantha said reverently. "She's the epitome of the new spiritual era and the symbol of our imminent evolution."

"So, she's an icon," I said, "like The Virgin Mary.

Not a real person."

"Mary was a real person," Passion objected.

"Kaylee is real," Samantha said with conviction. "Some people say she was the first person born with PSS. Some people say she will be the last person born with flesh. Some people say she is both."

And some people are cuckoo for Cocoa Puffs. Great. My agnostic father had painted a picture, and somehow it had become the pivotal icon for The Hold. Back in Greenfield he was probably rolling over in his unmarked grave.

"The first person born with PSS was Thea Frandsen of Norway," I pointed out.

"So we've been told," Samantha said. "Do you believe everything you're told?"

"No," I said. *Especially not by crazy cult princesses.* "What about the Pas Nova part? Is that her last name, or a place, or what? It sounds Latin."

"That's because it is." Samantha eyed me approvingly. "*Pas* means 'step' in Latin and *nova* means 'new' or 'next.'"

"So, she's Kaylee Step Next?" I asked, mockingly.

"I didn't expect you to understand," Samantha said, turning back to Passion, her voice earnest, "but Passion might. I believe this painting represents the next step in human evolution on earth, the *pas nova*, when everyone will be born as pure spiritual beings."

I stood there, staring at her, trying not to laugh in her face. How could people say stuff like that and not realize it was utterly ridiculous? My father had painted this picture with no religious or spiritual intentions whatsoever. He'd painted it for me, so I wouldn't feel alone. And these people had taken it, and changed the name, and twisted its very purpose to support some crazy theory they'd made up in their own heads. If I hadn't believed in Samantha's religious ranting before, I certainly didn't now.

"I think that sounds beautiful," Passion said, countering the silence of my disbelief. "What a wonderful thing to believe."

Was she really buying this? Or was she just courting Samantha like we were supposed to? Personally, I was getting kind of tired of playing nice. And with all the weird shit cropping up like Passion's PSS blood, my dad's painting, and the name Kaylee Pasnova, all I really wanted to do was talk to Marcus as soon as I could.

I looked down at my wrist and said, "I think it's time for us to go. My brother's going to wonder where we are." I didn't have a watch on. I had no idea what time it was.

"Doesn't he think you're at school?" Samantha asked, confused, but I was already moving out of the alcove and pulling Passion with me.

"I get claustrophobic," I said, racing toward the door.

"Hey, take it easy," Samantha called, coming after us.

"Olivia, calm down," Passion whispered. "You're going to give us away."

I glanced at her, looking away from our path to freedom for a moment, and felt my left elbow bang against something. It was a tall white pedestal holding a bronze sculpture of a young man, his right leg cast in blue translucent glass from the knee down. And the sculpture was wobbling, teetering on its perch.

"Oh my God! Don't let it fall," Samantha yelled, still too far behind us to do anything.

I reached out and grabbed the pedestal to steady it, but that was the wrong thing to do.

The sculpture pitched forward, careening off the edge like it was committing suicide.

My hands were too slow and too preoccupied with the pedestal, even though my brain was screaming at them, *Catch it! For fuck's sake, catch it!*

But they didn't listen.

And it fell.

And I missed it.

But Passion didn't.

She reached out and caught the bronze boy in mid-air, clutching him in her hands.

"I told you to be careful," Samantha hissed at me, charging up and grabbing the sculpture out of Passion's hands. "This is an Anita Rencraft, and it's the only sculpture she ever produced."

"Good catch," I said to Passion. "And, hey, at least we didn't set off the alarm," I told Samantha as she set the boy reverently back on his pedestal.

A split-second later, red lights began to flash from the ceiling, accompanied by a loud, shrill sound.

"Shit. Come on, we have to get out of here," I said, grabbing Passion's arm and heading for the door.

But there were already two armed guards coming through it, their guns drawn, the dogs barking up a storm out in the hallway.

"Put your hands up," the guy in the front said.

And we did.

"Oh, Jackson, be nice," Samantha said, stepping around us. "They're my friends."

18

MEETING MR. JAMES

"**W**hy doesn't someone explain to me why the three of you were in my private collection room in the middle of the school day?" Mr. James said, standing over us and looking from Passion to me to Samantha. The three of us were sitting on a leather couch in his very large, nicely appointed office, which is where the security team had escorted us right after they'd frisked Passion and me and taken our phones.

"Please don't be angry at Samantha," Passion said. "We begged her to show us. Anne is a real art buff and I—I was curious about the PSS."

"Daddy," Samantha said, "this is Passion Clawson, and this is her cousin Anne. It was their first day at

Edgemont today, but I noticed Passion right away. She has PSS of the blood." A significant look passed between the two of them.

"Cousins?" Mr. James asked, his eyes flicking to me and landing on my gloves, curious and calculating.

"I have a condition," I explained. "Severe eczema. The gloves are medicated and they protect me from exposure to infection."

Mr. James looked from my hands to Samantha, and she gave a slight shake of her head.

"I'm sorry to hear that," Mr. James said to me. "I have a very good doctor. One of the best. I'd be happy to have him look at your hands."

"Oh, Anne's been to lots of doctors," Passion interjected, probably because she'd felt me tense up at the mere mention of the word. "But thank you for the offer. It's very kind."

"Yes, thank you," I said, forcing a smile.

"You're welcome." He nodded. "And the offer stands if you ever want to take me up on it."

"Anne has an older brother," Samantha told him, another look passing between them. "Their parents are away overseas for several weeks, and he's been in charge of the family move to Indy."

"Well, that sounds challenging," Mr. James said, sitting down in a chair and appraising us. "You three must be very independent and responsible young people for them to trust you with a task like that."

"We are," I said, looking at him. *You have no idea, Mr. James.*

"Responsible young people who skip school and break into other people's valuable art collections?"

he asked, eyeing me pointedly.

"Daddy," Samantha scolded him. "I was the one who did that. Don't blame them."

"And what did you think of my collection, Anne?" Mr. James asked, placing his elbows on his thighs and pressing his hands together in a steeple.

"It's an extremely diverse and impressive collection," I said, which wasn't a lie. "But I'm not sure it proves what you think it does."

"Ah, a skeptic," he said, leaning back in his chair and smiling. "I was a skeptic myself once. I have a very soft spot in my heart for them. What about you Passion?" he asked, turning to her. "What did you see?"

"I'm not sure," Passion said. "I'd want to know more before I decide. But I know I saw beauty and power and I felt somehow—validated."

"Validated, yes. Very good word," Mr. James said, nodding at her. "Then I'm glad you saw it, both of you. And I'm sorry about your phones. You'll get them back, I promise. Just your typical security protocol for this sort of thing. Nothing to worry about."

He was afraid we'd taken pictures of his precious collection. Of *Kaylee Pas Nova*, to be precise. And his security team had probably already scanned and deleted whatever had been on our phones. Good thing Nose had wiped mine and Passion's was brand new, bought by Marcus as a part of her rich girl disguise.

"Now, is there a way I could contact your parents?" Mr. James asked Passion. "Because I'd very much like to talk to them. Not to get you in trouble or anything, but I have a special interest in young people with PSS, for obvious reasons," he said, looking adoringly at

Samantha, "and I'd love to talk with them about that in particular."

"Oh—I—" Passion stammered, looking from me to Samantha.

"Passion's parents are going through a bad divorce," Samantha explained to her father. "That's why she's staying with Anne and her family. They're her guardians at the moment."

"I see. Then your parents, Anne," he said turning to me. "What's the best way to contact them?"

"They're on a private cruise in the Mediterranean," I said. "Very remote. But they do check in now and then. Next time they do, I could give them your number."

"Very good," Mr. James said, retrieving a card off his desk. "This is my direct line. I always answer it," he said, handing it to me. "Tell them to call me anytime. Day or night." I wasn't surprised to see The Hold icon in the upper right hand corner of the card. "And, in the meantime, I'd like to extend the James hospitality to your entire household." He handed a card to Passion too. "If you need anything, give me a call. In fact, I'd like to have you all over for dinner tomorrow night."

"No, really, we couldn't," I said. "We've bothered you enough already."

"Nonsense," Mr. James said, "I'm sure with your parents gone you've been eating nothing but pizza and junk food, and Samantha and I could certainly use the company with her mother away on business. I'll send a car for the three of you tomorrow at six."

"The three of us?" I asked, confused.

"Your brother is invited too, of course," Mr. James said.

"Thank you, that's so nice of you," Passion said, smiling from Mr. James to Samantha, who was smiling broadly back. "And we were hoping Samantha could come over to our place this afternoon."

"I'm afraid not," Mr. James said, and I saw Samantha's face fall. "You see, Samantha is helping me organize a huge art gala event coming up this Friday evening, and we have lots of planning to do."

I honestly expected Samantha to argue. After the way I'd seen her handle that secretary at school, and everyone else, I was pretty sure that Samantha James was used to getting her way in just about everything. But she didn't say a thing, and that's when I knew that if Samantha's will was a thing to be reckoned with, then Mr. James's must be a force of nature. I had to keep reminding myself that this smooth, polite, charming man was the leader of a cult.

"Oh, okay," Passion said, sounding genuinely disappointed.

"We'll see each other at school tomorrow though, and when you come for dinner," Samantha promised, smiling at her.

"Now, I must get back to work," Mr. James said, standing up, "and the three of you will be taking a car straight back to class."

"But it's already two o'clock," Samantha protested. "By the time we get back to school, we'd have to turn right back around and head home."

"Good point," he said, glancing at his watch. "How about if I call a car around to take Anne and

Passion home? There's something new in the works for the gala I want your opinion on, Sam, but I have a couple of phone calls to make first. Girls, nice to meet you," he said, bowing a little at the waist, like a Chinese gentleman, and ushering all three of us to the door. "I look forward to some rousing conversations over dinner tomorrow."

"Thank you," Passion said. "Nice to meet you too."

We exited into the hallway where two large security thugs were waiting for us.

One of them handed Passion and me our phones, and the other one led us downstairs, leaving us in the foyer until the car came around to take us home.

Watching Passion and Samantha say goodbye was almost painful. I looked away, trying to ignore their cute flirty awkwardness.

When Passion and I climbed into the car and the driver closed the door, I turned to her and whispered, "You told me all that other stuff last night, but you couldn't tell me you had PSS blood?"

"A girl has to have some secrets," she said, smiling and turning to look out the window.

19

KAYLEE PAS NOVA

When the car pulled up to the McMansion, I could practically feel the eyes on us from inside the house. The guys probably all had their guns up and ready as we stepped out of the vehicle and it drove away.

Passion and I walked up the front path, and Marcus opened the door before we even arrived at it.

"Whose car was that?" he asked, gesturing us inside. "School isn't even out yet."

"That was Samantha James's car," I said, walking into the living room and slumping down onto a couch.

Passion sank down next to me and leaned her head on my shoulder.

"What happened?" Marcus asked, looking worried.

"Why didn't you bring her with you?"

"Well, we met her," I said. "Or, it's probably more accurate to say she met us. She was waiting for us."

"What do you mean she was waiting for you?" he asked, his voice low and still.

I looked at Passion for some help, but her eyes said it all. She wanted me to tell this story. "Samantha James has a power," I explained. "She can hear PSS."

"But you had the dog tags," Marcus said, making that leap of logic much more quickly than I had. "I mean, couldn't that block someone who could hear PSS?" He didn't even seem surprised that Samantha had a power. Then again, it was one more piece of evidence to support his CAMFer list theory, so maybe he'd been expecting it.

"Apparently, it can," I said, taking a deep breath, "because Samantha didn't hear me. She heard Passion."

"She heard Passion?" Marcus repeated, slowly turning his eyes to her, scanning her body almost like Samantha had, as if he would see it now—something he'd missed all these weeks.

Passion held out her arms, almost in surrender. "It's my blood," she said. "Only the white cells and plasma. My red cells are normal. At least, that's what they told us."

"Who told you?" Marcus's voice sounded dangerous.

"It was just Samantha and some of her friends," I said, wanting to protect Passion from that voice. "They tested it in the chemistry lab at school."

"You let Samantha and her friends test Passion's PSS in the school chemistry lab?" He was repeating us again. That was not a good sign. "Was it in front of the entire class? Did you announce it over the intercom and call for a pep rally? Who the fuck now knows that Passion has PSS? And why the hell didn't I?"

His tone was pissing me off. We'd done the best we could. "Mr. James knows too," I said. "We sort of accidentally met him and Samantha told him everything."

Marcus stopped in his tracks, staring at us both, his face paler than I'd ever seen it. "You met Alexander James?" he asked, his voice tight, his fists clenched.

"He was really nice to us," Passion said, but it was completely the wrong thing to say.

"Nice to you?" Marcus laughed, but it was not happy laughter. "Alex James was nice to you? Do you have any idea what kind of danger you were in?" he said, looming over Passion. "What kind of danger you've put all of us in? You were supposed to bring Samantha James back here, not surrender yourself into the hands of her father and give him a sample of your PSS."

"Hey, we did the best we could," I said, standing up and looming right back at him. "Samantha was all over us the minute we stepped into that school. And despite several major glitches in the plan, we managed to do exactly what you asked us to. We showed her some PSS, and we got into her inner circle. She and Passion are practically best friends now, and we're all invited to her house for dinner tomorrow, you included, so back the hell off because it's been a very long day."

He backed up a little and stared at us. "He invited you to dinner?" he asked, sounding very confused.

"He invited you too, because our parents are out

of town. And that was pretty nice of him considering we'd just been caught breaking into his private art collection."

"He keeps his art collection at the high school?" Marcus asked, confused.

"No, that was at Samantha's house after we skipped out of school," Passion offered. "She broke us in, and showed us all this amazing PSS art, and told us all about her spiritual beliefs, and that's when we found Olivia's painting."

"He has The *Other Olivia* in his art collection," I told Marcus. "I thought mine was the only one, but it isn't. My dad sold the original to Alexander James when I was four. But they don't call it *The Other Olivia*. They've given it the title *Kaylee Pas Nova*. It's their most valuable religious icon."

Marcus stared at us, his eyes shifting from Passion to me and back again. "You did all that, found out all that, in half a day?" he asked, his expression looking almost like he was afraid of us.

"Yes, we did," I said somewhat smugly, sitting back down next to Passion.

"I don't even know what to say." He sagged into the chair across from us.

"Um, good job. Or thank you very much, would be nice," I said.

"Good job," he said softly, his eyes still looking a little glazed over with shock.

"Marcus," I said. "Why would they title my father's painting the same name the CAMFers have last on their list?"

"*Kaylee Pas Nova* is on the CAMFers' list?" Passion

asked, leaning forward with astonishment.

"Not spelled like that," I explained. "The *pas* and the *nova* are run together. But it has to be the same thing. It can't be a coincidence. That combination of words isn't exactly common."

"No, it's not," Marcus said, and I could see the gears of his mind turning, making connections. "Maybe it isn't a name on the list. Maybe it never was. What if it's been the painting all along?"

"Why would the CAMFers want a painting by my dad?" I asked. "They can't extract PSS from it, and they don't exactly strike me as the artistic types."

"The CAMFers hate The Hold, and vice versa," Marcus said. "They've been at war almost as long as they've existed. It makes sense that the CAMFers would want to get their hands on The Hold's most valuable possession."

"The Hold?" Passion asked, looking confused.

"It's the name for the cult Samantha belongs to," I explained. "They worships PSS."

"'Cult' is just a term people use when they don't believe something," Passion said, crossing her arms over her chest.

Marcus raised his eyebrows at that declaration and turned back to me. "If Kaylee Pasnova is your father's painting, then we already have the last thing on the list."

"Holy shit," I said, shock running through my body. "It was right under their noses in Greenfield and they almost destroyed it. But they wouldn't have known that, would they? The CAMFers don't know that *The Other Olivia* is the same painting as *Kaylee Pas*

Nova. There are no public pictures or records of either one of them."

"If they have an agent in The Hold, they know," Marcus said. "Someone who's seen the original."

"You mean like a double agent?" I asked.

"It wouldn't surprise me," he said. "Maybe Dr. Fineman wasn't dating your mother just to get to you."

"Oh my God." The CAMFers hadn't only been after me. They'd been after *The Other Olivia* as well. Their double agent would have known my father's name, the painter of *Kaylee Pas Nova*, which would have led straight to me, my mother, and a completely unprotected version of The Hold's precious icon. But Mike Palmer must not have known the painting was important, or he never would have burned down my house—a fact that had really pissed off Dr. Fineman.

Now, the only one who knew *The Other Olivia* still existed, other than us, was Mike Palmer, and he didn't even know what he knew. Which meant if the CAMFers wanted to complete their list, they'd have to go for the original painting. "They're not only after Samantha," I said, looking at Marcus. "They're coming for *Kaylee Pas Nova* too. But that painting is alarmed and guarded like the Mona Lisa. They're never going to get it out of there."

"If they have a double agent they could," Marcus said, chewing his lip worriedly. "You two need to be more cautious than ever." He glanced down at my gloved hands. "If they don't know you have PSS, let's keep it that way. Fly under the radar as much as you can. They'll be less cautious around someone they don't consider an equal." He turned his gaze to

Passion. "And I'm sorry I yelled at you," he said to her. "What you both accomplished today is amazing. It just caught me off guard. Now, if you could take me through it a little slower, I promise not to freak out."

Then we told him the extended version, Passion and I taking turns filling in the details about Samantha, her friends, the reveal of Passion's PSS, how I'd managed to keep my ghost hand off the radar, and what we'd seen in Alexander James's art gallery, all the way through to a detailed word-for-word account of our interactions with Mr. James himself, which seemed to interest Marcus most of all.

But neither of us mentioned the connection we both knew was forming between Samantha and Passion. I didn't feel like that was my place to tell, and Passion seemed to want to keep it secret a bit longer.

At the end of our explanation, Marcus turned to Passion and said, "I get it now. I know what it's like to be confused about your PSS—to have it manifest in a way that no one's ever heard of, like you're a freak among the freaks."

Was that how he felt about his incredible chest?

"It's okay," Passion said. "I should have told you, or at least asked you. I have a habit of keeping things to myself."

"Yeah," Marcus said, nodding at her. "I think I can relate."

20

DAY TWO AT EDGEMONT HIGH

Tuesday, our second day at Edgemont, Passion and I had to navigate new classes, the huge campus, and our fellow students but, with Samantha at our side, we didn't really have any issues. The teachers and staff treated us like royalty by association. Samantha's friends welcomed Passion into the fold, with me as her accessory, and the other students seemed to view us with either awe or envy, or both.

At the end of the day, I found myself in Honors English, the same class I'd had last period at Greenfield High. We were supposed to be discussing Shakespeare's sonnets in small groups, but I was thinking about *Kaylee Pas Nova* and *The Other Olivia* and the fact that Marcus had been quiet and aloof ever since Passion and I had come home from the James' house yesterday. All last night and this morning, I could feel him retreating away from me into his own head. He was holding something back and that was scaring the shit out of me, because the last time he'd done that, he'd given himself up to the CAMFers for my best friend and we'd all almost died.

"Too bad your brother can't come tonight," Dimitri interrupted my thoughts, leaning across his desk toward me. "We need more guys." He nodded at the whispering and giggling group behind us, comprised of Samantha, Passion, Lily, Eva, and Juliana. Somehow, I'd gotten stuck in a group with Renzo and Dimitri.

"He wanted to come," I said, "but he was puking his guts out all night." The lie came easily. What didn't come so easily was the realization that I'd already been relegated to the status of "one of the guys" in Samantha's group. It had taken Renzo and Dimitri exactly one day to stop thinking of me as a girl. Perhaps this was my true superpower. Still, at least Samantha wasn't treating me like I was invisible anymore. I didn't have Passion's status of course. I was obviously ranked below the others in the group, but it was better than nothing. At least she hadn't tried to exclude me from the dinner party. And apparently the whole gang was invited, not just Passion and I.

"Some bug has been going around," Renzo said. "I had it last week." He had his sunglasses on. He rarely took them off, and I understood why. A PSS hand or ear were easy to look away from, but eye contact was conditioned into human beings from the moment we were born. After all, eyes are the windows to the soul. But Renzo had a bit too much soul in his eye. Plus, whenever I saw that blue milky orb, I couldn't help wondering what kind of beautiful music a PSS eyeball made.

I glanced at Dimitri, trying not to be too obvious. Where was his PSS? And what about the girls? I looked over my shoulder at the giggling group. Juliana always wore this cool pinky ring on her left hand. It was made of silver, and it was jointed, encasing her entire little finger like armor. It wasn't rocket science to conclude that she had PSS of the pinky. But I didn't see anything on Eva or Lily that gave theirs away. What I did notice is that Lily had stopped giggling with the rest of them. She looked pale and she was holding her hand up to her mouth.

Suddenly, she leaned over and vomited directly across Passion's desk and straight into her lap.

"Oh God, I'm sorry," Lily mumbled, jumping up and running from the room, while the rest of us tried to keep down our cookies.

"Mrs. Menkey," Samantha called, trying to help Passion get out of her desk without making it worse, but the haggard looking teacher was already handing out hall passes and dismissing the entire class thirty minutes early. It was the last period of the day. She was obviously tired of vomit and Shakespeare.

We did manage to get Passion to the bathroom, where we could hear Lily still going strong in one of the stalls. Eva tried to help her, though there was little to do but hold her hair out of the way. Meanwhile, Juliana, Samantha and I wiped Passion off with paper towels, washed her shirt in the sink, swabbed down the front of her pants, and made her stand under the hand dryer in hopes the heat would kill some of the germs and the smell.

When she was mostly clean, and Lily's stomach was empty, Samantha offered to call one of her dad's cars around to take Passion and me home, and we didn't refuse.

"But I'll see you tonight at six, right?" she said.

"We wouldn't miss it," Passion promised.

The ride home was uneventful, and Marcus greeted us at the door of the McMansion again. I had barely seen Nose, Jason, or Yale since Sunday. They'd been on night duty a lot, so they slept most of the day.

"What happened this time?" Marcus asked, looking at the wrinkled stain marks on the front of Passion's clothes.

"Someone threw up on her in English," I said. "Apparently, our lie about you being sick was the perfect alibi. Some nasty flu bug is going around."

"I'm going to go get cleaned up," Passion said, heading upstairs and leaving us in the foyer.

"Listen," Marcus said, taking my hand and leading me into the living room to sit down on one of the couches. "I've been thinking about this dinner tonight. Maybe this flu is a good alibi for all of us. I want you to call Samantha and tell her you can't make it. Tell her you and Passion are sick too."

"What? No. We need to go. This is the key to solidifying ourselves in her group."

"It's too dangerous," Marcus said adamantly. "We need to stick with the original plan to get

Samantha here. I need to talk to her."

"And what in the world do you think you're going to say to her?" I asked. "She's pretty wrapped up in her happy little Hold. And if you want to talk to her so badly, why not come to dinner with us tonight and let her hear your chest? I bet she'd love to talk to you then. I mean, you showed it to those guys at the gun club. How is this any different?"

"Because *he* will be there," Marcus said, practically snarling.

"You mean Alexander James? Yes, he'll be there." I shrugged. "But I really don't see what the big deal is. I mean he's smooth, but he seemed harmless enough when I met him."

"Harmless?" Marcus stood up and began to pace, his body coiled like an angry spring. He was pissed at me. I could tell. Pissed even more than he'd been the day before and that was saying something. "Yes, the man who drove my parents into an oncoming train and ruined my life forever is harmless. What was I thinking?"

"Alexander James was the one who chased your parents down?" I stood up too, completely appalled. "Him specifically?"

"Yes, him specifically." Marcus glared at me. "So, you'll forgive me if I have no desire to attend a dinner party hosted by the man who murdered my parents."

"Oh God, I'm sorry." I crossed to him and took his hand. "I had no idea Alexander James was the leader of The Hold when you guys were in it?" Of course, it made sense. It just hadn't occurred to me before.

"He wasn't the leader," Marcus said, looking

down at me, "but he was on his way."

"You knew him?" I tried to wrap my brain around it.

"Yes." Marcus nodded.

"And you knew Samantha too? Were you friends?"

"Sort of," he said.

"And that's why this entire plan revolves around Passion and me bringing Samantha to you?" An avalanche of understanding was thundering down on my head. "Because even if she hadn't recognized you physically, she would have recognized you instantly by the sound of your PSS."

"Yes." Marcus glanced away from me, unable to meet my eyes.

Because he'd been lying to me this whole time.

Again.

I'd fallen for it *again*.

"You knew about her power." I pulled my hand from his. "And you knew the dog tags would block it. And you didn't tell me?"

He didn't say anything. He didn't have to.

"What the fuck?" I stepped away from him and began pacing myself. "I don't get it? You told me about The Hold, and your grandparents, and your mom. Why not this? Passion and I went in there and got completely blindsided."

"I had no idea Passion had PSS," he protested. "And the very reason I gave you the tags was so you wouldn't be blindsided. I wanted you to be able to observe, to be off Samantha's radar until the timing was right and the two of you were alone."

"Fine," I shot back. "Then tell me that. Don't give me bullshit about the CAMFers and scare me into doing what you want. God, I thought we were past this. Why can't you just tell me the truth for a change?"

"I tell you the truth as much as I can," he argued, anger tingeing his voice.

"That's bullshit and you know it," I snapped at him. "You're always holding something back. And I've tried to be patient about it, because I understand why. But haven't I proven a thousand times over that you can trust me? That I would never use anything you tell me to hurt you?"

"It's not about hurting me," he said, those eyes biting into me. "It's about protecting you."

"Protecting me from what? I don't need protection from the truth."

"Yes, you do." He shook his head just like my mother did when she thought I was being naïve. "You don't have a clue how sheltered your life has been, do you?"

"My life? You're going to turn this around and try to blame your pathological lying on my life?"

"You think I'm a pathological liar?" He laughed bitterly. "Oh, that's a good one. People have been lying to you your entire life, and when I throw you the tiniest sliver of truth, you accuse me of being the liar. That's exactly why I didn't tell you." He turned his back on me and started to walk away.

"What the hell is that supposed to mean?" I demanded, going after him, grabbing his arm. "Who's been lying to me my entire life?"

"You wouldn't believe me if I told you." He yanked is arm out of my grasp. "I'm a compulsive liar, remember? You should probably look for your truth from a better source. You never know, you might find it's been hanging right in front of your face."

"Oh, great, thanks for more of your cryptic bullshit. That really helps."

"You want me to be more specific? Okay. Go ask *The Other Olivia* for the truth."

"*The Other Olivia?*" I asked, stepping away from him. "What has that got to do with—" I had been four when my father had painted the first *Other Olivia* and sold it to The Hold. Marcus would have been five. He and his mother and sister had been enmeshed in The Hold when he was that age. "You knew they had it." I stared at him. "You saw my father's painting all the way back then, when you were in The Hold, and you recognized my copy the moment you saw it. You've known all along the CAMFers were after it."

"Yes," he said, hope glimmering in his eyes.

"That's why you wrapped it carefully and kept it with us all this time." I felt my insides turn to stone. "So you'd have leverage with the CAMFers and The Hold. So you could use it as a bargaining chip." He'd kept this from me the entire time. All the nights we'd slept in his tent, *The Other Olivia* watching over us, he'd simply wanted it for this. "It was for you. For this fucking mission. That's all you wanted."

"Really? That's the truth you see in all this?" he asked sadly, his eyes glancing away from me, hollow and betrayed.

How dare he look betrayed?

"Obviously, whether I lie or not," he went on, his voice flat, "it doesn't really matter. Either way, it ends up hurting you. Honestly, I don't think I can do this anymore."

"Do *this*?" I repeated, glaring at him. "What is that supposed to mean?"

He stared back at me, a horrible finality written in his eyes.

I turned away, pain welling up in me. Really? After all we'd been through he was willing to bail over this? He had lied and deceived me, over and over again, and now *he* was breaking up with *me*? Yeah, that made sense. "You know what? I think you're right," I said, keeping my voice as steady as I could. "I'm pretty sure you can't do this." I turned and walked away, across the living room, up the stairs and down the hall, straight to the perfect room Marcus had made for Passion and me.

And I didn't even cry until my face hit the bed.

21

ASKING THE OTHER OLIVIA

Passion let me cry it out. She sat on the edge of my bed, her hand on my back. She didn't ask why I was crying. She didn't really need to. I cried, snot running down my face, until my pillow was soaked and my insides had turned into a puddle of nothing. Even when my dad had died, I hadn't cried like that, because he hadn't hurt me by choice. He might have been gone, but I knew he still loved me, and that he would have stayed if he could have.

But this. This was Marcus downstairs, still existing and choosing to hurt me and leave me. It was me upstairs, still wanting him, except now that want was an open wound I kept touching every few moments, just to see if the pain was still there, just to see if I could feel the part of me that belonged to him, even though I didn't want it to anymore.

When I was all cried out, I sat up, and Passion handed me a box of tissues to wipe the raccoon makeup off my cheeks.

"We broke up," I said, saying the words more for myself than for her.

"That sucks," Passion said. "Do you want to talk about it?"

"Not really." I glanced at *The Other Olivia* leaning against the wall. All this time I'd thought that Marcus cared about it because he cared about me. Turns out we were both just two more weapons in his arsenal. "I'd just like to be by myself for a while, if that's okay."

"Yeah, sure," she said. "We've still got a couple of hours before the car comes."

The car. Which was coming at six for the dinner party at the James' house. The same party that had started the fight between Marcus and me. Ha, I'd like to see him convince Passion not to go.

"I just need a few minutes," I said.

"No problem," she said, getting up and slipping out of the room.

The first thing I did was lock the bedroom door. Then I looked up to find the camera staring back at me from the corner of the room. Someone was on duty up in the security suite, and I wanted some fucking privacy.

I grabbed *The Other Olivia* and carried it into the bathroom, shutting and locking the door behind me. Once safely inside, I leaned it against the bathroom wall, sat down on the toilet seat, and stared at it. It did not belong to Marcus. It belonged to me. I got to say how it was used and what was done with it. If he'd wanted to use it as a tool against the CAMFers and The Hold, he could have asked me. Instead, he hadn't even bothered telling me.

Considering it had been through a house fire, it was still in decent shape. The frame was scorched some, and the canvas had a few small singe marks at the edges, but a slight trim and reframing and it would look as good as new. Now that I was looking at it closely, comparing it to the one I'd seen in Samantha's house, I was pretty sure my father had done this version on a slightly larger canvas. Trim it up and they'd be the same size and nearly indistinguishable from one another. Except for one thing.

I lifted the painting onto my knees and held my ghost hand up to it, only inches from the surface.

Immediately, in the lower right hand corner of the painting, a faint glowing letter "O" appeared in a dark swirl of paint. "O" for Olivia. For me. My father had shown me that special little feature when he'd hung the painting up in our house for the second time. He hadn't shown me before, so my guess was it had not been in the original. He had been thinking ahead, knowing that someday I might find out about the other painting. And he'd wanted me to be able to tell them apart. But why?

I turned the painting around, inspecting the back for damage.

My father always did his own framing and, as usual, he'd used a covering of brown paper to hide the unsightly metal hardware that held the painting inside its frame. The paper had been burned pretty badly in one corner, leaving a hole that exposed the frame and canvas inside it. With all the traveling and moving we'd been doing, the paper was starting to disintegrate even more. Probably better to remove it completely for now, until I could replace it.

I stuck two fingers in the burn hole and slipped them under the edge of the paper, feeling the brittle glue release a little at a time as I worked along the edge of it. A few places, the paper cracked and split, but I finally made it to the last corner and it came away in my hands.

I leaned the painting against the wall again and began to fold up the thin paper, but something on it caught my eye. There was faint writing in one corner on what had been the inside of the paper, not the outside where someone might write a public dedication or an artistic notation. The writing was small, done in pencil, almost as if its author had never meant for it to be seen. But I could read it by the glow of my hand. Just barely. But I could make out the words written in my father's beautiful swirly scrawl.

For Kaylee. We will always love you.

For Kaylee.

Oh, fuck.

My dad hadn't known a Kaylee. Our family had never known anyone by that name, as far as I knew.

People have been lying to you your entire life. Those had been Marcus's words right before he'd told me to seek answers from this painting. How could he have known about the inscription? He couldn't have. It had been on the inside of the paper. But he'd known about the other painting all along. The one titled Kaylee Pas Nova.

For Kaylee.

They couldn't be the same Kaylee.

Kaylee Pas Nova did not exist. She was a made-up religious icon.

So, who the hell was this Kaylee my dad loved? No, not just him. He'd written, *We* will always love you. That meant him and my mom. And maybe even me.

I looked at *The Other Olivia*—I stared at the ghost girl with the flesh hand and she stared back at me, her eyes as familiar as my own. To me, she had always been the sister I'd never had, a product of my father's imagination to keep me company. But one did not write painting dedications to products of one's imagination. What had I told Samantha in her father's art gallery? Artists paint ghostly figures to represent death, and grief, and their own immortality. What I hadn't said was sometimes they painted ghostly figures to represent people they'd loved who had died, so they could remember them.

Why would my mother be so upset by a painting my father had done? Why would she plead with him to destroy it, and leave him, and come back, and be devastated that he'd gotten rid of it only to make him paint another one? And why then hang it, like a shrine, in the foyer of our house? How had death forever become a taboo subject with my mother, while my father and I seemed to always be wallowing in its shadow? Death was something we'd talked about together since before I could remember.

Since before I could remember.

What happens to the memories you have before you can remember? Who keeps them for you? And how do you get them back if you find you suddenly need them to make sense of the world?

"Olivia, are you in there?" Someone was banging on the bathroom door. "Olivia, talk to me." It was Marcus, and he sounded scared. He wasn't knocking. He was banging so hard I could see the door shaking on its hinges.

"Just a minute." I folded the brown paper and stuffed it in my pocket. Then I stood up and opened the door only to find Marcus, Passion, Yale and Nose all standing there looking about as scared as I'd ever seen them. "What?" I said.

"What were you doing?" Marcus asked, glancing at *The Other Olivia* leaning against the wall.

"Having a moment alone," I said, picking up the painting and pushing past him, pushing past them all into the open room beyond. "What did you think I was doing?"

"I—we—Passion said you were really upset," Marcus stammered, "and then Yale saw you lock the doors and go into the bathroom, and you didn't come out."

I turned, noticing the looks of relief on their faces. The pink glow crawling up Passion's neck.

"You thought I was hurting myself?" I asked, setting the painting down and staring at Marcus. "Wow. Is your ego seriously so inflated you think I'd hurt myself because you broke up with me? God, get over yourself."

I shouldn't have said it. I knew it as soon as the

words were out, hanging in the air between us. But you can't take that shit back.

"My mistake," Marcus said stiffly. "I won't make it again." He turned and walked out of the room.

"I'm sorry," Passion said. "I got worried after I left you alone, and then when I went up to the security suite, and Yale told me you'd locked yourself in—"

"Why were you in there with a painting?" Nose asked, puzzled.

"None of our business," Yale said, grabbing Nose and guiding him from the room by his arm.

"Olivia, I'm really sorry," Passion said again. "But you have to admit, the way Marcus reacted didn't seem like the response of someone who doesn't care about you. He practically broke down the door."

I followed her glance. There were fist marks dented into the wooden bathroom door. And cracks.

"He's always the hero," I said, shrugging it off. "He would have done that for you too. Or for Nose. Or any of us."

"Maybe," Passion said. "But that's not what I saw."

"It doesn't matter. Even if he cares about me, apparently, I can't handle the truth. How did you guys even get into the room?"

"Marcus has a key," she said.

"And now he'll probably have one made for the bathroom too. So much for privacy. Whatever. I guess we'd better get ready for this party," I said walking into the closet, the brown paper from my father's painting crinkling softly in my right pocket.

For Kaylee. We will always love you.

I wanted to know what that meant. And I was

terrified to know.

One thing was for sure, Marcus wasn't going to tell me.

If I wanted to find out the truth about Kaylee, I'd have to look for it somewhere else.

Maybe Alexander James would tell me.

Maybe The Hold had the answers I needed that Marcus would never give.

22

THE DINNER PARTY

I made it through the dinner party at the James' house mostly in a daze. The food was probably amazing, but I barely tasted it. The conversation was all mindless small talk and social banter. I barely listened to it. Samantha and her father were gracious hosts, and if they noticed I wasn't all there, they didn't point it out.

Renzo was sitting to my left. His sunglasses were gone and his PSS eye was kind of mesmerizing. I mean it probably wasn't any freakier than Nose's nose or Marcus's chest, but I think I might have been staring at it, because I kept catching him looking at me. Once, his glance seemed to linger on my gloves until I tucked my hands under the table. Another time, he caught me fiddling with the dog tags through my shirt, and I dropped my hand in my lap again. It made me wonder if that eye had a power. What was Renzo really seeing when he looked at me?

Dimitri was there too, and Eva, and Juliana, but Lily was at home, still sick. And of course, Passion and Samantha were sitting as close as they could, and I suspected they were holding hands under the table. Well, at least two people in the world were happy in love, though I doubted it would last.

When the meal was done, and the dessert dishes cleared, Mr. James looked at Samantha and said, "Will you play for us?"

"Oh yes, please," Passion said, clapping her hands together like a little child.

As for me, I was sorely disappointed. I had expected everyone to talk about The Hold and try to suck Passion and me into it. I had hoped to have an opening to ask about Kaylee Pas Nova, the painting and the person who must have inspired it. And I desperately wanted to know how my father was connected to it all. But instead, no one had even mentioned The Hold, and there would be even less chance of it during a private concert.

We all followed Samantha into a large, domed recital room with acoustics so amazing you could hear your footsteps echo back to you as you walked in. Soft, plush chairs surrounded the piano in the middle of the room and we all found a seat.

Marcus was right. This party was very dangerous. First, they had tortured us with rich food and now a piano recital. I should run before evil Mr. James and his daughter corrupted my soul forever by teaching me ballroom dancing.

Passion was sitting in the chair closest to the piano, and Samantha turned to her and said, "Can I play you?"

"I'd be honored," Passion said shyly, blushing.

Even though I'd heard Passion's music before in the practice room, it wasn't any less spectacular the second time around. In fact, it was more so. This time it was louder, flowing and ethereal and yet confident. This time the end was different, full of visions of Passion. Passion meeting Samantha. Passion hearing her play. Passion stabbing her thumb and revealing her PSS for the first time. Passion seeing the art in Mr. James's collection, the music swelling to a heart-wrenching crescendo of strength and finality.

"Wonderful!" Mr. James exclaimed when Samantha stopped playing, and I opened my eyes to find Eva staring at me from across our little semi-circle of chairs. I stared right back, but she didn't look away, and without even thinking, I stuck my tongue out at her.

Eva cocked her head to one side, smiled, and stuck her tongue out at me.

Her PSS tongue.

It was a quick in and out, but there was no mistaking it.

How in the world had I not noticed that before?

Of course, Eva didn't say much. She was quieter and more introverted than even Passion and me. She barely ever opened her mouth, and now I knew why.

"Eva, can I play you next?" Samantha asked, turning on the piano bench.

"Sure," Eva said, smirking at me.

Eva's music was quiet and subtle and sweet, and even though I didn't see images of her in my head the way I had with Passion's, by the time the music stopped and I opened my eyes, I felt like I knew Eva. Like we'd been friends for a very long time, even if I didn't know her middle name, or her birthday, or if she had any siblings. I felt like I knew who she really was.

After that, Mr. James was called away for a phone call and the room, with no adult in attendance, got slightly more casual.

Samantha played Renzo, and his music was very bouncy and spicy and Spanish-sounding. It made you want to get up and dance, though no one did.

Then Samantha looked at Dimitri, and he nodded his head, but instead of starting to play him, Samantha turned to Passion and said, "You asked me yesterday if I'd ever known anyone else with PSS blood, and I haven't. But I also told you I can hear PSS no matter where it is, or how deeply it is hidden."

"Yes," Passion nodded.

"Everyone knows that PSS is very rare," Samantha went on, "but it isn't as rare as it seems. PSS doesn't only manifest outwardly as an eye, or an ear, or a tongue. When I was a little girl, I knew a boy with both external and internal PSS."

I clutched the arms of my chair. She was talking about Marcus. Samantha James was referring to Marcus.

"And that was when I first realized why I could sometimes hear PSS from people who didn't appear to have it. I was hearing the sound of the PSS inside of them. You see, sometimes PSS manifests as an outward limb, where it is visible. But sometimes it manifests on the inside of us, as blood, or an organ, or a bone, where it can't be seen. When that happens, the music is usually much softer, and muffled, and sometimes I can barely hear it, but over the years my ear has gotten better and better."

"That's incredible," Passion said, looking around the circle, her eyes landing on Dimitri.

"I have PSS of the right bicep," he said, pulling his right sleeve up and presenting his formidable gun to us. Even as we watched, he flexed his PSS, his arm bulging to Popeye-on-spinach proportions and back down again.

"And I have PSS of the medial phalange," Juliana added, waving her armored pinky at us. "That's just the middle bone, not even the whole finger," she said, sounding almost embarrassed.

"And what about Lily?" Passion asked.

"Oh, Lily's PSS is very external," Renzo said, grinning from ear to ear.

"Hey," Dimitri said, punching him in the arm. "Be nice."

"She has PSS boobs," Juliana piped in. "And the guys find that very entertaining to imagine. But they'll never get to do more than imagine it, because Lily doesn't like boys."

"Such a waste," Renzo said, shaking his head.

"Hey!" protested Samantha. "Take that back."

"I wasn't talking about you," he said. "You're bi. Bi is not a waste; it's a blessing."

At about that moment, I realized my mouth was hanging open and I clamped it shut. Was I shocked?

Yes. But not as much by the revelation of internal PSS as you might think. I mean, it made sense. If humans were being born with PSS on the outside, they were probably being born with PSS on the inside. If nothing else, Passion's blood proved that.

No, what shocked me was the fact that I was sitting there with a group of teenagers who were just like us. Just like Marcus, Yale, Jason, and Nose, right down to the member with the embarrassing PSS that everyone joked about. They weren't evil, or elitist, or fanatics. They were a group of friends with something in common, just like we were.

"Wait a minute," I said, and all eyes in the group fell on me. "Wouldn't this internal PSS be seen on X-rays, or discovered when someone had surgery? I mean, I've never heard of it before. Why isn't it common knowledge?"

"It's been covered up, to a large extent," Dimitri answered. "Mainly to protect the innocent. Most people aren't even sure what they think of the PSS they can see. Imagine the reaction if this got out. People would be lining up for X-rays and demanding to have their children screened."

"And PSS organs and bones don't break or get sick," Juliana pointed out. "They get discovered much less than you'd think. Neither Dimitri or I had a clue we had PSS until Samantha found us."

"Until she found you?" I asked and couldn't resist adding. "Were you missing?"

"Not so much missing, as lost," Dimitri said. "We didn't have a place or really know who we were until we joined The Hold."

"What's The Hold?" I asked, playing dumb. Finally, the conversation was going the way I'd hoped it would, but Passion was frowning at me. She knew I knew more about The Hold than I was letting on.

"It's just a group of people who believe the same thing," Samantha said proudly. "Like I explained before, we believe that PSS is a special gift and a crucial development for the future of humanity. But those are just empty words if we don't back them up with action. The Hold, under my father's leadership, has worked for years to protect people with both external and internal PSS. It's one of our missions."

Passion was now staring at Samantha with utter adoration, and I knew exactly why. She'd just found out Samantha was a pastor's kid, just like she was. It was one more thing they had in common. And after the way Passion had hidden her PSS blood all her life, cutting away at herself, only to have her family reject her, The Hold and its mission must seem like the answer to everything.

I, on the other hand, seriously doubted it was. Still, I couldn't see all the evil and danger Marcus had been warning us about.

"And on that note," Samantha said, grinning at her own cheesy pun and turning back to the piano, "I'll play you Dimitri."

No. Dammit. What about Kaylee Pas Nova and my dad? I needed answers, not music.

But I was quickly swept away by Dimitri's melody. It was strong and compelling, almost like a march. And Juliana's was light and airy, like something you'd hear at the ballet.

As I listened, I found myself wondering what my PSS would sound like. What music did my ghost hand make and how would Samantha play it? I could reveal myself to them right there. Explain that I'd been afraid, and I was used to hiding. Make up some story about where I'd gotten the dog tags. Or even tell them the truth about my hand and its power. I was sitting in a circle with some of the only people in the world who would truly understand.

But then the music stopped and Mr. James came back into the room.

The party began to break up.

And the moment was lost.

23

ALL GYM TEACHERS ARE EVIL

Almost immediately after we got home from the James' party, Passion started heaving her guts out and, from what I gathered, expensive party food wasn't any better coming back up than a cheap burger and fries would have been. Apparently, the flu makes no class distinctions; whether you're rich or you're poor, it's all the same leaning over the edge of a toilet bowl.

Marcus tried to debrief me about the evening, but there wasn't that much to tell, and I wasn't really in much of a mood to tell him. He already knew people had internal PSS. He was practically the poster boy for it. Besides, every time I told him something new, I found out he'd known it all along anyway. And I was busy helping poor Passion, so eventually he gave up and left us alone.

Of course, Passion was in no shape to attend school the next morning, and Marcus tried to convince me not to go on my own. It was a short conversation. He told me not to go. I told him I was going. He refused to drive me. I took the bus. Unfortunately, it was the wrong bus, so I ended up missing first period, and wandering in halfway through Music Symposium.

Samantha was obviously bummed to hear that Passion was sick. Lily still wasn't at school, and it looked like Dimitri and Eva had succumbed as well. We were a small group that day, and I kept glancing over my shoulder, looking for Passion, because I could feel her through the tags.

Calculus was uneventful. The fourth period cafeteria was like a ghost town. Renzo, Samantha, Juliana, and I sat down at a table to eat, but about five minutes later a guy puked into the lunchroom trash and we all pretty much lost our appetites.

"This is going to ruin everything," Samantha said, shoving her food aside in frustration. "People are canceling their tickets to the art gala." She lowered her voice to a hushed whisper. "And if the adults don't go to that, how will we ever pull off the Eidolon."

"It will be okay," Juliana said. "It's only a twenty-four hour bug. Better to get it over with now. Everyone will be fine by Friday. Besides, your father would never cancel the gala, not this year. He's going to have security amped up tighter than ever."

"She's right," Renzo added, lowering his voice too.

"We have to have the Eidolon, even if some people are missing."

"What's an Eidolon?" I asked, and they all turned to look at me.

Samantha regarded me for a moment, and I could tell she was weighing whether to tell me or not, whether I was worthy.

"You know Passion will want to bring her," Juliana pointed out. "And groupies are allowed."

Groupies? Was that how they thought of me? As Passion's groupie?

"The Eidolon is a rite of passage for teens in The Hold," Samantha said softly. "We have one every year in October, usually on the night of my father's art gala, because the parents are all distracted and so is most of my father's security team."

"Your father lets you go without security?" I asked, surprised.

"Not completely, no," Samantha said. "Leo and his team follow us, but they keep their distance."

"So, the Eidolon is a religious thing?" I asked.

"It's like nothing you've ever seen," Juliana said, grinning. "The adults all think it's a rave or a party, and they look the other way. And we do keep the location a secret, but you have to come to really understand what it is."

"And people without PSS can come too?" I asked.

"A select few," Samantha said. "If someone with PSS invites them."

Marcus hadn't mentioned anything about an Eidolon when he'd told me about The Hold. Then again, he hadn't been a teenager when he'd been in it.

"I can't wait to see this guy Eva is bringing," Juliana said. "Who would have thought she could snag a college boy? She's so quiet."

Eva was bringing a college guy? Did that mean the Eidolon required a date? Was it a cult version of the prom or something?

"That's probably exactly why she snagged him," Renzo said. "Men like a mystery."

"And what do boys like?" Juliana asked him, teasingly.

"Big tits and a nice ass," Renzo said, smirking, as the bell rang.

We got up and headed into the hallway, and I started to turn left to the American Government class we had fifth period.

"Wrong way," Samantha said, taking my arm and pulling me in the other direction. "We have P.E. on Wednesdays."

"P.E.?" I asked, puzzled, but following along. "Why only on Wednesdays?"

"It's a trade we make for Music Symposium," Juliana explained. "We get to opt out of either freshman or sophomore gym class to practice our instruments, but then we have to make up for the missed credit our junior and senior year. So, every Wednesday we have P.E., and we get notes from Am Gov e-mailed to us."

"But I hate P.E.," I moaned, stopping in the middle of the hall and letting the tide of students rush by me.

"Come on," Samantha said. "It's not that bad. We're playing volleyball." She sounded like she genuinely wanted me to come. And volleyball was about the only sport I wasn't absolutely terrible at.

"We have an all-girls tournament going," Juliana encouraged. "We make the boys play by themselves."

"Okay," I said, letting them propel me onward to Auxiliary Gym Two.

Of course, there were locker rooms involved, and an ugly P.E outfit to be donned—bright blue basketball shorts and white t-shirts with *Edgemont Pride* printed boldly across the front.

I felt really awkward changing alongside Samantha and Juliana. If I hadn't felt different enough compared to their statuesque beauty, my black gloves just added to the effect.

"I like your dog tags," Juliana said, as I was pulling my shorts on.

"Thanks," I said, tucking them inside my white shirt.

"Where'd you get them?" she asked.

"A friend gave them to me as a going away present." That was mostly accurate. Marcus had given them to me, and then he'd bailed on our relationship.

"Well, we'll meet you out there," Samantha said, and I realized they were both ready and I still didn't have my shoes and socks on.

"Yeah, okay," I said, sitting down to put on my footwear as they went out into the gym.

I was feeling kind of sluggish, maybe because I hadn't slept much since Passion had started puking. I stuffed my clothes in a locker, slammed it shut, and leaned my head against the metal, reveling in its coolness. Shit. Did I have a fever? Maybe a slight one, but my stomach didn't feel upset. I hadn't eaten any lunch, so hopefully there wasn't much in there to be upset about. I could make it through the day. No problem.

I was the only one left in the locker room, and I could hear the sound of shoes squeaking on the waxy gym floor and a volleyball being smacked back and forth as girls called out "Got it" and "Set" and "Coming your way" to one another.

That sounded fun, right? I wove my way between the locker room benches, marched out the door, and ran smack into a stocky, squat woman with short hair and a trollish frown.

"Sorry, I'm sorry," I said, stepping back from her.

She was holding a clipboard, she had a whistle around her neck, and her white shirt had the words Coach Blazen embroidered on the lapel. She might as well have had 666 stamped on her forehead as far as I was concerned. There is nothing more evil, in my experience, than a high school gym teacher.

"You must be Anne Clawson," she said, looking at her clipboard and checking off my name. "And why are you wearing gloves?" She gave my hands a stony glare.

"I have a medical condition," I stammered. "I can't take them off. It should be in my file."

She looked less than thrilled, but she shuffled through the papers on her clipboard and stopped at one, frowning even more. "Fine," she said. "I don't know how you're going to play volleyball in gloves, but go ahead." She gestured at the court where Samantha and Juliana were already playing.

I started to step away, but she wasn't done with me yet.

"Clawson," she said in a booming voice, calling me by my ill-fated fake last name and stopping me in my tracks. "No jewelry allowed on the court," she said, stepping in front of me and holding out her hand.

I looked down to see the chain of my dog tags peeking out from the collar of my shirt.

"Oh, it's not jewelry," I said. "They're dog tags and they're really sturdy. They make them that way, you know, for war and everything." I was babbling. *Shit. This was not good.*

"No jewelry on the court," she insisted, her hand still out.

I didn't know what to do, but a million things went through my head at once: Run. Tell her to fuck off. Tell her she can pry your dog tags from your cold dead hands.

I looked up and saw the volleyball game playing out before me—saw Samantha and Juliana who thought I was Passion's groupie, a tag-along. They would never tell me anything important about The Hold and *Kaylee Pas Nova* unless they thought I was one of them. Yes, they might tell Passion, but I was beginning to wonder if Passion would pass that information along. She was becoming more and more enamored with The Hold every day. And then there was Marcus, who had no perspective at all. Maybe it was finally time to take my fate into my own hands, or my own hand, to be precise.

"Clawson," Coach Blazen growled, sensing my

inner turmoil like an animal smells fear. "Hand them over."

I reached down and took hold of the dog tags, slowly pulling them over my head, my warm skin grieving the loss of the cool chain.

On the volleyball court, the team playing Samantha's had the ball and they were setting it to the front row. Samantha was bouncing on her feet, anticipating the opposing teams attempt at a spike over the net. She was the tallest one on the team and the perfect pick to block it.

I put out my hand and dropped the tags into Coach Blazen's waiting palm.

The moment I released them, Samantha's head snapped in my direction, her PSS ear practically pointing at me, utter surprise and confusion flooding her eyes.

The volleyball came over the net, hard and fast. It hit her directly in the face and took her down.

People cried out as she hit the floor.

Coach Blazen muttered, "What the—" and shoved the clipboard and the dog tags in my hands, running over to check on Samantha who was now laying prostrate on the court, a group of concerned girls swarming around her.

I grabbed the dog tags, bent down, and stuffed them into my right sock, the cold metal snug against my ankle.

Then I wandered over to the crowd surrounding Samantha, still holding Coach Blazen's clipboard.

I was relieved to see that Samantha was conscious. And I was mortified to see the huge red mark on her face. Her nose and left eye were already starting to swell. I felt bad. Really bad. What had I been thinking? Of course, she'd react that way. God, I was an idiot. Then again, I hadn't really had a choice thanks to Coach 666.

On the floor, still a little dazed, I saw Samantha searching the crowd, looking for something, looking for what she'd heard only moments before.

Someone stepped to the side, and her eyes found me, locking onto me, listening and straining and finding nothing.

24

SHOWING MY HAND

"**Y**ou have a fever of a hundred and one," the school nurse said to me. "And you need to keep ice on that and take ibuprofen for the swelling and pain," she said to Samantha, who was sitting next to me with an ice pack pressed to her face. "You both need to go home. Do you want to make the calls or should I?"

"We can do it," Samantha said, pulling out her phone.

"Yeah, we're fine," I said, pulling mine out too.

"Good," the nurse said. "Because I've been called over to the Junior Campus. This flu is hitting hard today." And she slipped out the door, leaving Samantha and me alone.

"How are you doing it?" Samantha turned to me immediately, peering at me with her one good eye. "How are you blocking me?"

"I don't know what you mean," I said, avoiding her gaze.

"Cut the bullshit. I heard you," she said, looking down at my gloves. "Is it one hand, or both?"

There was no point in pretending anymore. "Just my right hand," I said, holding it out.

"And the gloves block it?" she asked, sounding more fascinated than pissed, which was good.

I could lie to her, pretend it was the gloves. But I was kind of tired of lying. Besides, hadn't I railed at Marcus for never telling the truth? "No, it's not the gloves," I said, reaching down and pulling the dog tags out of my sock. "It's these. Coach Blazen insisted I take them off."

"No jewelry in gym class," Samantha said, impersonating the coach's voice perfectly.

"Exactly." I nodded, trying not to laugh.

"But how do they work, and where did you get them?" Samantha asked.

"Someone made them for me, a friend. As for how they work, I don't really know. But they block PSS from being detected by you. And by minus meters."

"Minus meters?" she said, her look piercing. "What do you know about minus meters?"

"Well, I know the CAMFers use them to detect and extract PSS. I've been hunted using one, and I've even had one used on my hand, briefly, which is something I never want to experience again. Ever."

"They tried to extract you?" Samantha asked, appalled. "When? Why?"

"It was a few weeks ago," I said. "Where I lived before, in Illinois. And they did it because that's what they do."

"No wonder your parents moved here," she said. "And I guess I can understand why you and Passion have been so guarded. But The Hold would never let that happen in Indy. We protect our own."

"There aren't any CAMFers in Indianapolis?" I asked, wondering if she was really that naive.

"Oh, I'm sure there are," she answered, "but they don't move openly, and they wouldn't dare try to extract someone. If they did, my father would take care of it." The way she said "Take care of it" had undertones of *The Godfather*. And it was strangely comforting. Maybe The Hold really was a place we could all be safe. Maybe we could stop running from the CAMFers and fight back for a change.

But there was no way Marcus would ever side with The Hold after what they'd done to his parents, even if it had completely changed since then and become less constrictive. He would never buy it. I wasn't even sure I bought it. Samantha, and her friends, and her dad had been nice so far, but it was the kind of nice that felt like it had a very specific purpose behind it. I wasn't sure how I felt about Mr. James suddenly finding out I had PSS that I'd been hiding from him. That was certainly weighing heavily on my mind, but so was something else.

"What does my hand sound like?" I asked a little shyly. "Is it nice?"

"I only got a short blast before the volleyball hit me in the face," Samantha said, eyeing my dog tags. "Put those down for a minute and let me listen."

"Okay." I hung the dog tags over the arm of my chair, careful not to let any part of me touch them.

Instantly, Samantha cocked her head to one side like a dog listening to a whistle, peering at me with her one unbruised eye. "It's strong, and loud, and a little bluesy," she said. "I like it." She smiled her approval.

I didn't think it would thrill me so much that she liked the music of my PSS, but it did.

"But it's going to be damn distracting until I can get home and play it," she added, her fingers twitching as if they were already at the keyboard.

"How do you handle all that music coming at you all the time?" I wondered out loud as I grabbed the dog tags and slipped them back on over my head. "It must be overwhelming."

"It's not that bad. The new stuff can be a little distracting, but as soon as I sit down and compose it, it fades into the background with the rest."

"But it's always there in your head? That must be awful."

"It's not awful," she said, grinning at me. "It's wonderful. It's like having a soundtrack for your life. I don't know what I'd do without my music."

I found myself wishing I felt that positive about my own PSS power. But my ghost hand didn't pull out something nice like a soundtrack.

"You and Passion don't have to hide anymore," Samantha interrupted my thoughts. "No one at Edgemont is going to bother you for having PSS.

You'll see when you come to the Eidolon. People admire us because we're different. They want to be with us. They wish they could be us."

"You mean your 'groupies?'" I couldn't completely keep the distain out of my voice.

"Yeah, so what?" she said, not missing my tone. "People admire and follow other people for all sorts of reasons. I have groupies who follow my music. My dad is a groupie who follows PSS art. We're all someone's groupie."

She had a point. Hadn't I become somewhat of a Marcus groupie when I'd left Greenfield?

"Anyway, I know you'll love the Eidolon," she said. "It's a very freeing experience. And you should invite your brother and his friends. It would be good for them." She pulled out her phone and started tapping out a text. "Do you want a ride home?" she asked. "I can call you a car."

"Yeah, that would be great." Relief flooded over me. I'd thought she might press me to go back to her house and talk to her dad. I slipped my phone back into my pocket. "And I'm sorry about your face. Does it hurt a lot?"

"Not too bad," she said, "but the headache is getting worse. How's your stomach? Should you take a barf bag in the car or something?"

"Nah, I should be fine. My mom says I have a cast-iron stomach. I can count the times I've thrown up on one hand."

"Okay," Samantha said, getting up and bringing the ice pack with her. "Let's go. The cars should be waiting for us."

Sure enough, outside the front of the school, a familiar dark-windowed car was pulled up to the curb with Leo sitting in the driver's seat.

"Leaving school early again?" he asked dryly.

"I got hit in the face with a volleyball," Samantha explained, giving him a glimpse under the ice pack, "and Anne has the flu."

"Well, I'm going to have to drive you both," he said. "The other cars are in for service and getting prepped for the big night." Then he turned to me. "You gonna be sick in my car?"

"No," I promised, as Samantha pulled open the door and we climbed in, settling into the plush leather seat.

"Thanks for the ride again," I said, smiling at her. There was something compelling about Samantha, this rich, musical girl with the PSS ear, and as much as I'd tried to dislike her from the very beginning, I couldn't.

"No problem," she said, smiling warmly back as Leo pulled away from the school. He took the first right onto the main road, heading toward Samantha's house. But that didn't surprise me. Her place was much closer than the McMansion, and he was getting paid to keep her safe, not me.

We pulled up to a red light and I glanced out my window, looking across the intersection, and noticed a VW bug in the oncoming lane. It was the exact same color as my mom's and, for a moment, my heart skipped a beat and my entire body tensed. But the lady driving it was way thinner than my mother, and she also had a shaved head and was wearing a pair of ridiculously large sunglasses my mother wouldn't have been caught dead in.

Still, it was weird. And as I stared at her, cars speeding by flashing her in and out of my vision, something began to sink in. I don't know if it was the familiar shape of her face, or her perfect upright posture, or the way she tapped the steering wheel impatiently as she waited for the light to change, but a bolt of recognition suddenly zapped me to the core. This wasn't a lady that looked somewhat like my mom driving a car like my mom's.

It was my mom.

In Indianapolis.

A thin, shaved-head, sunglassed version of my mom who was about to drive right past me the moment the light turned red.

As if she could read my thoughts, she turned her head slightly, glancing in my direction.

Instinctively, I ducked down, peeking above the edge of the window like a little kid.

"Hey, are you okay?" Samantha asked. "Are you going to be sick? Leo, pull over."

"No," I barked, sitting up but still looking out the window. "Don't pull over. I'm fine." My mother couldn't see me because of the tinted windows. She had already turned back to watching the light, bored and impatient. The last thing I wanted was for Leo to pull off the road and draw attention to us.

"Don't you dare puke in my car," Leo said, as the light changed to red and we surged forward.

I watched my mother drive by, her car mere feet from me, her familiar profile slipping past me and out of sight. She had no idea I was there. In that car. So close to her.

There was only one reason I could think of for my mother to be in Indy; somehow she had found out where I was. But how? Emma couldn't have told her.

No one knew I was here, except for those of us following Marcus. Oh, and Mike Palmer. Shit. Mike Palmer knew exactly where I was. But how could it possibly serve him to tell my mother? And if he had told her, why hadn't she gone straight to the McMansion and confronted me? Oh my God. What if that's where she was headed right now? What if she'd just arrived in Indy and she was driving to the McMansion to get me? Well, I wouldn't be there. And Marcus would lie to her and send her away. And I had no idea how I felt about that.

I turned in my seat, looking out the rear window, and watched the pale blue VW recede into the distance, tears prickling at the corners of my eyes.

"Are you okay?" Samantha asked, concern in her voice.

"Yeah, I'm good." I turned back to the front. "Just got something in my eye," I said, brushing the moisture away with a fingertip.

Why had my mother shaved her head? She'd had beautiful chestnut hair down past her shoulders. She'd always worn her hair long, because my father had liked it that way. Why in the world would she hack it all off like that?

But even as I asked it, a little voice in my head was already answering. *You know why. She did it because of you. You were all she had left, and you abandoned her.*

25

MEETING MR. JAMES AGAIN

When we pulled up to Samantha's house, Leo parked the car and looked over his shoulder at her.

"I'm running low on gas," he said. "I'm going to have to let you both out here, and I'll come back and get Anne after I've filled up. I wouldn't want to make you feel worse," he said, speaking to me, "by exposing you to all those fumes."

It wasn't a question. I wasn't being given a choice. And that's when I realized that Samantha had been on her phone texting almost the whole way in the car, and I'd been too distracted about my mom to realize what that meant. Until now.

I had a sinking feeling I was about to have another

talk with Alexander James, and that Leo would not be back to take me home until Mr. James was satisfied with my answers. That whole thing about the other cars being in the shop—probably a load of bullshit. And I'd been having such warm fuzzy thoughts towards Samantha only minutes before. Dammit, I was sick and feverish. Why couldn't they just take me home and leave me alone? Except, if they did that, I might run smack into my mom. Maybe it was better to go along with this and see what I could find out.

"Come on," Samantha said, hopping out of the car. "We can get you something to help with that fever while you wait."

I looked at Leo and he stared back at me, his dark eyes framed in the rear view mirror.

I slowly opened my car door and climbed out.

As we entered the house, I grabbed Samantha's arm and said, "Listen, you can cut the crap. I know why I'm here."

"You're here because we care about you," Samantha said earnestly. "You have nothing to be afraid of, Anne. My father just wants to talk to you. That's all."

"Okay, fine," I said, letting go of her arm. "Let's get this over with. Honestly, I have a few questions of my own."

Ten minutes later, I found myself sitting outside Alexander James's office in a comfy chair with a glass of water in one hand and several Advil in the other. Samantha had handed them to me when she'd come out after briefly chatting with her father, and then she'd been whisked away so the family doctor could check out her face. Before she'd gone though, she'd assured me again that I was perfectly safe and would be returned home as soon as her father and I were done talking. Even so, one of the security goons had remained behind, looming over me.

"Cheers," I said, raising my glass to him and downing the painkiller.

He didn't even blink.

"Anne," Alexander James said, making me jump and inhale the water down the wrong tube. I hadn't even heard him open his office door, but there he was holding it open for me. "How nice to see you again. Please, come in."

I stood up and handed the half-full glass to the security guy, coughing the water out of my lungs as I followed the spider into his parlor like an obedient fly.

Mr. James took a seat at his desk and indicated that I should sit in the chair on the other side of it, facing him, which I did. He sat back, scrutinizing me, his eyes lingering on my gloved right hand, and he put his fingers in that familiar steeple.

"I understand that you have had a hard time of it," he began. "Samantha has shared some of your story with me. I'm sorry to hear that you and your family had a run-in with CAMFers in Illinois. I want to assure you that this will never happen to you in my city. The Hold protects its own."

"I'm not a member of The Hold," I said, letting my snarkiness get the best of me.

"Of course you are." He smiled patronizingly. "The day you were born with a PSS hand you became a member. The Hold is not a religion or cult, as some would describe it. It is a genetic family. You don't have to sign up, or even believe in your own heritage to join. You are born into it and you belong to it, whether you like it or not. It isn't a matter of belief. It just is."

"So, I don't have a choice?"

"Oh, you have all kinds of choices." Alexander James leaned forward. "Probably more today than you've ever had before," he said, opening up a thick file on his desk and shuffling through it.

Was it a file on me? Or was he using it to ignore me and tip the balance of power in his direction? I looked away, not wanting to give him the satisfaction of seeing my curiosity.

"What is it you really want, Anne?" he asked, his voice earnest. "To be surrounded by people who understand you? To live without fear? To live without being feared? The Hold can offer you that."

I looked up at him. Fuck. This guy was good. He'd only met me a couple of times and he'd already sized up my biggest insecurities. But why such a hard sell? He hadn't gone after Passion like this when he'd found out about her PSS. He'd been playing it cool until now. Either something had changed, or he wanted me for his little people collection even more than he wanted Passion with the PSS blood. And that didn't make sense.

"What I really want are some answers," I said. "I want someone to be honest with me for a change."

"I see," he said, sitting back. "People have lied to you. They have betrayed your trust. And you think I'm lying to you now. That is understandable. So, let us be honest with each other, *Olivia*."

I jerked my head up and found his eyes boring into

mine. He had called me Olivia. He knew who I was.

"This," he said, holding up the folder he'd been looking at, "is a very thorough file on a missing girl from Illinois with a PSS hand named Olivia Black."

"Where did you get that?" I blurted, but I already knew.

"Your mother gave it to me." He dropped the file onto his desk with a heavy thwack. "She was here, only half-an-hour ago, begging me to find you."

"Why would she come to you?" Shit. I was screwed. This guy knew everything about me. My mother hadn't been heading to the McMansion. She'd been driving away from Samantha's house.

"Several reasons," Mr. James said. "First, because I am the leader of The Hold and I make it my business to find and protect all members of my family. Second, because I was once business acquaintances with your father, and your mother remembered this and thought I might be willing to help her. And finally, I believe she was offering me a chance to redeem myself, because your parents once asked this very favor of me, long ago, and I failed them. I could not find your missing sister Kaylee for them, and it has haunted me ever since."

I couldn't move. I couldn't think. I couldn't stop that last sentence from bouncing around in my head. I had a fever. That could make you hear things, right? Or hallucinate? Or go stark raving mad?

"I don't have a sister," I exhaled, looking around the room for some way to escape this. "I've never had a sister."

"They decided not to tell you," Alexander James

said gently. "It happened six years before you were born. And they didn't want that pain and grief to cloud your world. They wanted you to be happy."

"Happy?" I said, and it came out all mangled and shrill. Six years before I'd been born, my parents had lived in Manitou Springs, Colorado. That's where they'd met. They'd told me stories about how my mom had worked in an art gallery, and my dad had displayed some of his earliest work there. She'd bought one of his pieces, mainly because she thought he was cute, and when he found out, he'd asked her out. A year later, they were married. Then the story always flashed forward to moving to Greenfield and having me. All that time they had been lying to me. All my life. This is what Marcus had been talking about. But how in the world had he known?

"Your sister was born with PSS two years before Thea Frandsen in Norway," Alexander James went on assaulting me with the truth. The truth I'd demanded. The truth I'd been begging for. "Doctors knew nothing about PSS back then. It had never been seen before. And she had it on over 80 percent of her body. Her birth was kept very tightly under wraps. They didn't expect her to live. And they didn't know what to do with her when she did. So, they kept her at the hospital. Your parents were in shock. It didn't help that they were barely allowed to see her.

Then when she was seventeen days old, someone took her. We don't know who or why. But she was never seen again. The authorities didn't ever want the story of the ghost baby getting out. It was too unbelievable, and they thought they'd be made a laughing stock. And so, they tried to erase it. They tried to erase her.

That is when your parents came to me. I followed every lead. For years, I followed every rumor or hint of a rumor, but when your father sold me the painting, he asked me to stop looking. They wanted to forget and move on. They wanted to love you without the ghost of your sister hanging over you."

Hanging over me. Yes, the truth had been hanging over me all my life. But Alexander James didn't know there was another copy of his precious painting. That my father and mother had changed their minds about letting my sister's disappearance haunt us all; *Kaylee, We will always love you.*

"It was a very difficult decision," he went on. "That painting was all they had to remember her by. It was your father's depiction of the girl he hoped she'd grow up to be."

"Wait," I said, glaring at him with a hatred I didn't even know I could feel. "You put a painting of my missing sister in your collection, and encouraged people to worship it as some mystical religious icon?" I stood up, shoving my chair back. "What kind of fucked up psycho are you?"

"I have never misrepresented that painting," he said, standing up too and towering over his desk, his voice low and dangerous. "People bring themselves to every piece of art and they see what they want in it, what they need from it. *Kaylee Pas Nova* is everything The Hold stands for, the very reason we exist: so a child born with PSS will never be erased again. Who do you think The Virgin Mary was? Just a poor girl who got pregnant before her wedding. And what about Buddha? A nobleman's son who gave up his wealth to become a monk. I didn't make your sister represent anything. She simply does. She is our Kaylee."

"This is crazy." I backed away from him, stumbling against the chair behind me. "You're lying to me. My father would never have kept this from me. He would have told me I had a sister."

"What purpose could I possibly have for telling you this if it weren't true?" Alexander James asked, coming around his desk toward me.

"I don't know," I said, glancing at the door, thinking of making a run for it.

"You asked me for the truth, and I gave it to you," he said, pausing in his advance. "And now it's your turn. Am I going to have Passion's mother on my doorstep tomorrow looking for her?"

"No." I shook my head. "Passion's parents—they don't care about her. They're practically CAMFers."

"Good." He nodded. "That makes things less complicated, since she seems to have a strong affinity for my daughter and The Hold already. And what about these boys you're with? Are they going to give me trouble?"

Shit. I'd exposed us all. I'd caused Alexander James's discerning eye to turn toward Nose and Yale and Jason. And Marcus.

"They're just foster care runaways," I said, trying to sound casual. "Passion and I weren't very street smart, and they've been helping us out."

"Foster care runaways staying in a house in Hunterwood Estates?" Alexander James raised a skeptical eyebrow.

"One of them is a hacker," I said. "He broke into the rental home data base. It wasn't that hard."

"I see." His eyes appraised me. "Well, there's no question that you are a very resourceful young lady. What about these tags? Samantha says they blocked her from hearing you. Let me see them," he commanded, moving toward me.

I reached inside my shirt and slipped the dog tags out. My hands were shaking.

Alexander James stopped only inches from me and peered down at them.

"Where did you get these?" He reached out, laying his fingertip lightly on the top one.

"My father gave them to me right before he died." I pulled the lie from thin air. "I don't know where he got them, but he said they would protect me. That I should always wear them."

"And he put your fake name on them?" Alexander James asked, his eyes drilling into me.

"No. I did that. In the garage at the Hunterwood house."

"Clever girl," he said, like I was his new pet. Then he put his hand on my shoulder. "I am very sympathetic to your situation, Olivia. I know all about your mother's issues with your hand, her inability to accept your PSS as the gift it is. And though I am sure she loves you, I doubt very much she will ever overcome those hang-ups, deep-seated as they are. She blames your sister's loss on PSS. That can't have been easy to deal with all your life. Frankly, I'm impressed you're as well-adjusted as you are, given the circumstances. And that is why I'm going to leave the next step completely up to you." He removed his hand from my shoulder, and I was glad. I didn't want him to feel me shaking, to know my fear of him. "I can call your mother right now," he said, "and she can come and get you. Or, I can advocate for you, try and convince her to put you under the legal guardianship of The Hold, which means you could stay here in Indy, under my roof, until you come of age. I would gladly do the same for Passion."

"And after I'm eighteen?" I asked cautiously.

"The Hold has college funds for our wards. You could go to school wherever you wanted. Or not. Once you're of age, you're free to do whatever you choose."

"Even leave The Hold?"

"You could leave Indy," he said, smiling. "But you will always be a member of The Hold, remember?"

How could I forget? I was marked. If Alexander James didn't keep reminding me, my hand would. "Can I have some time to think about it?" I asked. "It's a big decision, and with everything I just found out, I'm—I need some time."

"Of course," he said, taking a step back and giving me room to breathe. "You're overwhelmed. This must have been quite a shock. And Samantha said you weren't feeling well. I can give you some time to recover and think. I will have a car take you back to the house in Hunterwood Estates. But you need to make your choice by Sunday evening. I'll be meeting with your mother again on Monday, and it would be cruel to make her wait any longer than that."

"Thank you," I said, nodding my numb head at him. He was going to let me go. I was going to get away. What an idiot. Did he really think I was going to stick around "thinking" about his proposal?

"You're welcome." He put his hand gently on my shoulder again, the weight of it settling into my bones. "Just remember this, because it is very important." His voice was deep and full of menace. "If you run, I will find you."

26

DISSENSION IN THE RANKS

"**W**e need to leave. Now. Tonight," Marcus said, pacing the spare upstairs bedroom like a caged big cat, stopping every two or three passes to peek out between the vertical blinds at the dark car parked across the street from the McMansion. Alexander James was now monitoring our every move, thanks to me.

When I'd gotten back to the house, Marcus had been in the midst of gearing up to come after me. Apparently, Passion had sensed my distress through our connection with the tags, and she'd told him something was seriously wrong. And my explanation of what had happened hadn't calmed him down any. In fact, it had done the exact opposite. But at least Passion was calm now, more than calm, she seemed almost serene. Obviously, she was feeling better physically too.

"I'm not going anywhere," she said firmly. "I'm not leaving Samantha or The Hold. He offered to pay for our college. I don't get why you're so freaked out. If he knew you had PSS, he'd offer you the same deal. All of you," she said, looking around at Nose and Yale and Jason. "You'd be safe from the CAMFers. Isn't that what you've wanted all along?"

Marcus whirled around to face her. "You don't even know this man or what he's capable of. He's a murderer."

"She doesn't know because you haven't told her," I said, my head throbbing. "You can't expect people to know things you've kept secret." Like my sister. How had Marcus known about my sister? And why hadn't he told me?

"Okay, fine," he said. "Passion, Alexander James chased my family down into an oncoming train and killed my parents. I was seven. And I was a member of The Hold. How's that for taking care of family?"

"I don't believe you," she said, staring at him.

"What?" His fists were clenched. He looked like he might launch himself at her.

"I'm not saying you're lying," she said. "I can see you think that's what happened. But I don't believe Mr. James is an evil villain, or a murderer. And I'm sorry if your parents were killed in an accident. But maybe it was just an accident."

"You think I don't know what happened to my own family?" he said, his face red, his eyes flaming with anger.

"I think you've had a very hard life," Passion said calmly, "and you see everyone and everything through a lens of mistrust."

Go Passion. I had no idea she had such insight into Marcus, let alone the balls to call him on it. If I hadn't felt like a pile of crap, I might have stood up and given her a standing ovation.

"Besides," she went on. "You heard what Olivia said. If we run, he'll come after us. If that car out there isn't proof of that, I don't know what is."

"You guys could probably run," I pointed out, looking at Marcus. "He may have believed me about you. But he might not have. I don't know."

"We're not splitting up," he said. "We're not leaving you to The Hold."

"I could go back with my mom," I said, shrugging.

"And that's what you want?" He sounded hurt, really hurt. And I couldn't help feeling a little thrill because of it.

"I don't know," I said. Because I didn't. My brain was mush. I was still running a fever, and I could barely string two coherent thoughts together. All I'd wanted to do after my little talk with Alexander James was come back to the house and crawl into bed. Instead, I'd had to tell everyone that we'd been found out, and not only were we not going to extract Samantha from The Hold, Passion and I were very likely going to be absorbed by it.

"What about this art gala thing on Friday?" Yale asked. "Didn't Samantha say her dad uses most of his security for that? We could probably sneak away then."

"That's the night of the Eidolon," Passion said.

"I'm not missing it. And I'm not running."

"So you actually want to join The Hold?" Marcus asked, incredulous.

"Yes," Passion said. "I'm taking Mr. James up on his offer. I'm going to tell Samantha on Friday."

"And the rest of you?" Marcus asked bitterly, looking first at Jason, then Nose, then Yale. "You want to go to college too? You want to join his cult and live in his mansion and have people worship you like a god?"

"I don't trust any of it," Jason said. "What's in it for him?"

"If it sounds too good to be true," Yale said, "it probably is."

"You know we're with you," Nose said to Marcus. "Just tell us what to do."

All his good army men in a row. Well, at least Marcus still had that.

"We'll come up with something," Marcus said, looking back at Passion. "We always do." But he wasn't going to share it in front of her. His traitor. His Judas. *Maybe he wouldn't tell me either. Then again, what else was new?*

"Well, I'm going to bed," I said, getting up and walking down the hall toward my room.

I heard Marcus coming after me long before he called my name or grabbed my arm.

"What?" I said, turning and looking up at him.

"Listen—I—I'm sorry you found out that way," he said, guilt in his eyes. "From him. About your sister."

"How did you know?" I asked, feeling numb, too tired to rage at him anymore.

"I didn't know for sure. At first. But my mom's

entire time in The Hold was dedicated to separating fact from fiction. When I went looking through some of her old notes and journals, the pieces were all there."

"When?" I asked. "When did you know?"

"A week ago," he said. "But how could I tell you? What if I was wrong? You'd think I'd lied to you again. Even if I was right, I knew how badly it would hurt you. I didn't know what to do. And then when you saw the other painting, I knew you were close to figuring it out yourself. I wanted you to, and I was terrified you would blame me for not telling you when you did."

"So you broke up with me and let Alexander James do your dirty work? Yeah, that was ballsy of you," I said, pulling my arm from his grasp and walking away from him.

I went into my room and closed the door, and this time when my face hit the pillow I didn't cry. Instead, I fell into a fevered sleep and dreamt of Alexander James, cradling my baby ghost sister in his arms, smiling down at her, and when I saw her face in the dream, it wasn't a face at all; it was the round symbol of The Hold, two fists clenched in the middle of it, forever in conflict.

Passion was fine by the next morning, but she stayed home to take care of me, and to appease Marcus, who was adamant she not go alone after what had transpired between me and Alexander James.

She did a good job of nursing me. She kept me hydrated, even though I wasn't throwing up, and made sure I had saltines and 7-Up next to my bed. I had a feeling she was keeping Marcus at bay as well, because I'd woken up once to the murmur of voices and found her shutting the door firmly in his face and locking it. Of course, Marcus had a key if he really wanted to push things, but I doubted he would. If he was smart, he'd give me some time and space, especially while I was sick.

At about three in the afternoon, my fever broke, and an hour later I started feeling good and hungry, so Passion went downstairs to make my favorite comfort food: macaroni and cheese.

I was lying there, trying not to drift off, when my phone started buzzing like crazy on the nightstand. I picked it up and looked at the screen. It was Emma, but it wasn't the time for our prescheduled call. I jabbed the answer button, put it to my cheek and said, "Hello?"

"Hey Liv, can you talk?"

"Yeah, sure. What's going on?"

"He woke up," she said. "Dr. Fineman woke up from his coma."

"When?" I asked, a coldness traveling down my body.

"I'm not totally sure. Last night or this morning, I guess. Anyway, he's still in the hospital."

"Emma," I said, "listen to me. When we get off the phone, I want you to go straight to your parents and tell them everything that happened. Tell them about my hand, and Passion, and the blades, and the PSS guys. Tell them about Mike Palmer and the CAMFers. Most importantly, make it very clear to them that you are in a lot of danger. If he's awake, you all need to get out of Greenfield. Now."

"What? No, I can't tell them all that. They'd never believe me."

"I don't care if they don't believe you. Make something up. Figure out a way to get them to leave."

"But what about your mom? If I tell them anything, it's going to get back to her eventually."

"It doesn't matter. She's going to know where I am by Monday anyway."

"What? How?"

"It's a long story. And I don't have time to explain. Emma, just get your parents to leave Greenfield. Think of a way. I know you can do it."

"Well, okay. They have been talking a lot about going to visit Grant in Indy, especially my mom. She really misses him."

"Good." Emma should have no problem convincing her parents to visit her brother Grant, who was a freshman at Indianapolis University. And then all the Campbells would be in Indy. Along with my mom. And me. Why not make it my whole damn hometown while I was at it?

Still, Indy was better than Greenfield with Dr. Fineman on the loose. "Push for this weekend," I told Emma. "And get them to stay until Tuesday, if you can." Hopefully, by then I could carve out a deal with Alexander James that would keep me and everyone I loved safe under the grand umbrella of The Hold. It was the only thing I could think of to do. Did I trust the benevolence of The Hold or Alexander James? No, I did not. But if I could use it to my advantage,

I would. And I wasn't sure I had any other choice at the moment.

"I'll try." She still sounding unsure.

"No, don't try. Do it. They already want to go. Em, promise me you and your parents will be in Indy by tomorrow."

"My dad has a work thing tomorrow. He can't miss it."

"Then by Saturday. Please."

"Yeah, okay," Emma said. "I'll text you when we're heading out of town."

"Thank you." I exhaled a sigh of relief.

"You're scaring me, Liv. What's going on? Are you okay?"

"I have the flu," I said, laughing weakly. "And I'm thinking of joining a cult."

"Come on, be serious," Emma scolded.

"I am being serious. But I'm going to let you go now so this call doesn't get traced. Be safe, Emma. I love you."

"I love you too. Be safe yourself."

Five minutes later, Passion came in with a warm bowl of macaroni and cheese, and I scarfed it down. I had a feeling I was going to need all the strength I could muster very soon.

"Do you think you'll be up to school tomorrow?" Passion asked hopefully when I handed her the empty bowl. "And for the Eidolon?"

"I think so," I said, "but do you really think Marcus is going to let us go to that?"

"Oh, he changed his mind," she said, looking pleased with herself. "When I explained to him that

Samantha really wanted him and the guys to come, he said they would."

"What?" I said, sitting up and throwing off my blankets. "What about their PSS? Samantha will hear them coming a mile away?"

"Why would that matter?" Passion asked, sounding puzzled.

"Does she already know? Did you tell her about them?"

"No, I didn't tell her," Passion said defensively. "I thought it would be a really cool thing to surprise her with."

Yeah, Samantha was about to get a very big surprise.

Marcus, Nose, Jason and Yale were going to crash the Eidolon.

27

BAD PLANS AND WILD THINGS

I went downstairs to find Marcus. Alone. I told Passion we needed to talk about our relationship but what I really hoped to do was talk him out of his plan. His very bad plan. Because if he crashed the Eidolon it might mess up my very bad plan to cut a deal with Alexander James.

I found him sitting out on the back deck. It still had the slight smell of gasoline, but it wasn't too bad. He was stretched out in a wooden lounge chair, staring out at the immaculate lawn and the woods and stream beyond. He looked good. Too damn good.

I sat down in a second chair, and he glanced at me briefly, then resumed staring off into the distance. "You must be feeling better," he said.

"Yeah, I was feeling better," I agreed. "And then Passion told me that you're planning to attend the Eidolon."

"Did you know they have a problem with coyotes around here?" he asked, completely changing the subject. "They build these big houses, and they surround them with fields and woods and water. It's the perfect habitat for wild things to flourish, and then they're surprised when the coyotes take up residence and eat their cats."

"They eat cats?"

"Of course they do," he said. "Some little girl came by yesterday with a flyer for her missing cat, Snowball. Beautiful picture of a fluffy white Persian with a red collar and a heart-shaped tag. Only problem was I'd seen that collar and tag before, the night you saw Mike Palmer and we scoured the property."

"You saw her cat that night?"

"Not her cat, no. Not exactly." He looked at me. "I saw a pile of white fur and bones with the collar in the middle of it out there in the tall grass."

"Oh, ick! Poor thing. Did you tell her?"

"No," he said, shaking his head and looking away. "I'm not into breaking little girls' hearts."

Well, I beg to differ.

"Besides," he said. "If you create the perfect place for wild things to thrive, you should be prepared to encounter the consequences that come with wild things."

"And that's your rational for this?" I asked, finally making sense of his little interlude. "Samantha James is throwing a party for domesticated cats with PSS, and you're the wild coyote that's going to rush in and eat them all up?"

"No metaphor is perfect," he said, shrugging. "But as they go, it's not bad."

"What are you even going to do? Passion isn't going to change her mind about The Hold, and Samantha isn't going to come with us willingly."

"Not willingly, no," he said, not looking at me.

"You'd take her by force?" I asked. "Isn't that the exact reason you're pissed off at The Hold? Because they tried to keep your mom against her will?"

"You think a kid has any choice when they're raised in a cult?" he asked vehemently. "Brainwashed by their own parents into believing something? She's never had a choice."

"If she's never wanted one, how does it even matter?"

"She has wanted one," he said, his brown eyes falling on me, pools of intensity. "She wanted to come when we left. She begged to come. But my parents said no. They couldn't risk charges of kidnapping, on top of everything else. But I promised I'd come back for her."

"You promised Samantha James you'd come back for her when you were seven?" I stared at him, my mind racing like a hamster wheel. This thing with Samantha went way deeper than I'd ever suspected. It wasn't just about redeeming what had happened to his mom. He had some kind of damsel-in-distress childhood fantasy about Samantha James that he'd been harboring all these years. Had they been in love? No, that was ridiculous. She'd been six and he'd been seven. Kids that age didn't fall in love; they had crushes. But would a boy yanked away from his childhood crush directly before he'd watched his parents violently die, hold onto that crush like a lifeline? Would he believe in it like a fairy tale and pursue it like a dream he barely remembered?

Shit. Was this why he'd broken up with me? Because we were getting close to Samantha, and when he finally confronted her, he wanted to be available?

"You know," he said, completely oblivious to the jealousy that was rolling over me like waves of the ocean. "I never thought you'd flip so easily and buy into The Hold. It's no different than the CAMFers. They're two sides of the same coin."

"That's bullshit," I said, unable to keep the heat out of my voice. "They're exact opposites. You said so yourself back at the gun club. And for your information, I haven't bought into The Hold. But I don't see any other viable option at the moment."

"I'm not a viable option anymore?" he asked. "This group we've made, it doesn't mean anything to you?"

"Those are two different questions," I pointed out. He was really starting to piss me off. He'd kept this secret about Samantha, and broken up with me, and now he was complaining that I didn't consider him an option. "Besides, I don't even know what this group is once we've crossed off everything on your list. We've found Samantha. We know who Kaylee Pas Nova is. But now what? Even if Samantha comes with us, and we get away from The Hold, what then? We can't keep driving around on ATVs and living in the woods the rest of our lives."

"What about your sister? You don't want to try and find her?"

"You mean my sister who went missing twenty-three years ago? The one Alexander James looked for with unlimited resources and couldn't find?"

"You're satisfied to know she disappeared and that's it?" he asked, sounding completely disappointed in me.

"I'd have no idea where to even start looking," I said. But honestly, I hadn't thought about it. She wasn't real to me. I couldn't wrap my mind around her existence.

"I certainly know the first place I'd look," Marcus said. "The CAMFer compound where Danielle and I were held had numerous holding cells. I doubt we were the first prisoners there."

"And you also said it was secured like a fortress after you escaped. You couldn't even get near it."

"Yeah, but that was eight months ago. And I was by myself."

"Fine. Why don't we tell Alexander James where it is, and let him bang at the doors with the power of The Hold?"

"No." Marcus glared at me. "I'm not aligning myself with that man. Ever. And neither should you."

"And that leaves me going back home with my mother," I said. I couldn't imagine going back to Greenfield after all I'd been through. Maybe it had only been a few weeks since I'd left, but it felt like a lifetime. So much had changed. I had changed. My mother had changed. And I couldn't imagine navigating the whole issue of my long lost sister with her.

I couldn't fit back into that small-town world again. Too much had happened.

"If that's what you want," Marcus said coldly, looking back out toward the woods.

What I wanted was him. I wanted us back. I wanted that feeling when I'd wrapped my legs around him in that steamy bathroom and we'd almost lost ourselves in each other.

But now Samantha and all his other secrets were standing between us, and he was going to have to figure that shit out on his own. God, I was glad I hadn't told Passion he'd known Samantha. Or told Marcus that Passion and Samantha were becoming a thing. But if he came to the Eidolon he'd see it. Seems Samantha wasn't the only one who was going to get a surprise when he showed up. How upset would he be when the dream of rescuing his childhood love came crashing down?

"You're bringing guns to the Eidolon, aren't you?" I asked, fear stealing into my heart.

"Of course not," he said, his voice dripping with sarcasm. "We thought it would be better to go into an unknown situation like that completely unarmed."

"It's a bunch of teenagers throwing a party," I said. "Come talk to Samantha if you have to. Find out if she still wants to leave The Hold, but please don't bring guns."

"You don't remember what happened last time you asked that of me?"

"You are such an idiot," I said, starting to get up from my chair, but he put out a hand and said, "Shhh, don't move."

I followed his gaze, and saw what he saw; a lanky dog-wolf creature, wheat-colored with the sun shining golden on it, loping along the manicured path, moving quickly and stealthily, but completely without regard for us.

The hair on the back of my neck stood up and goose bumps blossomed on my arms, as the lone coyote loped out of sight around a bend in the path. He was so like Marcus. They were so like each other.

"Promise me something," Marcus said, after a long stretch of silence.

"What?"

"Wear your dog tags to this Eidolon thing."

"Why? Everyone already knows about my ghost hand."

"Just in case," he said. "For me."

"Sure. Whatever," I said, and I left him on the deck to make my way back to my room.

"How did it go?" Passion asked, hopefully. "Did you guys make up?"

"Um, no," I said. "But it's fine. Probably better this way."

I was almost as bad of a liar as Marcus was.

28

FRIDAY

Friday morning, Passion and I got ready for school and went out to the car sitting across the street.

"Good morning," Leo greeted us as we walked up. He looked fresh and well kept, so they must have switched surveillance detail sometime in the early morning. "You girls hoping for a ride?"

"We thought you might as well," I said, "since you're going to follow us anyway."

"Hop in then," he said, and we did.

There were a lot more people at school than I'd expected. Everyone from Samantha's gang was back in commission and very amped up about the impending Eidolon. And from what I could tell from their enthusiastic, glance-at-my-right-hand greetings, Samantha had informed them of my new status in the group. I was no longer a groupie; I was an equal. Renzo even started openly flirting with me, which was both flattering and a bit disconcerting. I couldn't even chant "I have a boyfriend," in my head to disarm the effects of it. Because I didn't. So, I might have flirted back a little.

Passion was thrilled to see Samantha, and vice versa, and I was happy to see that Samantha's eye was only a little puffy. Both Passion and I tried to extract more information from the group about what the Eidolon was, and what to expect, but everyone just smiled and said, "You'll see." Samantha did tell us that Renzo would pick us up at our house at dusk, that we should wear comfortable, warm clothes and shoes, and that we'd be home by dawn.

"Oh, I have good news." Passion told Samantha "Clay and his friends decided to come. They can drive and follow Renzo, if that's okay?"

"Awesome," Samantha beamed, turning to me. "Anne, did you talk your brother into it?"

She was still calling me Anne, even though I was sure her father had told her who I really was. But whatever. I'd play along.

"No, I actually tried to talk him out of it," I said. "He's a serious buzz kill."

Everyone laughed at that, even though it hadn't been a joke. Then Samantha said something about how family members could be the most challenging when it came to understanding our PSS, and she put her arm around me like we were best friends or something. It was weird.

Thankfully, the rest of the day flew by, even though I was a little jumpy, worrying that my mom was going to show up any minute and drag me out of there by my ear. What if Alexander James had a change of heart and decided to tell her before Monday? And what if he felt so guilty he took back his offer about The Hold?

In reality, according to Samantha, he was consumed by preparations for the art gala. He probably wasn't thinking about me or my mother at all.

Apparently, he wasn't the only one distracted by the upcoming event. The teachers certainly were. And the students. Even the janitorial staff was, whose job appeared to be plastering the school hallways with James Foundation Annual Art Gala Posters and cleaning them up when they fell down to be trampled by the student body.

I'd been seeing the posters all over Indy since the first day we'd arrived in the city, long before I'd known anything about Alexander James or The Hold, but there was a newer version up now. *Never Before Seen Art Collection Unveiled*, it said. Wow. Was Alexander James going to unveil his PSS art collection in public? Was he going to let *Kaylee Pas Nova* out to play? Why would he do that after all these years of hiding her? And was this, perhaps, the chance the CAMFers were counting on to get their hands on The Hold's iconic painting? No wonder Mr. James had beefed up his security this year.

After school, Renzo and Samantha walked Passion and me out to the car that was waiting to take us home.

"See you tonight," Renzo said, leaning in

my window and smiling cockily like we had a date or something.

"Yep," I said, blushing and rolling my window up so he had to jump back to avoid being reverse-guillotined by it.

I turned to Passion in time to see her and Samantha exchange a cute little kiss goodbye through her open window.

"I'm glad that your cousin and his friends are coming," Samantha said. "They're going to love it. I know it."

I doubted she'd be nearly that excited if she realized they'd all be coming armed and with significant ill intent.

"I can't wait," Passion said, and we pulled away, the two of them waving at one another until we were out of sight.

It was a long impatient wait until dusk back at the McMansion.

Marcus was in a foul mood and barely spoke to me, let alone shared any of his plans for the evening. I guess our role as fake brother and sister at the Eidolon was going to be as siblings who didn't get along very well. I did hear Yale talking excitedly about finally getting to drive the Porsche, and I was tempted to ask him if it bothered him that the trunk would be full of guns, but I didn't work up the nerve. Yale, Nose, and Jason had been Marcus's friends first, and I hadn't gotten too close to them. Maybe that was my fault for pairing up with him. Maybe it was because I wasn't a guy. Maybe it was because I still couldn't bring myself to trust the three of them after they'd turned on me in Mike Palmer's garage. Whatever the reason, they clearly belonged to Marcus, not me.

When a dark blue Mercedes pulled up outside the McMansion at dusk, Passion, Marcus and I made our way out to it.

The driver's side door opened and Renzo stepped out. He'd opted for an eye patch instead of his sunglasses, and I had to admit he looked like some kind of handsome modern-day pirate. "Hey, Anne." He sidled up to me and, for a moment, I thought he might embrace me. "You look beautiful tonight."

I glanced down at what I was wearing: black Docs, dark jeans, and a bomber jacket over a t-shirt. Fashion that, at its best, could only be described as combat chic.

"What about me?" Passion teased. "How do I look?"

"You look great too," he said. "And you must be Anne's brother." He held out his hand to Marcus. "I'm Renzo."

"I'm Clay," Marcus said, putting his hand in Renzo's.

There was a nervous moment while they shook hands when I thought Renzo might force Marcus into The Hold handclasp like Shotgun had at the gun club, but he didn't. Renzo obviously didn't know Marcus from his long lost past. Thank God.

"So, what's the deal with the rides?" Renzo asked. "I've only got room for Passion and Anne, 'cause I'm picking Dimitri up on the way out of town."

"No problem," Marcus said, "We have a car." He nodded toward the garage where the Porsche was emerging, a grinning Yale behind the wheel with Jason and Nose in the back.

"Nice car," Renzo said. "It might even keep up with mine."

"In case it doesn't," Marcus said, "where exactly are we going?"

"Out of town," Renzo said. "Way out of town to a little state park called Shades."

"Shades?" Marcus and I blurted at once.

Oh, shit. *Don't go to Shades.* That is what Mike Palmer's matchbook had told us. The matchbook that was tucked in my jeans pocket at that very moment along with the torn scrap of backing paper from *The Other Olivia* with my dad's dedication to my missing sister on it. I'd gotten into the habit of keeping them both with me like weird souvenirs of places I'd never been.

"Yeah, you know it?" Renzo asked.

"No," Marcus said, looking at me, glancing at my neck to make sure I had the dog tags on, which I did. "Never heard of it."

"That's a weird name for a state park," Passion said. I'd never shown her the message on the matchbook. It seemed I was as good as Marcus at keeping things to myself.

"Oh, you have no idea," Renzo said. "It used to be called Shades of Death by the early settlers and Native Americans, but when Parks and Recreation took it over in the forties they shortened the name to Shades. I guess they thought it had a nicer ring to it."

"Why was it called Shades of Death?" Passion asked, starting to sound a bit concerned.

"You'll see," Renzo grinned wickedly. "I wouldn't want to spoil the surprise."

"Yeah, I don't think we should go," I said, stepping away from Renzo and looking at Marcus. We had to abort this fucking mission. Somehow, Mike Palmer had known a week ago that the Eidolon was going to be at Shades, and he had warned us not to go. Granted, he was my sworn enemy, so maybe we should do the exact opposite of what he'd told us. But if he'd known where the Eidolon was going to be, that meant the CAMFers knew as well. Better to hide in the McMansion than risk this. I had lost my enthusiasm for the Eidolon completely.

"What? Hey, come on," Renzo said, frowning. "Don't let a little name thing freak you out." He reached out and put his arm around my shoulder, pulling me into him. "It's one of the most beautiful parks in Indiana, I promise. Besides, I'll be there to keep you safe."

"Stay home if you want, Sis," Marcus said, his eyes piercing into me as I stood there with Renzo draped all over me. "But I'm going. We'll see you there," he said to Renzo, turning on his heel and walking stiffly up the driveway to the Porsche.

"Well, he seems a little hostile," Renzo purred in my ear. "What's up his ass?"

"Let's go," I said, slipping out from under his arm and heading to his car, where I made a point of climbing in the back and letting Passion sit next to him in the front. If Marcus was going to be that pig-headed, so could I.

"Where's Samantha?" Passion asked as he revved up the engine. "I was hoping she'd ride with us."

"Nah. She always goes ahead to get things ready," Renzo explained. "And Lily is driving Eva and her groupie in her car."

"Oh," Passion gave a sigh of disappointment.

As we pulled away from the curb and the Porsche pulled out as well, I didn't miss the flash of a third car's lights, obviously following farther behind us. Leo's car had never left the McMansion, and it gave me some comfort to know he was still on duty. We weren't completely on our own.

What had Marcus been thinking? Did he assume that because he had guns, we'd be fine? Or was he so obsessed with talking to his long lost Samantha that he thought it was worth the risk? Or maybe, once again, there was some crucial piece of information I was missing that would help all this make sense. A piece of information he was withholding from me.

I had no idea. And as we drove into the night, the moon rising early over Indianapolis, I rolled down my window and let the winds of fate swirl around me.

29

THINGS GET WORSE

We picked up Dimitri and he climbed into the back beside me, the lights of the Porsche hitting us like a spotlight through the rear window.

"Those your boys back there?" Dimitri asked.

"They don't belong to me," I said grumpily, and he laughed.

"Then you're doing something wrong," he said, and I was pretty sure he was right.

We took off and soon we were out of town and driving on a wide highway, the lights of other cars flashing past us and the Porsche humming behind us. I tried not to fall asleep like I always do on long car rides, but I must have zoned out or drifted off, because the next thing I knew Dimitri and Passion were in the middle of a conversation about Alexander James's art gala.

"It's a real big deal this year," Dimitri said, "because he's finally managed to purchase this collection he's wanted for years. It only became available in the last few days, and I guess the paintings are going to officially change hands at the gala."

So, the unveiling wasn't going to be of his special PSS collection then, but of some new acquisition.

"Who's the painter?" Passion asked perkily.

"Stephen Black," Dimitri said. "He's the guy who painted *The Kaylee*. You've seen it, right? Anyway, I guess his widow finally decided to unload his entire body of work. Isn't that incredible timing?"

"What did you say?" I asked, turning my head in what felt like slow motion. My eyes panned past Passion's face, noticing the look of shock frozen there, then went on to fall on Dimitri's, the look of excitement and elation on his in stark contrast.

"I said Alexander James is buying this collection at the gala tonight," Dimitri reiterated for me. "And the deal's only been in the works for a couple of days."

I could guess exactly how many days. I could guess it right down to the exact hour in fact. I'd be willing to stake my life on it that this deal had been struck on Wednesday afternoon about half an hour before I'd been summoned to Mr. James's office. My mother had come begging for him to find me, and she'd cut the only deal she could, with the only thing she had that he might want. And Alexander James had jumped on that business proposition like the bastard he was.

Which would have been bad enough, but that wasn't all.

He'd located me, the missing girl, thirty minutes later. I'd walked right into his office, but he hadn't told me about that deal, and he hadn't called my mom, because the legal paperwork for the sale of my dad's collection probably hadn't gone through yet. Which was exactly why he'd given me the generous offer of not informing my mother of my whereabouts until Monday—when the deal would be sealed.

Every painting my dad had ever painted except *The Other Olivia* was about to become the property of Alexander James and his precious Hold. And he'd screwed over both me and my mom to get it. He'd never cared about me, or my hand, or redeeming himself over my sister's loss. This had been his game all along. He'd wanted to take everything I had left of my father from me.

"Stop the car," I said to Renzo.

"What?" Dimitri said.

"Stop the car." Was I whispering? Was I mumbling? Were the words coming out of my mouth some foreign language no one else could understand?

"Olivia, it's going to be okay," Passion said, forgetting to use my fake name, her face gone white as a sheet.

"Stop. The. Car. STOP THE FUCKING CAR!" I screamed, surging forward and trying to grab Renzo around the neck from the back, but Passion caught my gloved hands, holding them, squeezing them.

"What the fuck?" Dimitri yelled.

"Stop the car, please," Passion pleaded with Renzo.

She was literally blocking me from climbing over the seat and throttling him. "Stop the car," she said again, almost a sob. "She's having a panic attack." And it was true. A truer thing had never been said.

Renzo swerved, throwing me off Passion and into Dimitri's chest, and then we were on the side of the interstate and I was clawing at the car door, fumbling at the handle, throwing it open and stumbling out. The cool night air hit me like a smack in the face, but it didn't clear my hysteria. If anything, it made it worse, made me feel sharper, made me know harder what a complete idiot I'd been and that I'd ruined everything. For my mother. And for me. My choices had led to this complete and utter ruin.

I walked to the shoulder of the road, halfway between the Mercedes and the Porsche which had pulled up behind us, its light blinding me from looking the way I needed to look. The way I needed to go. Back to Indy. Back to stop my mother from throwing everything away for nothing.

"Is she okay?" someone asked from behind me.

"Olivia," Marcus called as he opened his door, his silhouette stretched huge and gruesome in the light of the oncoming traffic. "What's the matter?"

Voices.

"Why does everyone keep calling her Olivia?"

"Shouldn't we help her?"

"Let her brother do it. She's completely wacked."

"Olivia," Marcus said, grabbing me, taking hold of both my arms. "It's okay. Are you still sick? Do you need to throw up?"

He sounded concerned. But he didn't know anything.

"No," I said, shaking my head. How could I make him understand? "She's selling it all," I said. "He's taking it all. Tonight. That's why he let me go."

"Who's selling what?" he asked, confused. "I don't understand."

"My mom," I said. "She's selling my dad's art to pay for him to find me. She's giving it to him at the gala tonight. Right now."

"What are you—" He froze, understanding dawning in his eyes. "You mean Alexander James?"

"Yes," I sobbed, burying my head in his chest, feeling his arms come around me like they should have in the first place. "We have to go back," I cried shamelessly into his shirt. "You have to take me back. I have to stop her. Please. Please help me stop her."

"Shhhh," He stroked my hair with his hands, crushing me to him. "It's going to be all right. I promise. Calm down. It's going to be okay."

"No," I gasped and shook my head, gripping his shirt in both my hands and wiping my dripping nose on it at the same time. "We have to stop it. We have to go back."

"Listen to me." He took my face in his hands and made me look at him. "Going back won't accomplish anything. He's probably told his security specifically not to let you into the event. Even if we went back, the deal would be done before we ever got there. We can't stop this by going back. We can only stop it by going forward."

"But how?" I cried, tears streaming down my face.

"I don't know." His eyes were on mine, dark and true. I hadn't seen him look at me like that since the night in the bathtub. "I have no idea, but I promise you, I will help you fix this."

"I don't believe you." I tried to pull away from him. "You always lie to me."

But he wouldn't let me go. I was trapped. Forever trapped by him and his lies and my own stupidity.

"Let go of me!" I screamed, struggling against his hold, battering my fists against his chest and kicking at his legs. The harder I struggled, the harder he held me, until I was pinned against him, crying and limp.

"I'm sorry I hurt you," he murmured, and I could hear the rumble of the words through his chest, accompanied by the Thu-bump of his amazing heart, just like I had so long ago on a hill overlooking Umlot Memorial Hospital when I'd first fallen for him. "I should have told you about your sister as soon as I'd guessed," he went on. "I should have been there for you in that moment, but I was too afraid."

"I'm afraid now," I whispered. "I'm so afraid."

"Me too," he said, squeezing me until I could barely breath. "Because I think I love you."

"What?" I looked up at him. I could not have heard that right. He had not just told me he loved me while I threw a hysterical tantrum on the side of the road with people watching who thought we were brother and sister.

"I'm pretty sure I love you," he said again, only a little louder, looking down at me.

"What about Samantha?" I blurted.

"What about her?" He sounded completely confused.

"I thought—I mean she seemed really important to you. You're not in love with her?"

He stared at me, his eyes first puzzled, then almost amused. "Um, no. I'm not in love with Samantha. It's—I—don't be mad at me, okay, but I didn't tell you everything about my connection to the James family."

"Of course you didn't," I said stiffly, starting to pull away.

"Olivia, please," He pulled me back. "I'm trying to come clean here. I'm trying to tell you the whole truth."

"Okay, tell me."

"Samantha is my cousin. And Alexander James is my uncle. He's my mom's brother."

I stood there for a moment, absorbing that. Samantha and Marcus were cousins. They'd grown up together in The Hold. And when he, and Danielle, and his parents had left, she'd wanted to leave with them, probably because she was six and didn't understand their disenchantment with The Hold. But I understood why he had to make sure. Why he needed to talk to her.

"And what else?" I said.

"There's nothing else," he answered. "That's it. No more lies or surprises. I'll tell you anything you want."

"Anything?"

"Fire away."

"Do you only think you love me? Are you pretty sure you love me? Or are you absolutely positive?" I asked. "Because it's kind of an important distinction."

"I think I'm pretty positive I love you." He grinned down at me.

"Good, because I'm pretty positive I love you." I looked into his chocolate brown eyes. "I want to kiss you so hard right now."

"That would be nice," he said, "but probably very confusing for some of the bystanders."

And that's when I remembered we were on the side of an Indianapolis interstate with six people looking on.

I glanced behind me and saw Dimitri and Renzo standing on one side of the Mercedes, confused and concerned looks on their faces. Passion was leaning against the bumper, and she gave me a tentative, questioning smile when I caught her eye.

I turned and looked past Marcus to the Porsche, its lights now off. Yale, Jason, and Nose were still sitting in it and looking on, their faces interested but carefully neutral.

"We'll figure this thing out with your mom and the paintings," Marcus said, pulling my attention back to him. "Samantha has lots of sway with her father. Let me talk to her, and we'll see what we can do. This isn't over yet. Not by a long shot."

"Okay." I nodded.

"But come in the car with me," he said. "I want you near me."

"What about Passion?"

"She'll be fine," he said, taking my hand and turning toward the Porsche.

"Hey," I turned back, calling out to Passion. "I'm going in the other car. I—we'll see you there."

"Okay," she called back, waiting for a minute and then ushering Renzo and Dimitri back into the Mercedes. I was pretty sure there'd be a discussion in that car about what had just happened, and I didn't envy Passion having to explain it.

Marcus opened the back door of the Porsche for me, and I climbed in next to Jason.

"Hey," Jason said in way of greeting.

"Hey," I said back, as Marcus crammed himself in next to me and shut the door.

When I turned to Marcus, he took my face in his hands, his eyes sparkling and speaking to me almost as well as his lips did when they fell on mine.

And then we kissed a lot, which might have made the other guys in the car a little uncomfortable.

But neither of us really cared.

30

THINGS GET COMPLICATED

About fifty miles northwest of Indianapolis, a huge forest of giant oaks and hemlocks rose out of the flat, over-farmed landscape in front of us. The trees looked completely out of place in the Midwest, like some dark, magical woodland had been plucked right out of an old English fairy tale and plopped in front of us. I could see the twinkle of other headlights between the braches, and when I rolled down the window, I could hear voices, drifting to us on the cool night wind.

Yale followed Renzo's Mercedes into the park, navigating the small winding road to an old brick gatehouse and through the open gate, even though a sign clearly stated that the park was closed for seasonal trail repairs. We pulled up into the dark parking lot, populated with ten to fifteen other cars. Yale turned off the engine and we all sat, looking at Marcus, waiting for him to tell us what to do.

"Let's do this," he said, throwing open his car door and pulling me out by the hand after him.

Passion, Renzo, and Dimitri were getting out of the Mercedes next to us.

"You okay?" Passion asked, brushing up against my shoulder as we walked away from the cars.

"Yeah," I answered, feeling such a jumble of emotions that I didn't know whether to smile or cry. "He's going to do something about the paintings. We're going to talk to Samantha."

"Good," she said nodding, "I can too, if you think it might help." Then we were suddenly standing in a group of about thirty people, all teenagers like ourselves, girls and guys, none of them with obvious PSS that I could see—but that was easy enough to hide. Everyone was talking, loud and excited, and I caught sight of Lily briefly, but I didn't see Samantha anywhere.

"Okay, everyone, listen up," Renzo barked, standing on a large rock, his pirate patch gone, his PSS eye piercing us into silence. Dimitri was standing next to the rock, his arms piled high with the black cloth I'd noticed him pulling out of the Mercedes trunk when we'd first parked. "We have robes for you to put on," Renzo explained. "Dimitri will be handing them out. If you don't want to wear one, that's fine. Go back to your car and wait for the rest of us to come back because the robe is only the beginning of what we're going to ask of you tonight. This is the Eidolon, and it's a sacred ritual, so deal with it."

Sacred ritual? I glanced at Marcus, but he wasn't looking at me. He was scanning the crowd for Samantha.

"Here you go," Dimitri said, holding out robes to us and eyeing me cautiously as if he thought I might whack out again.

"Where's Samantha?" I asked.

"She's waiting for us further up the path," he said, nodding to a trailhead that started beyond Renzo's rock perch.

"Oh, okay," I said, taking a robe. It was more like a cloak or a cowl than a robe, black and heavy with a large hood and wide sleeves. It didn't have an opening at the front but simply pulled over your head. And they must have been one size fits all, because Passion and I were swimming in ours while the guys' robes barely fell below their knees.

I pulled my hood up over my head, and noticed others doing the same, and in a matter of moments the parking lot looked like a convention of Sith Lords.

"Next step," Renzo said, now cloaked as well. "Get rid of all your phones and electronics. Lock them in your cars. We're not going to frisk you, but trust me when I say you'll be sorry if you bring them."

"I'll take the phones back to the car," I said to Passion, pulling mine out. She handed hers to me, and I grabbed the keys from Yale. None of the guys had brought phones apparently, or they'd decided to risk taking them. I mean, what was sneaking in a phone compared to sneaking in a firearm? I knew Marcus was carrying because I'd felt his gun holstered inside his jacket when we were making out in the back of the Porsche. At this point, I was assuming the only one who wasn't armed was Yale.

Phones and keys in hand, I wound my way back to the car through a sea of robed strangers, and unlocked it to toss the phones in the glove box. Then I relocked the car and stepped away from it, ready to wade back into the crowd. It was pretty cool wearing the robe, the way it flowed around my legs when I walked and gave me a feeling of anonymity and power that my normal clothes just didn't.

"Hey, Anne," someone said to my left, and I turned to see Eva's pale, freckled face peeking out at me from her hood, a taller robed figure standing behind her and holding her hand.

"Hey, Eva," I said, smiling in greeting. This must be her college boy I'd heard so much about. I glanced at up at him, his hooded head turning so we could finally see each other clearly.

"This is Grant," Eva said, beaming, as she introduced me to my best friend's brother. "And this is Anne." She introduced me to him. "She's new to Indy. Her family just moved here."

Grant and I both stood there stunned, staring at one another. What were the chances we would meet like this? That he would be the groupie Eva had hooked up with out of all the college guys in Indy? First I'd run into my dad's painting, then my mom, then I'd had to urge Emma and her parents to flee to Indy, and now Grant was here. It was like my old life in Greenfield was stalking me, each new event a tightening noose of coincidence determined to snare me and pull me back as I struggled forward. Supposedly, the universe was expanding, but I was beginning to feel like it was closing in on me.

"Olivia," Grant blurted, coming out of his shock with brute force, and grabbing me by the arm. "What the hell are you doing here? Your mom is worried sick about you. Everyone in Greenfield is frantic about your disappearance. Does Emma know you're here? Because I'm going to kill her if she does. She swore to me she had no idea where you were."

"No, she doesn't know." I glanced at Eva who looked very confused. "Let go of me, okay? Don't make a scene."

"Don't make a scene?" he asked, his voice rising. "You disappear without a trace, leave behind everyone you love, and you ask me not to make a scene? No, I'm getting my phone back right now and we're calling your mom." He pulled me by the arm and turned to run smack into Marcus.

"Is there some kind of problem?" Marcus asked, flanked by Nose and Jason with Yale behind them. They all looked extremely imposing in their black robes.

Standing across from each other, even clothed exactly the same, Grant and Marcus were as different as the sun and moon. Grant was taller and slimmer, a shock of his sandy blonde hair showing from under his hood, his blue eyes locked on Marcus's brown ones. Marcus was shorter but he seemed more substantial, as if he were somehow bigger than his own body. But despite the differences, both of them were exuding testosterone like bulls at a bullfight.

"No, there's no problem," Grant said, "In fact, the problem is solved if you get the fuck out of my way. This is my sister's best friend, and she's been missing for a month."

"Aha," Marcus said, "then you must be Grant."

"Yes, I'm Grant. And who the hell are you?"

"Stop it. Both of you," I said, pulling out of Grant's grip and stepping between them. "In case you hadn't noticed, I'm right here, and I can speak for myself, thank you very much. Grant," I turned to him, "this is Marcus. He's my friend, and I left Greenfield with him of my own free will." I don't know why I called Marcus my friend. Probably because, for those still under the impression he was my brother, friend was a slightly easier adjustment to make than boyfriend. Besides, we'd only recently re-established that status. Or, maybe I just didn't want to overwhelm Grant with too much information at once. I don't know. "And if you want to call my mom when this is over tonight," I went on, "and tell her you found me, then fine. But not now."

"Well said," Renzo praised me, walking up to us. He and Dimitri had joined the fray. In fact, a crowd had gathered around us, the whole parking lot focused on our little drama, probably hoping for a fight. "The Marked never have to explain themselves at an Eidolon, but Fleshmen do." He looked at Grant and then at Marcus. "And if your answers aren't good enough, neither of you will be coming with us tonight."

Great. The last thing I needed was one more guy staking his claim to me.

"Is this answer enough?" Marcus turned to Renzo and reached up, pulling down the front of his robe and unzipping his leather jacket underneath, a small triangle of his PSS shining out the top.

Renzo stared at it for a moment, then glanced at me and back to Marcus. "You people keep a lot of secrets," he said. "You could have told me you were marked hours ago."

"If you'd been through what we have," Marcus said, leaving his jacket open and ignoring the murmurs of the crowd, "you wouldn't go around telling just anyone. I wanted to be sure I could trust you first."

"And how do we know we can trust you?" Renzo countered. "Paranoia breeds mistrust, and you both reek of it," he said, including Grant in that evaluation.

"I thought you said the Marked never have to explain themselves at an Eidolon," Marcus challenged him. "As for him," he said, glancing dismissively at Grant. "He's not with us. I have no idea why he's here. All I know is he was manhandling Anne and trying to drag her away against her will."

"She's not Anne," Grant argued, growing red in the face. "She's Olivia. She's my sister's best friend. And I wasn't trying to take her. I was trying to get her back."

Renzo turned and looked at me, his blue eye drilling into me as if it could discern the truth. And maybe it could, because all the flirty interest from earlier in the evening was gone. He was all business now, and I was just an annoying glitch in his Eidolon.

"My name is Olivia," I admitted, "but recently I've been going by my middle name, Anne. And I am his sister's best friend, but that doesn't mean I want to go with him."

"Do you hear that?" Renzo asked Grant.

"She doesn't want to go with you. You're here as a guest," he said, glancing at Eva, who was standing behind Grant. "So act like one and have some respect, or we'll leave you here. Do you understand?"

"Yeah," Grant said, his jaw clenched. "I understand."

"Let's clear out, people," Renzo said, turning away and moving through the crowd, drawing it after him. "We have places to go and people to see."

"Do we still have a problem?" Marcus asked Grant.

"No, we're good," Grant said, even though his body language said differently. "But I'd like to talk to Olivia for a minute. Alone. If that's okay with you?"

"That's completely up to her," Marcus said, keeping his face carefully neutral.

Grant was standing there angry and confused. And yes, he was my friend and my best friend's brother, and I knew I owed him an explanation for where I'd been and why I'd left. But we also had an Eidolon to get to, and I didn't want to face Grant's questions alone.

"Can't we talk after?" I asked hopefully.

"No," Grant insisted. "It can't wait."

"I—um—okay, then go ahead. I trust these guys," I said, nodding at Marcus and the PSS guys still standing around him.

Everyone's eyes were on Grant. Eva was staring at him, a look of half-confusion, half-dread dawning across her face. Marcus almost looked sorry for Grant. And I was looking at him too, because I had no idea what could be so important he needed to say it right there, right then.

Grant's eyes fell on me as if I were the only person

in the world, and he inhaled a deep, shaky breath before he began, "When you went missing," he said, the shock of finding me still a quiver in his voice. "I didn't know what to do. I couldn't study. I couldn't sleep. I couldn't eat. I couldn't stop thinking about the horrible things that might be happening to you. Or worse, that you might be dead." His voice broke a little on the last word. "That's when I realized what an idiot I'd been to never tell you how I felt about you. I thought I'd lost that chance forever. I was a wreck, Liv, and I'd pretty much decided to quit school and go back home, but then I heard about this thing, this Eidolon, and I knew I had to come. I thought I might find some answers here, or some closure or something," he said, his voice raw with emotion, "but I never dared to hope I'd actually find you."

I stood there stunned. In all the days since I'd left Greenfield, I'd never once thought about how it might have impacted Grant. In fact, I'd assumed it hadn't. Out of all the things I thought he might say, a confession of his feelings for me had not been one of them. Last time I'd checked we'd been friends who'd made out once in his garage. Yes, I'd had a massive crush on Grant for years, but I'd never thought it was remotely mutual.

I looked up to find Marcus staring down at me, his eyes dark and guarded.

I glanced across at Eva and saw jealousy and barely contained hurt blazing from hers.

And when I looked at Grant, I saw a friend, someone I cared deeply about who was in shock and on the edge of an emotional breakdown because of me.

Even if I didn't feel for him the way he felt for me, how could I just leave him there in the parking lot and go on my merry way?

"I'm sorry," I said to Grant. "I don't even know what to say."

"How about you figure that out on the way to the Eidolon," Marcus said, his voice flat, "or we'll get left behind."

He was right. The parking lot was starting to empty out.

"And you're sticking with us," Marcus said to Grant, pretty much a command. "I don't trust you not to turn around, come back here, and call the authorities right down on our heads."

"I'm not going to do that," Grant said, shooting daggers at Marcus with his eyes.

"Good," Marcus said. "Then you can come as Olivia's guest."

"But he's with—" I looked around for Eva, but she was gone, disappeared into the dissipating crowd. Shit. I'd made an enemy there without even trying.

"Okay, everybody follow me," Renzo called, moving up the trail near his previous rock perch. Where was Passion? I couldn't see her amidst the dark sameness of the robes. But it didn't matter, because I could feel her up there near Renzo, eager to get to Samantha and the Eidolon.

"Let's go," Marcus said, turning to follow, and Yale, Nose, and Jason went with him.

"Olivia," Grant said, his eyes searching my face, his hands held out, as if he wanted to grab hold of me again. "I'm sorry if I messed this up.

You have to understand. I can't believe I found you."

"You don't owe me an apology," I said, "If anything, I owe you one. And I'll try to explain. It's complicated, but I'll do the best I can. Come on. They're getting ahead of us."

"Okay." He nodded, but I could tell he was still in a daze.

Then Grant and I followed the robed crowd into the woods up a winding trail, moonlight mixing with the occasional flash of PSS as various people took turns lighting the way.

31

GRAPPLING WITH GRANT

"So, you've been in Indy all this time?" Grant asked as we entered a narrow ravine, the path we were on changing from a well-defined nature trail to a slightly damp creek bed full of slippery rocks and dark shadows. We were following the group, and a trail marker assured us we were on our way to something called The Devil's Punchbowl.

"No," I said, looking ahead at the crowd, trying to pick out Marcus and the guys. "We've only been here for a week. Before that we were in the woods, traveling on ATVs." Obviously, Marcus had suddenly decided Grant was my problem to deal with. It was probably better that way anyway. I hadn't expected Marcus to get all clingy and jealous on me, but I was a little surprised he hadn't hung back with me to keep his eye on Grant.

Still, perhaps it was a vote of confidence and trust that he thought I could handle it on my own. And, if Grant thought he had feelings for me, it was my job to let him down easy. Having Marcus standing there while I did it would have just added salt to the wound.

"But why did you even leave?" Grant asked. "I mean, I know the fire was devastating and things weren't great between you and your mom—"

"It wasn't that," I interrupted, slipping on a rock and almost falling flat on my face. I would have too, if Grant hadn't reached out and caught my hand, holding me up.

"Just a minute," I said, pulling my hand from his and stripping off my gloves.

Immediately, the blue glow of my PSS lit up the area we were in, a deep gully with towering, multi-layered sandstone cliffs on either side of us. Based on the incline we'd been walking, we were obviously moving up the gorge.

The group had stalled in front of us, and now I could see why. Up ahead, the ravine we were in ran right up against a rock wall made of something harder than sandstone, the creek trickling over it into a giant bowl-like formation, which we were now standing in, hugging the edge to keep our feet dry. Leaning up against the sheer rock face ahead of us was a thick wooden ladder, and I could see people clambering up it, hiking their robes up around their knees so they wouldn't trip on them. But with only one person on the ladder at a time, we were in for a wait. I glanced behind us. We seemed to be the end of the line, the last dregs in The Devil's Punchbowl.

"Listen," I said to Grant. "I left Greenfield because I was in danger. The house fire wasn't an accident. People were trying to kill me, or at the very least kidnap me. Mike Palmer was one of them, and that doctor my mom was dating. They're CAMFers."

"Mike Palmer and Dr. Fineman are CAMFers?" he asked, incredulous and looking at me like I was crazy.

"Yes." I suddenly wished Marcus or someone was in on the conversation to back me up. "I'm on a list of people they're trying to take, because we have PSS, and Marcus is too. He basically rescued me." And then I'd had to turn right back around and rescue him and Emma. But I really didn't want to go into that. Better to tell Grant that story when Emma was on hand to confirm it, because it was really going to freak him out. But I could tell him something. "Emma knew that part, but we swore her to secrecy because it would have put her and us in danger."

"Dammit," he said, his face going red. "I knew she knew something. She was so quiet about it, but I could tell she wasn't—I mean she wasn't a basket case—she was doing better than I was and that didn't make sense. I'm going to kill her the next time I see her."

"Don't blame her. She was being the best friend ever." It sounded like Grant didn't know Emma and his parents would be in Indy tomorrow to see him. Maybe they were keeping it a surprise. Well, at least they'd be there to support him after I crushed his heart under my feet. Shit. This wasn't going to be easy.

"Grant," I said, reaching out and touching his arm. "When I left, I didn't think about how it would be for anyone else. I didn't have much of a choice. I was running for my life."

"It's okay," he said, exhaling as if he'd finally remembered to breathe. "You're okay, and that's all that matters."

I didn't even see it coming, the hug that crushed me to him and threatened to crack my ribs.

"God, you're really here," he sighed against my hood.

I'd be lying if I said that hug didn't feel good, if I pretended that I hadn't imagined him embracing me desperately like that a thousand times, but it was too late for us, for Grant and me. That ship had sailed, and I kind of hated the universe for throwing it in my face at the most inopportune moment possible.

"Yes, I am," I said, gently extracting myself from his arms and stepping back. The line of robed figures in front of us had dissipated, the last of them disappearing up the ladder. We were alone—about to be left behind—and it was probably as good a time as any to tell Grant about Marcus and me. "But a lot has changed since you last saw me." I tiptoed toward it. "I'm not even that person anymore. I've learned things about my ghost hand, and my family, and myself that you wouldn't even believe."

"Is that why you're here at this Eidolon thing? Are you joining The Hold? Because that would be great. You could be here in Indy, and we—"

"No," I said, cutting off that line of thinking as fast as I could. Yes, it was something I'd considered, but if I told Grant that he'd get the wrong idea. "I'm not here for that. I'm here for Marcus, I'm here *with* Marcus. We're together."

"You're with Marcus?" Grant echoed, as if the words made no sense.

"Yes." I nodded, and in case that wasn't clear enough. "I love him."

"You love him?" Grant asked angrily. "You've known that guy like three weeks, and you love him?"

"We've been through a lot together," I tried to explain. "He saved my life."

"Okay, whatever Olivia, that isn't love; that's gratitude. It might even be Stockholm syndrome considering he took you away from your home and everyone who cared about you and isolated you in the woods for weeks. Maybe you were in danger, I don't know. But I know a narcissistic asshole when I see one. He doesn't love you. He barely knows you. There's no way that guy cares about you half as much as I do," Grant said, moving toward me, grabbing me, kissing me, his lips half-angry, half-desperate, and completely determined to prove something.

I fought it, trying to pull away, even as my body remembered the sweetness of that day in the Campbells' garage with him. Even as my mind reminisced about how much I'd wanted this and for how long, I knew I didn't want it anymore.

"Get off me," I said against his lips, trying to turn my head. How dare he force himself on me like I owed him something? This was Grant, my friend, Emma's brother. And I had clearly told him I loved someone else. What the hell did he think he was doing?

My hands were pinned between us, and as I struggled to leverage them against his chest, my anger and helplessness building, I could feel my ghost hand wanting to reach into him. It would stop him. It would hurt him. It would help me.

"I believe the lady is saying 'No,'" Marcus said from behind us.

Startled, Grant let go of me and stepped away.

I turned to see Marcus and Jason standing at the bottom of the ladder. Jason was holding a handgun, and he wasn't pointing it at Grant, but he was certainly showing it to him.

"What the fuck?" Grant said, staring at the gun, and the guys, and then at me. "Are these the kind of people you hang out with now?"

"Yes, they are," I said. "I told you, a lot has changed." Like the fact that Jason was using a gun to defend me, instead of threaten me.

"So what? You're going to shoot me in the woods now and go to your PSS rave with a clean conscience?" Grant challenged them.

"Sure," Jason said, smiling wickedly.

"No." Marcus shook his head. But if he hadn't been pissed off before, he was now. "What about you? Were you just going to rape Olivia in the woods and then go back down to the parking lot and call her mom with a clean conscience?"

"Rape?" Grant said with surprised disgust. "It was a kiss, and it wasn't like that at all."

"For you, I'm sure it wasn't. But why don't you ask her?" Marcus nodded at me.

"Olivia, tell him. It wasn't like that," Grant said, looking at me.

I didn't want to hurt him. I truly didn't. But I also never wanted him to kiss me like that again.

"I didn't want to kiss you," I said. "And I clearly said 'no' when it started."

"Maybe your mouth said no," Grant said mockingly. "But your body definitely said—"

And that is when all hell broke loose.

Marcus charged at Grant, grabbing him by the robe and smashing him against the rock face closest to us, pinning him there.

Jason had the barrel of the gun against Grant's cheek before I could even squeak out a protest.

"Listen to me, you college prick," Marcus said, his voice dripping with rage. "If you ever touch her again, or any other female, for that matter, without their explicit consent, I will fucking hunt you down and hurt you in such a way that you will never be able to do it again. Do you understand what I'm telling you?"

Grant's eyes were bulging out of his face. Marcus's arm was across his throat, so I'm not even sure he could speak, but he nodded his head. Vigorously.

Jason lowered the gun and Marcus let go of Grant, who stayed plastered against the rock looking truly terrified.

I was appalled. And I was thrilled. But I also had enough sense to know this wasn't just about me. Marcus had watched his sister get raped while he was handcuffed to a police car. It wasn't surprising he had a very low tolerance for that sort of thing. But I wasn't Danielle. And Grant hadn't raped me.

"You're fucking crazy," Grant rasped, rubbing his neck and looking from Marcus to Jason to me. "All three of you."

"Maybe a little," Jason quipped, shrugging, his gun still pointed at Grant.

"Take him up," Marcus said to Jason, nodding at the ladder. "But don't let him out of your sight."

"Let's go," Jason said to Grant, gesturing at the ladder. "Ladies first."

And Grant went, without any argument, up the ladder and into the dark without even a fleeting glance back at me.

Well, that friendship had completely tanked. And what would Emma think when she heard the circumstances? Would she side with Grant? Even if she believed me, Grant was her brother, and I was just her friend. Would I lose her too?

"Are you all right?" Marcus asked, coming to my side and wrapping his arms gently around me. "I never should have left you behind with him. I thought you might need some space. But when I noticed that the two of you hadn't come up the ladder, I got a bad feeling in my gut. God, I'm so sorry."

"It's not your fault," I said, wanting to comfort him as much as he wanted to comfort me. "He's normally not like that. I think it was the shock of seeing me or something."

"I don't fucking care what it was," Marcus said. "He does it again, and I hurt him. Badly."

"I'm okay." I tucked my head under his chin, feeling him tremble. "Thank you for coming back. I almost stuck my hand into him."

"Hmm. Then maybe I came back a little too soon," he said.

"No," I scolded. "Don't say that."

"You're right," he whispered, kissing the top of my head. "I will always come back for you."

We stood for a moment, embracing in The Devil's Punchbowl. "Come on," he said, taking my hand in his and tugging me toward the ladder. "Let's get to this Eidolon and talk to Samantha."

32

VIVA LA REVOLUTION

Jason and Grant were nowhere to be seen on the trail above the ladder, but there was only one direction they could have gone. Marcus and I glanced up at the steep sides of the box canyon, rising a hundred feet above our heads. I'd had no idea there was landscape like this anywhere in the Midwest, and it was both beautiful and eerie, the way the shadows and frigid air gathered in those deep cuts in the earth, secreted in pockets, caves, and crevices carved into the limestone by eons of trickling water. I was beginning to understand where Shades had gotten its name.

We were hiking quick, trying to catch up with the pack, and we didn't really talk, conserving our energy for the rough trail. But Marcus held onto my hand, guiding me and helping me over some of the bigger pools as the creek increased in girth and volume.

The next time I glanced ahead, it looked like our path just ended, blocked off by a wall of rock. But then I saw the stairs to the left and Grant and Jason moving up them, other dark forms above them, and the faint echo of voices drifting down to us. We were catching up.

A few minutes later, we arrived at the foot of the wooden stairway, and I read the sign at the bottom. *Devil's Drop*, it said, with an arrow pointing upward. Great. And my mom thought I was obsessed with morbidity. I had nothing on the Satan worshippers who'd named all these park features.

The steps in front of me went straight up the side of the ravine, attached to it with huge rusty bars embedded straight into the rock. The staircase tacked back and forth, disappearing into the darkness above.

I started trudging up and Marcus came after me, our feet pounding out a rhythm together. As we climbed higher, we began stopping at every landing to catch our breath, but we finally came out at the top, winded and leg-sore.

We were standing on the top of a rounded plateau or tableland which ended on all sides in rocky jagged cliffs. The landscape was flat with low shrubs and only a few smaller trees poking out between the cracks of rock and boulder. Groups of robed teenagers dotting this strange landscape, milling around and talking excitedly. Beyond them was the vast backdrop of the night sky spread out before us in an incredible display, the moon hanging there, a mere sliver of silver laced with clouds. And the stars were amazing, stars upon stars upon stars, overpopulating the universe with points of light mixed in dark milky galaxies.

As my eyes drank it all in, I noticed Grant and Jason standing to the side with Nose and Yale. Jason's gun was tucked back inside his robe, but it was obvious he'd enlisted the help of the other two to keep an eye on Grant. And it must have been obvious to Grant too, the way he was standing with them, sullen and resigned.

Jason saw us and came over, a worried look on his face. "This is a shitty location," he said to Marcus. "It's completely indefensible. We've got a flight of stairs at our back and that at our front," he finished, pointing at the cliff.

"You're right," Marcus said, addressing Jason's concern. "But we haven't seen any sign of CAMFers, and if they were here, they would have taken us in those canyons, not waited until we had the high ground."

In all the mess with my mom, and my dad's paintings, and Grant, I'd almost forgotten the real threat to us, the one we'd been running from for weeks. Mike Palmer, a CAMFer, had warned us not to come here. It still made no sense that he'd leave us a message at all. But my dog tags were completely silent, which meant there probably weren't CAMFers anywhere in Shades.

"Maybe," Jason said, but it was obvious he didn't agree with Marcus. "Unless they're waiting for something."

"Stay in the trees then," Marcus said, nodding toward a stand of scraggly hemlocks. "They're not coming up the cliffs, so keep your eyes on the stairs. We'll make this as quick as we can."

"Got it," Jason said, turning back to join Nose, Yale, and Grant, and motioning them back into the shadow of the trees.

"Welcome to the Eidolon," Renzo's voice cut through the night air, silencing the chatter of the crowd. He had climbed up onto a flat boulder toward the edge of the cliffs, and everyone was gathering around him.

As Marcus and I moved to join them, I looked for Samantha. Where was she? I'd thought this Eidolon was her thing.

"Far below us, at the bottom of this cliff," Renzo began, like an actor on a stage, "is the Sweet Water River. And upriver, only a hundred feet or so, is a rock formation known as The Devil's Backbone."

What was he, a park ranger? I thought this was some kind of religious ritual, not a geology lesson. I glanced at Marcus and he shrugged.

"Where's Samantha?" he asked softly, searching the crowd.

"I don't know," I whispered back in frustration. "But Passion is up there." I pointed. "I can feel her. So, Samantha probably is too."

"Are you positive she's even here?" he asked.

Shit. No, I wasn't sure. Samantha had invited me. She'd told me she'd be here, and everyone else had told me she'd be here. But they could have all been lying. I pulled my dog tags out and clutched them in my ghost hand, getting an instant flash of Passion and an impression of giddy happiness.

"She's here," I told Marcus.

"The unique positioning of that feature," Renzo was saying, "has carved out the river bed directly below this cliff and made the water extremely deep. Which is why, throughout history, people have come here to cliff-dive. That is how it got its name, The Devil's Drop, and that is exactly why we've brought you here tonight. We are going to dive this cliff."

"What do you mean by 'we?'" someone called out nervously as chatter and murmurs of excitement broke out amidst the group.

"If you came here for the Eidolon," Renzo answered, quieting the crowd, "then you came here to dive."

"I thought we came here to party!" someone hollered, eliciting a few cheers of agreement.

"*This* is not a party," Renzo corrected the heckler passionately. "We didn't drag you all the way out here to get drunk or wasted, and if that's what you came for then you might as well take the stairs back down to the parking lot. This," he said, gesturing toward the cliff behind him, "is about claiming our power and what belongs to us. We are the first generation of The Hold. Our parents don't have PSS. They aren't marked. They are Fleshmen, and yet they run everything for us. Why?"

"Because we're underage," someone suggested timidly from the crowd.

"Exactly!" Renzo said, pouncing on the answer. "Because they consider us children. Because we have no rights. Because nothing can legally belong to us. But that time is coming to an end."

Now I was really lost. What did jumping off a cliff

because Renzo said so have to do with the unmarked parental control of The Hold? This was getting weirder by the minute.

"How many of the Marked here are no longer underage?" Renzo asked.

A handful of robed figures raised their hands, but Marcus didn't join them. He was scanning the crowd again, searching for Samantha.

But Renzo continued to run the show with no sign of her. "This year, many of us turned eighteen," he said. "Next year, even more of us will. Soon, enough of us will be of age to take The Hold for ourselves. It is time we grew up. It is time we grasped what is inherently ours. But, to do that, we need two things. We need power. And we need a leader. Not an unmarked adult who doesn't even understand who we are, what we are—but someone from our own generation. It is time to put the fate of The Hold into the hands of the Marked!"

The crowd went wild, cheering and cat-calling in agreement.

Samantha had better show up quick, because I was pretty sure she had a mutiny on her hands. Renzo was talking about overthrowing her father. He was talking about generational revolution within The Hold. And it sounded like he was grooming the crowd to jettison him straight into the position of The Hold's new leader.

This didn't make any sense. If Samantha was at the Eidolon, wouldn't she be speaking up against this? Not only that, wouldn't she have heard Marcus's PSS the moment we arrived at the top of the stairs? Hell,

I'd kind of been expecting her to be waiting for us. She'd certainly heard Passion and me easily enough in a school practically crowded with PSS. But, she'd only heard mine after I'd taken off the tags. The tags I was currently wearing while holding onto Marcus's arm. Shit. I was blocking him. Had I been touching him this entire time? Probably.

I quickly let go of him, breaking contact and stepping away.

Renzo had stopped talking and was pulling someone up onto the rock from the crowd.

Marcus glanced at me, puzzled, wondering why I'd moved.

The new figure on the rock turned, Samantha's beautiful face revealed to everyone in the crowd as she swiveled her head, staring directly at Marcus, her mouth falling open.

The night filled up with silence as the crowd waited for Samantha to speak, their new leader, the one Renzo had been amping them up for. He wasn't the new Messiah. He was just the prophet paving the way. Samantha was the one setting herself up to replace her parents. She was the true leader behind this little revolution. And I had not seen that coming. Not at all.

But I obviously wasn't as surprised as she was.

The silence expanded, her eyes blazing into Marcus, her ear turned toward him. Her glance flicked to the glimmer of his chest, and her mouth opened a little wider. Then she looked at me, standing next to him, then back to Marcus, realization dawning in her eyes.

As for the crowd, they slowly pivoted as one in

their black robes, white faces seeming to float in the darkness as they turned to see what Samantha was staring at, what had stopped her in her hot revolutionary tracks.

Everyone was looking at us now, and I recognized Passion's pale face toward the front where she'd been standing with Samantha before Renzo had pulled her up on the rock.

Marcus didn't move, but I could feel the tension radiating off of him. If my reunion with Grant had been a little rocky after only a few weeks, what was this one going to be like after ten years?

"David?" Samantha said, his childhood name slipping from her lips like a strangled cry.

"Hey, Sam," Marcus said, his voice breaking as well.

Samantha leapt from the rock, the crowd clearing an aisle for her as she ran toward Marcus. She didn't stop or even slow as she approached him, but slammed into his arms at full speed, a sob of joy expressed from her lungs as she did so. "David," she kept saying over and over again. And then she pulled back and looked at him. "You're alive," she whispered, tears painting wet tracks down her face. "They told me you were dead. That the accident—"

"I was dead," he whispered, his face wet too.

"But you aren't. You aren't," she said, as if she were still convincing herself. "I don't understand."

Then she pulled back, and her glance fell to the glimmer of his chest, and she looked at his face again, her eyes swimming with wonder, and he nodded. "You came back?" she asked, incredulous.

"Yes," he said.

It was as if they were by themselves, not standing on a cliff under the moon with a sizeable audience. As for that audience, they were transfixed. Even if they didn't know what was going on, it was obvious it was something meaningful, and moving, and important.

"But—what about Danielle?" Samantha's eyes flicked to me, falling to my ghost hand. "You aren't—" She turned back to Marcus, confused and desperately hopeful. "She's not Danielle," she said, the loss in her voice cutting into my heart.

"No." He shook his head. "Danielle is gone. But not at the accident. It was in February."

"This February?" Samantha moaned, laying her head into Marcus's shoulder and openly weeping.

He held her, and comforted her, and the crowd watched, a few whispered murmurs rippling through them like the wake of a pebble dropped in a pool.

Renzo was still standing on his rock, and he looked both unhappy and confused, as if he wasn't quite sure if all this had been staged by Samantha for the sake of the Eidolon, or if our little group was disrupting it once again.

Finally, Samantha raised her head, pulled herself out of Marcus's arms, and seemed to become aware again of where she was.

"Sam, we need to talk," Marcus said, gently. "I have a lot to tell you, and some of it is going to be very hard for you to hear."

"I understand," she said, nodding, though I seriously doubted she did. "But we can't postpone the Eidolon. Everyone is here." She turned toward the crowd. "Everyone is waiting."

"Sam, you have to trust me," he said, "This is more important."

"No." She shook her head. "There's nothing more important than this." She stared at him, some hidden message in her eyes. "I need this before you tell me. We all do."

Holy crap. Was it possible that Samantha James was aware of her father's questionable practices and what he'd done to Marcus and his family? That somewhere, deep down, she had always been aware? Did she remember why her cousins and aunt had run from The Hold? Had their influence stayed with her all these years, growing and manifesting itself into this; a young woman determined to overthrow him and lead The Hold in a new direction for a new generation?

But even if that were true, it was going to take a hell of a lot more than some made-up ritual on the top of a cliff to remove Alexander James from his position as leader of The Hold. He was an adult with money and power and a whole lot of security. We were a handful of teenagers with PSS, and a smattering of groupies without it. If this was the revolution, it was a pitiful one. Still, Samantha might be able to get my dad's paintings back, so I was willing to hang around and find out.

"I can hear your people," Samantha said to Marcus, nodding at the shadows of the PSS guys and Grant standing in the trees behind us. "I can also hear that they haven't manifested yet."

Of course, she could hear Nose, Yale and Jason's PSS. But what did she mean by that last part?

And then it hit me. Samantha James had a very

discerning ear, and she was saying, that with it, not only could she hear PSS, she could differentiate between PSS that had manifested a power, and PSS that hadn't.

Which meant she knew my ghost hand had a power. She'd known since that day in PE. And she hadn't let on or mentioned it to her father.

"They haven't," Marcus said, "but I don't see what that has to do with anything. We think it's only triggered by need."

"Or fear, or stress," she said, "or the adrenaline rush produced when you jump off a cliff and, for a split second, your body is sure it's going to die."

Marcus stared at her. He looked past her at the crowd and Renzo on his rock, and beyond that to the cliff.

"We've been doing it for three years," Samantha said to Marcus.

"And it works?" he asked, sounding skeptical.

"Every time," she assured him.

33

GO JUMP OFF A CLIFF

"**Y**ou can't seriously buy this shit," Jason said, staring at Marcus. "This cult princess tells you that jumping off a cliff will give you superpowers, and you believe it?"

We were huddled on the rocky edge of the cliff itself; Marcus, Jason, Nose, Yale, me, and Grant, standing next to one of the many signs that clearly said in bright bold red lettering *NO DIVING OR JUMPING, $2000 FINE.*

And we weren't the only ones checking out The Devil's Drop. All along the cliff's ledge little groups had formed as people took a look over that precipice and tried to decide if they were going to jump or not. After her reunion with Marcus, Samantha had gotten back up on her rock and encouraged everyone to consider it, including the groupies and any Marked who'd already jumped at a previous Eidolon. But she'd also made it clear that no one had to participate, and those who opted out could make their way back down the stairs after it was all over and meet the jumpers at the bottom.

"She's not just a cult princess," Marcus said. "She's my cousin."

"I don't give a rat's ass who she is," Jason said. "I don't trust her."

"You have to admit, it sounds pretty crazy," Yale agreed.

I was only half-listening to them argue, because the rest of me was fixated on the ominous presence of open space a mere step away, and the fifty-foot plunge to the winding river below us. Part of me wanted to take that step, right there, right then, and freak everyone the hell out. Another part of me wanted to run away as fast as possible.

"It does," Marcus said to Yale. "Except it fits what we already know. My sister got her power at a very young age. She had meningitis and almost died and probably would have if she hadn't healed herself. Samantha got that same virus, and the antibiotics they had to give her would have left her completely deaf. Instead, her PSS kicked in and gave her an ability to compensate. Olivia's hand manifested its ability the day the CAMFers came after her. It does seem like a pretty convincing pattern. If a threat to one's life or well-being triggers the power, I can see how cliff-diving might simulate that."

"Yeah, but what about Jason?" Yale argued. "His entire life has been one big threat to his well-being. If anyone should have a power, he should."

"I don't know," Marcus frowned. "Maybe he has a much higher tolerance for fear than the rest of us, like he got desensitized or something. In which case, this probably wouldn't work on him anyway. Or the theory is wrong. There's really only one way to find out," Marcus finished, looking pointedly at Yale and Nose.

"Oh no, come on," Yale groaned.

"I'm up for it," Nose said, a grin breaking out on his ski-masked face. "I've always wanted to sky dive, so why not cliff-dive?"

"Then you're on your own," Yale said. "I'm not a big fan of heights."

"Aw, come on, man," Nose pleaded. "Grow some balls. It'll be a blast. Don't make me do this solo."

"Yeah, okay," Yale said, a grin breaking out on his face too. "What the hell. You only live once."

I would have never guessed it would be that easy to convince them. Then again, they'd been hiding in a basement for a week bored out of their minds. Maybe after that, this actually sounded like a good idea. Either way, I had to admire their guts. The small part of me that thought jumping would be amazing had already been majorly outvoted by the many parts of me that knew it would be terrifying.

I looked up and caught Grant staring at me.

He quickly glanced away, glaring at Marcus and said, "I'm jumping too."

Marcus stared back, unflinching, both of them like a pair of dogs with their hackles up. Then Marcus shrugged. "Saves me the trouble or throwing you off," he said. "But you'll go after Yale and Nose," he clarified. "That way they can keep an eye on you at the bottom and make sure you don't call anyone."

"You guys aren't jumping, are you?" Passion asked, her voice full of anxiety as she broke into our little huddle, eyeing the cliff's edge with barely contained terror.

"Yale and me are," Nose answered excitedly.

"Please, don't do this," she begged them. "Don't let them do this." She turned her desperation on Marcus. "If I'd known this was the Eidolon, I never would have brought any of you. I never would have come myself. And Samantha won't listen to me." She was almost in tears. No, her eyes were so red she'd obviously already been crying. Now she was trying not to, but she wasn't doing a very good job. I'd never seen Passion this upset about anything. And then I remembered; her twin sister had drowned. Maybe even in a river. I didn't know the details, but it was obvious Passion was currently caught in a living nightmare where everyone she cared about was about to jump off a cliff into a river and die a horrible watery death.

"Passion?" Grant said, staring at her. "I thought you were—what the hell is she doing here?" he asked, looking from Marcus to me accusingly.

"Grant?" she said, her face growing even paler. "I—what are you—how did he—" she stammered, looking to me for help.

"He came with Eva," I explained to her. "And Passion came with me," I said to Grant. "We both left Greenfield with Marcus."

"Is she your girlfriend too?" Grant asked Marcus snidely.

"Hey!" Passion said, startling us all with the sudden power in her voice. "You shut the fuck up!" She advanced on Grant, making him stumble back a little. "Leaving Greenfield was the best thing I've ever done. And Olivia and Marcus have helped me more than you could possibly imagine. And for the record, I don't like guys. I like girls. You got that?"

Grant just nodded, wide-eyed.

I couldn't help noticing the smirks on the faces of the other guys, and honestly, I'd never been more proud of Passion myself.

"And if you're stupid enough to jump off a cliff," she said, including Nose and Yale in her scalding wrath, all sign of tears gone, "you're bigger idiots than I thought."

"We need to find out if this really works," Marcus explained to her gently. "If it does, then Nose and Yale will manifest powers, and we'll be less at the mercy of the CAMFers."

"No," she insisted. "It's too dangerous. They could die. They could drown. You really believe it's worth that?" She looked from Nose to Yale.

"To get a power like Olivia or Marcus have?" Nose asked. "Hell yeah."

"Your power is never going to be that cool," Yale said. "You'll probably get PSS snot or something."

"Oh, look who's talking, Casper ass," Nose shot back. "Don't even make me guess what your power is gonna be."

"Wrap it up, people." Renzo's voice cut through the chatter of the various groups. "I need my jumpers over here, experienced ones in the front," he said, pointing to the largest most prominent rock jutting out over the river valley.

People began to separate, some lining up under Renzo's watchful PSS eye, others hanging at the back, curious to watch the proceedings.

"I can't even watch this," Passion said, her voice full of distress as the jumper line grew longer and longer. "This is crazy. People are crazy."

"I'm not going to stand here gawking," Jason said to her. "I'm going to hang back by the stairs if you want to come with me."

"Yes," Passion said, relief flooding her voice.

It was a nice gesture, especially for Jason, but I also knew he wasn't hanging by the stairs; he was guarding them. There wasn't a moment in time when Jason didn't expect us to be ambushed by CAMFers, and I was beginning to appreciate that. It helped me let my guard down occasionally, knowing that no matter what, he never would.

"Okay then," Nose said, "looks like it's time to go jump off a cliff."

"Be safe," Marcus said, gripping Nose's arm and clapping Yale on the back.

"Watch yourself at the bottom," Jason added. "You'll be completely defenseless down there."

"Not if we get a power," Yale pointed out.

No one was saying anything to Grant, and despite the jerk he'd been, he was my friend and Emma's brother. Even if he was only jumping to get away from Marcus and me as fast as he could, I still wanted him to be safe.

"Be careful," I said, reaching out and touching his arm.

"Yeah." He glanced away, his jaw clenched. "You too."

Then Nose, Yale and Grant moved away, heading through the crowd to the jumper line, and Passion and Jason moved into the shadow of the trees near the stairs leaving Marcus and me standing at the back of the watchers.

"Children of The Hold," Samantha's voice rang out strong and melodic. She was back on her rocky perch, ready to lead the Eidolon in all her glory. "We are no longer children."

"Damn straight," one of the jumpers called out.

"We are new adults," she said. "New, because no one has ever seen the likes of us before. We are a new generation of humanity, in every sense of the word. And tonight we take up our power."

There was no doubt that Samantha James had the same charisma her father possessed. She was captivating. The way she spoke was like music, the way she moved and gestured like a graceful dancer. And it seemed she was just as resolute as her father in her belief in The Hold, though perhaps a different Hold than he'd imagined. Nothing had swayed her from that course: not finding her long-dead cousin, and not the desperate pleas from her newest girlfriend and follower. Samantha James was a force to be reckoned with, and I was hoping that reckoning would play out in my favor.

"It is important that you understand what we have come here to do," she went on. "Whether you jump tonight to claim your power, or to show solidarity with those of us who do, or whether you stand in witness on this cliff, together we are The Hold."

"Long live The Hold," a voice yelled from the crowd, and other voices rose in agreement.

"Yes, long live The Hold," Samantha agreed, nodding. "Because it has kept us safe until we can claim what is rightfully ours, both our power and our place. Here tonight," she said, her voice rising in a crescendo of conviction, "we will take up that power. And when enough of us have it, we will take our place. We will take The Hold for ourselves!"

Cheers rang out from the crowd, pumped up as they were with nervous excitement.

"Now," Samantha directed, "if you are jumping, Dimitri will give you instructions and Renzo will jump first to demonstrate exactly how it's done. Please pay close attention to them. Sometimes powers manifest during the actual jump itself, and this can be very alarming for the jumper. It is important to keep a cool head. But don't be too disappointed if that doesn't happen. The first year, Renzo's power didn't manifest until a week after he jumped."

Renzo had a power? Of course he did. He was an experienced Eidolon jumper. I glanced at him, remembering that night at Samantha's when he'd barely taken his PSS eye off of me. God, what if he had X-ray vision or something?

"And if you're not jumping," Samantha continued, "there's an excellent viewing area there." She pointed to her right. "You can see both the jumpers and the river from a slightly lower ledge."

"You're sure you don't want to jump?" Marcus asked, looking down at me.

"Yes, I'm sure," I said. "Why? Do you want to?"

"Maybe a little." He grinned, steering me toward the viewing ledge as I used my hand to light our way.

A handful of others joined us on the terraced rock ledge, huddled in their own little groups.

We picked a spot close to the lower edge, the river valley plunging down in front of us. To our right and up a little higher was the ledge people would be jumping from, though several large boulders blocked our view of the preparation area.

Marcus sat down and I sank down too, leaning against him. He wrapped his arm around me and said, "We'll talk to Samantha. We'll get your father's paintings back. And again, I'm sorry about the Grant thing."

"Shhhh," I said, putting my finger to his lips, looking out at the incredible night sky and the dark horizon stretched out before us. "Let's just enjoy this for now. It's my first Eidolon."

"Mine too," he said, smiling and nuzzling my neck, kissing it gently.

"Geronimo!" someone yelled, and Renzo, recognizable by the glow of his PSS eye, went hurtling off the cliff above us, arms and legs flailing, completely naked.

"Oh my God," I said, bursting into laughter as I watched his pale body plummet, splashing into the dark blue water of the river. "They're doing this naked?"

"Yeah," Marcus said, as we both watched Renzo's head break the surface far below us. "I figured they might. It's much safer that way. Clothes can drag you down in the water, or you can get tangled in them during the fall and hit the water badly."

"Wait," I said, staring at him. "You knew and you didn't warn the guys?"

"They won't back out now," he said, smirking. "They wouldn't risk looking like complete pussies in front of everyone. Especially the girls."

"And you wanted to do this?" I asked, staring down at the Renzo speck which was now swimming to the rocky back of The Devil's Backbone. Two figures were standing there waiting for him, one holding what looked like a towel.

"Well, more specifically," Marcus said, smirking, "I wanted you to do it."

"You perv." I pulled back from him in mock horror. "This entire mission to Indy to find Samantha and infiltrate The Hold was all so you could get me naked?"

"Pretty much," he said. "You got me."

"Yes I do," I said, kissing him gently and feeling his body respond, his arms pulling me to him, his lips growing urgent. I pulled away a little and whispered against his mouth. "And I got you naked long before tonight."

"Pocahontas!" someone yelled from the cliff and another diver, a female with the tiniest flash of PSS on her hand, went plummeting downward much more gracefully than Renzo had.

"That was Juliana," I told Marcus. "She has a PSS pinky."

"What's her power?" he asked. "And the guy with the eye, what can he do?"

"I have no idea. None of them have revealed anything obvious. I didn't even think they had powers until tonight. Your cousin has been playing this card game very close to her—"

"Stop." Marcus held up his hand and cut me off. "Do you hear that?"

I cocked my head, straining to listen, but all I could hear was the low chatter of the watchers around us and the wind picking up in the trees.

"I don't hear anything," I said.

"It's a hum," he said, looking at me. "Are your dog tags doing anything?"

"No," I shook my head, reaching up and touching them through my robe and shirt. "Nothing."

"They hear it too," he said, nodding up to the jumpers' ledge where Samantha, Dimitri, and several others, still in their robes, had come to the edge and were gesturing up the gorge.

Then I heard it, finally, a low thrumming that reminded me of the sounds the blades had made when a minus meter had triggered them.

I did not like that sound. It made terror rise up in my heart.

But not as much as the sound that came next.

It cut through the night and the thrumming. A lone burst, sharp and ballistic, the solitary, devastating crack of a single gunshot.

Marcus and I jumped to our feet.

His gun was out and ready.

Someone screamed.

Someone fell from the cliff, plunging down and tumbling head over heels over head, her robes flapping like broken bat wings around her.

Samantha fell and landed with a splash in the dark swirling water below.

34

THE DEVIL'S DROP

Marcus yanked his robe off over his head, and his shirt came part way with it, giving me a blinding flash of his chest before it fell back down and he tossed the robe aside.

"Here, hold this," he said, handing me his gun and stepping to the very edge of the ledge.

"Stop!" I said, grabbing him and clinging to him, holding him back from jumping after his cousin. "It's not safe." I pointed down at the river where several large submerged rocks lurked directly below us. There was a reason our ledge was a viewing spot, not a jumping spot.

"Look," I said, pointing again, this time drawing his attention to the middle of the deep pool.

Renzo and Juliana were in the water, almost to Samantha already. And we could see her flailing and splashing: not floating, not dead. She was still moving.

"She's okay," I told him. "They've got her."

Gunfire filled the air, not a single shot this time but the repetitive rattle of multiple automatic weapons.

There was more screaming, and then, as we stood there, stunned, a mob of people were hurling themselves off the cliff. Some were robed, others half-naked, and they jumped not one at a time but en masse and colliding with one another as they scrambled to get away from something behind them much more deadly than a cliff-dive.

"What the fuck?" Marcus said, grabbing his gun back from me and whirling around, scrambling up the rocks toward the top of the cliff. And I followed him, the other watchers with us doing the same. I don't know why. I think we couldn't comprehend what was happening. We could hear the danger, and we had seen others fleeing it. But our friends were up there, and we had to see and know that danger for ourselves before we could react to it in any sane way. And although running toward it wasn't sane, none of us were exactly thinking straight.

Marcus crested the plateau, me close behind him, and what lay before us was so different from the landscape of stark beauty we'd stepped away from fifteen minutes before, it was as if we'd entered another world entirely.

The cliff-top was shrouded in green smoke, billowing here and there, seeping up from the very ground, it seemed. Within that smoke, figures darted, weaving in and out, sometimes visible, sometimes not. I could hear people moaning. Someone crying for help. It was like a war zone.

Another volley of gunfire shattered the air to our right.

"Get down!" Marcus said, grabbing me and throwing me to the ground between several small boulders. Then he was down too, practically on top of me, his gun held out in front of us and trained in the direction the gunshots had come from.

The wind gusted, swirling some smoke in our direction, and my eyes began to sting and water.

"Shit," he said. "That's tear gas."

I could feel him scrambling in his jacket for something, and then he handed me a pocket knife.

"Cut off some of your robe," he directed. "Two pieces, big enough to tie around our faces. And something to cover your hand too." He nodded at my glowing ghost hand.

I took the knife, popped the blade, and curled myself around so I could hack at the hem. Once I had a hole in the material, the rest was a matter of ripping it into a long strip, and tearing that in three.

I handed Marcus his knife and then his piece of cloth, and we both wrapped our mouths and noses, tying them behind our heads. Then I wrapped my hand, masking my PSS as best I could.

"Hold it right there," a voice boomed.

I froze.

Marcus froze too, his gun aimed at the silhouette of an armed, combat-ready CAMFer standing about ten feet in front of us.

"Don't shoot!" someone called from right behind me. "We surrender. Please don't shoot."

"Come forward with your hands in the air," the CAMFer commanded.

Gravel crunched and feet shuffled past me, our fellow watchers from the viewing ledge stumbling toward the CAMFer, only inches from where Marcus and I lay.

I thought they'd all gone by, when something heavy slammed into the back of my leg, grinding it into the dirt. I felt an awful popping sound from my knee as a groupie in a robe literally tripped over me. I bit back a cry of pain, and the guy glanced down, greeted by the slightest shake of Marcus's head and the dark barrel of his gun.

"Come on, you. Get over here," the CAMFer barked, and knee-stepper looked up and moved away, joining the rest of his group to stand in a line before their captor, hands on their heads as directed.

I don't know how Marcus knew, how he understood before I did, but just as the guy raised his gun to mow down that line, Marcus raised his gun and tagged him right in the throat.

Blood spurted from his neck once, twice, three times before the guy toppled over onto his face.

Marcus jumped up, leaving me lying between the rocks, and grabbed the dead man's weapon, handing it to the guy who'd stepped on my knee. "Get your group to the cliff," Marcus told him. "Shoot anyone who tries to stop you."

The guy took the gun, but none of them moved.

"Go, now," Marcus said, shoving knee-stepper

toward the cliff, and he shambled away into the dissipating smoke, his little group of stunned lambs following after him.

"We need to move." Marcus was already back to me, trying to haul me up by my arm.

I tried to stand, but instead I fell against a rock, pain exploding in my knee.

"What's the matter?" he asked, looking me up and down with concern.

"Knee," I said through gritted teeth. "Popped out of joint, I think."

"Can you walk?"

"I don't think so."

"Okay." He bent over and scooped me up in his arms.

"Fuck!" I said, grabbing his shirt and twisting it in my hands. Just having his arms beneath my knee hurt, but probably not as much as walking would have.

"Sorry." He looked down at me. "But we can't stay here. We have to find the others and get the hell off this cliff. Can you take the gun? I can't shoot and carry you at the same time."

"Yeah, okay." I took it from him.

"If someone's coming at us, take a shot," he said. "Otherwise, we need to conserve ammo."

More gunshots cut through the night, coming from the area of the stairway.

Then a shadow was charging us, the outline of a gun jutting out in front of it.

I scrambled to aim the gun, to even get my shaking fingers on the trigger.

"Don't fuckin' shoot," Jason called out, running up

to us, gun in one hand and dragging Passion behind him with the other. They each had one of Jason's camouflage bandanas tied over their faces, but their eyes were red and swollen. "They have the stairs," Jason huffed, trying to catch his breath. "I held them off as long as I could, but there were just too many. They kept getting through."

There was no question of who "they" were. But why would CAMFers shoot Samantha? It didn't make sense. If she was on their list, they didn't want her dead—they wanted her PSS. Then again, they hadn't killed her; they'd injured her and knocked her off the cliff.

"We have to jump," Marcus said.

"I can't do it," Passion whimpered, her eyes pools of fear.

"What if they're down there too, waiting for us?" I asked. "What if this is a way to funnel all of us into a much easier extraction point?"

"So, what? We stand here and let them take us instead?" Marcus asked, turning toward the jumping cliff. "We have a better chance of getting away down there than up here."

"I can't jump. My knee is fucked," I reminded him. "And I can't swim with one leg. Leave me here with a gun." I tried to remove myself from his arms. "I can distract them and give you more time."

"No." He gripped me even tighter. "I can jump with you and help you swim. We're not leaving you. Let's go," he said.

And then we were moving, with Jason and Passion behind us. The terrain was rough, and we had to weave and stay low for cover. Pain blossomed in my knee with every jostle, but I pressed my face into Marcus's shirt and tried not to cry out. This was a bad idea. My injury was going to get us all killed or captured.

Suddenly, Marcus stopped, staggering back, his legs going weak under us both.

"Put me down. I'm too heavy for you," I pleaded softly, looking up to find him staring at the ground to our right, a look on his face that stopped my heart cold.

"What?" I craned my neck to see.

Five robed figures lay strewn out in a line looking almost asleep, except for the blood wetting their robes to a slick sheen and pooling on the rocks beneath them. They'd all been shot in the back multiple times and fallen where they'd stood. The one in the middle had his head angled to the side and his hood pushed back enough for me to see his face, Yale's face, Yale's eyes open and staring at nothing. Yale who had hated guns and would never have his power.

Jason crouched down next to him and touched his neck. He looked up at Marcus and shook his head. I don't know why he even did it. We all knew.

"No, not Yale," Passion moaned next to us, just before she bent over and vomited.

"When the first few got past me, they must have shot into the back of the line," Jason whispered.

"Where's Nose?" Passion asked desperately, standing up and wiping her mouth on her sleeve.

But I already knew what was coming. Yale and Nose would have been standing together, side-by-side, waiting for their chance to jump.

Jason moved to the body on Yale's left and pulled back the hood, revealing a strange ski-masked face and, for a moment, my heart sang with hope and I thought, "That's not Nose."

The face looked sunken, like a skull, the nose caved in where his PSS had blinked out of existence the moment he had. He wasn't Nose without his Nose. He wasn't anything, anymore. Ever again.

Passion moaned again, and I think she would have fallen down on them both and stopped right there, but Jason pulled her away, putting her hand in mine. She clung to Marcus as she silently wept.

"Check for Grant," Marcus said and a shock went through me. I'd forgotten Grant. Marcus had remembered him, but I hadn't.

"Oh God, what about Samantha?" Passion scanned the remaining bodies, her face gone utterly white. "Did you see Samantha?" she asked me and Marcus.

"She's okay," I said. "She went over the cliff." I was surprised Passion didn't know what had happened. Maybe she hadn't been able to see from the woods, or she and Jason had been too occupied with the oncoming CAMFers, but wouldn't they have noticed that first lone gunshot?

"She got away?" Passion asked, relief in her voice.

"Yeah," I nodded. Hey, it was true. Sort of. And at that moment it was more important to keep things together for Passion than to provide her with the details of Samantha's "escape".

"He's not here," Jason said, stepping back from the bodies. He'd pulled their hoods back and I saw the empty, staring faces of another guy and two girls, none of them Grant.

Jason returned to Nose's body and reached within his robe, pulling out Nose's handgun. He checked the clip. "Fully loaded," he said, looking at Marcus, some silent message passing between them.

"We need you and the ammo with us," Marcus said, glancing at Passion.

Gunfire sounded again, behind us but moving closer, and under it all the strange humming sound still grew.

"I'll lead," Jason said, taking Passion's hand back.

And then I understood. Jason had wanted to take Nose's gun, leave us, and exact some calculated revenge on the murderers of our friends. But we needed him and that gun to make sure we all made it to the cliff ledge alive. Marcus had to carry me. And Passion wasn't going to make that jump under her own power. Revenge would have to wait.

Marcus stumbled, following Jason and Passion now, and this time when he crushed me in his arms, squeezing me until it hurt, I didn't cry out or say anything. It felt good compared to the stabbing pain inside of me. It was all one pain. Mine. His. Ours.

Finally, we came to the jumping cliff, that flat slab of rock jutting out over the river.

Even as we stood there, two more robed figures rushed past us, hurling themselves down into the gorge, hand in hand.

Shots rang out behind us, very close.

Marcus turned and I raised his gun just as two CAMFers came charging out of the smoke.

My fingers didn't fumble this time. I pulled the

trigger, not once, but over and over again, feeling the satisfying kick back of the gun against my hands, the sound echoing down into the river gorge. The closest guy collided with the ground, his dropped semi-automatic skidding across the rock and straight off the edge of the cliff. I looked up to see that Jason had tagged the other guy but he wasn't quite dead. It took one more bullet to finish him.

I had killed my first human being. Blood was now pooling from under his chest.

Marcus spun me around toward the cliff so I couldn't see anymore. "Take off your robes," he demanded, his voice urgent, setting me on my feet next to a rock I could lean against. He took his gun from me, checked the clip, frowned, and set it on the rock next to me.

The humming was much louder on the ledge, barreling down the gorge like a train coming through a tunnel. And my tags were still absolutely silent. Why would CAMFers come with guns but no minus meters? Why would they shoot Yale and Nose? And where was Grant? Had he jumped already? Was he captured? Was he dead, lying alone in a pool of his own blood somewhere?

"I don't like water," Passion whimpered, as Jason stripped her robe over her head for her, then took off his own, letting the wind pull both of them out of his hand and over the cliff.

As I watched them spiral down, I noticed tiny forms below in the river. Most splashing and moving toward the shore. But one or two floated peacefully in place, their robes like black angel wings, floating around them. Thankfully, Passion was too scared to look down.

I scanned the shore for any signs of men with guns, but I didn't see any. I didn't see Samantha either, or Renzo or Juliana. Hopefully they'd gotten her back to a car and were on their way to a hospital.

"Olivia, take off your robe," Marcus barked and then he was yanking it over my head and tossing it to the wind, the wrap around my ghost hand coming undone and flying after it.

Jason was throwing his guns down, letting them fall with a clatter onto the rock.

"What are you doing?" I asked, appalled.

"No more bullets," he said, Nose's gun the only one left in his hand.

"You and Passion go first," Marcus said to Jason, glancing behind us. "I may need you to help me with Olivia in the water."

"Then take this," Jason said, handing Nose's gun to him.

"I can't do it," Passion cried, trying to bolt, but Jason still had her hand and he pulled her back, wrapping both his arms around her in a vice hold.

"Okay, here we go," Jason said and then he stepped off the cliff as casually as if he were stepping off his front porch, a thrashing Passion trapped in his arms.

But they didn't fall.

They didn't even go down.

They went out, Jason's feet treading the air like solid ground, his first step turning into another and another, legs moving forward, propelling him and Passion out into space about ten paces where they finally stopped, just hanging there facing away from us like a pair of lost human helium balloons whose strings had tangled.

"What the fuck?" Jason said, glancing frantically over his shoulder at us, and that small motion seemed to turn him in mid-air slowly, until he was facing us again, still standing out there in the middle of the gorge.

It was his ability. Jason's PSS leg had finally manifested a power. Apparently, he could air-walk off a cliff and defy gravity.

Passion didn't move. She was frozen in Jason's embrace, looking back at me, her eyes gone beyond terror to where terror hides from things. And then she went limp in his arms.

Gunshots rang out behind Marcus and me, and something whizzed past my head.

Marcus turned, firing into the dark, aiming for the shadows moving toward us.

The humming sound coming from the gorge was growing louder and louder, chopping at the air, grinding into my bones.

I looked back at Jason and he was still there, clinging to Passion and hanging in space, and then something huge and metallic and bug-eyed rose up behind them.

It was a helicopter, a gunned helicopter, closing in on us and obviously lining up Passion and Jason in its sights.

"Marcus!" I cried, and he turned back to me, taking it all in with one glance.

"Grab on to me. Now!" he said, tossing Nose's gun

aside and running at me.

And I did. I didn't even think about it. I reached out to him, extending my ghost hand and winding long ethereal bands around the both of us like rope, binding us and pulling us together as one the moment he reached me.

We flew off the cliff edge, air whooshing past and wind buffeting us as we went hurtling out over the river and collided with Jason and Passion.

The helicopter was so close that I could see the look of concentration on the pilot's face as he took aim. I could feel the cut of the blades as they displaced the air, thrusting it at us and trying to blow us apart.

I looked up, saw Jason and Passion hanging above us, Marcus now clinging to Jason's left leg.

And still, we didn't fall.

Marcus's hand was slipping. I could see it slipping, so I wound a PSS tendril up his arm and around Jason's leg, binding us all together as one.

The helicopter made a sound, a blast of sound, and then the world dropped out from under us, my stomach jumping into my throat.

I looked down to see the river rising to meet us.

35

WAITING AND OTHER THINGS THAT SUCK

Pain.

Smacking, cold, drenching pain.

The impact was hard, knocking the air straight out of me.

Someone kneed or kicked me in the chin.

Water surged up my nose, clawing its way to my lungs.

I opened my eyes and every direction was dark and murky.

How was I supposed to swim to the light when there was no light?

And then I saw something. A dark person-shaped shadow moving away from me. Not swimming. Not moving. Just sinking.

So, that way was down.

And the other way was up. The way to air and light and life.

I kicked, ignoring that logic, trying to push myself down toward that shadow and catch hold of it.

Pain instantly shot through my knee and up into my thigh, the agony making me gasp in a little water and whole lot of panic. Shit. I'd forgotten about my fucked-up knee.

I collided with something and turned to face it.

It was Marcus, his eyes wide open, two bullet holes in his shirt, which was drifting around him revealing the empty gape of his chest.

Without air in its lungs for buoyancy, the human body sinks. And Marcus no longer had lungs because his PSS had been disrupted. Even now, he was drifting away from me into the deep dark black.

I reached out and grabbed his wrist with my ghost hand. I willed it to wind around him, to bind him to me like it had up on the cliff, to never let go of him even if he dragged me down into the blackness with him forever.

But my ghost hand refused to obey me. It didn't like the cold wet world.

And then someone grabbed my other arm, yanking me up, practically pulling my shoulder right out of its socket and I lost my grip on him. I was being pulled away. He was going down. I was losing him.

I struggled against the hold on me, thrashing, and then someone's arms were under both of mine, wiry arms wrapped under my armpits and over my shoulders, pulling me, pulling me.

My head broke the surface, and I gasped for breath, hacking water out at the same time, spewing the river from my throat—not so I could breathe, but so I could scream.

"No," I cried, but it came out more like a cough. "He's down there," I tried to say. "I need him."

The wake of the water rippled behind me as my savior pulled me toward shore. My heels banged against rock, jarring my knee with hot pain. Then we were standing up, waist deep in water, Passion clinging to me, her skinny, pale arms practically holding me in a head lock.

"Let go of me," I said.

"No," she said in my ear. "You can't save him."

"We have to get out of here. Now," Jason said, his hands on me too, dragging me further up on the rocks.

"He's not dead," I struggled against them both, snot and river and tears running out of my eyes, and nose and mouth. "He can reboot."

"It's too deep," Passion insisted. "You can't pull someone up from that deep. You'll die trying."

"I don't care," I said, struggling against Passion again, but her grip was relentless and my knee was so wacked, I couldn't get leverage. "We can't leave him down there."

"They're coming," Jason said.

I could hear it, men crashing through the brush and trees behind us, calling out to one another.

"We have to go," he said, yanking me up on my feet as Passion let go of me.

"I can't run." I looked Jason full in the face, willing

him to understand, telling him with my eyes, with my soul. "I can't even walk. And I can't leave him."

"I can carry you," he said.

"No," I shook my head. "Then we're all dead. Go," I said to him. I looked at Passion. "Please, go," I begged.

"Come on," Jason said, grabbing Passion's hand and pulling her up the rock. She was still looking back at me as they disappeared into the woods.

And then a strange peace descended over me, a calm so deep and dark it was as if I was seeing everything from the bottom of that deep pool of the river, lying down there next to Marcus, waiting for us both to wake and rise.

I saw the scattered groups of wet, terrified teens, huddled on the rocks, some injured, all in shock.

I saw the bodies floating, one bumping up against the rocky shore.

I saw the armed men up on the cliff, milling around and pointing down at us.

The helicopter was there with them, the flat top of the plateau making almost a perfect landing pad.

I saw it all. Saw the army of men emerge from the woods on all sides, yelling at us, telling us "Don't move. Put your hands in the air."

But I did not comply like the others. My hands were clamped between my thighs, what little warmth my body had left slowly but surely seeping into them.

"I said, 'put your hands in the air,'" a man said, planting the barrel of his gun on the back of my neck, the cold circle of it biting into my vertebrae.

"No," I said, my teeth chattering. "I'm freezing. I need to get warm."

"You won't be warm if I fucking kill you," he said, pressing the gun even harder into my neck.

"Kill me then," I said, shrugging and watching the water. How long had it been since we'd jumped? How long had Marcus been down there? Five minutes? Ten? Fifteen? I would not leave this shore until he came back up, no matter how long it took. No matter what they did to me.

"Stand up, minus bitch," the guy with the gun said, pulling the barrel away from my neck and grabbing me under the left arm, trying to pull me upright.

I let him, let him pull me up and pin me against him, ignoring the agony in my knee as I sank my ghost hand into him, my fingers searching even as I felt the puff of his breath in my face, even as his eyes went wide and vacant and I realized that if he collapsed, I'd go crashing down with him.

"Don't fall," I whispered, pushing my hand upward and seeing him jerk upright with it, like a hand puppet. He was young, maybe not much older than me.

"Hey, Paulie, what the hell are you doing?" someone called from behind us. "Bring her over here."

My hand found what it was looking for, Paulie's burden, something perfectly round and smooth that would answer my need. But if I pulled it out, we'd both fall.

"Paulie?" the voice was closer, the other man almost on top of us.

I yanked my hand out of Paulie and felt him begin to crumple against me.

I tried to move as he went down, tried to hop away on one leg, even as I looked down at the magic eight ball gripped in my fingers, its glassy wisdom staring up at me, *Reply hazy, try again*. Yep, that was helpful. I'd been hoping for a gun, or a knife, or a cane. Or a grenade.

"What the fuck?" the new guy said, catching Paulie in his arms, which also pretty much rendered his gun useless, pressed against his side. He was much bigger and older than Paulie.

Teetering, I tossed the eight ball over my shoulder into the river, and took its advice, sinking my hand into the new guy.

The three of us went crashing down like a one-legged tripod.

They broke my fall, which was good, but my hand was still fishing around inside of the big guy when I looked up to find ten or fifteen guns trained on me, cocked and ready.

"Hold your fire," someone commanded.

"She's got her fucking hand inside Gary," another one said, his voice breaking with panic, his finger twitching at his trigger.

"He wants this one alive," the commander said. "Hold your fire." Then to me, "Take your hand out of him. Slowly." He reversed his gun and placed the butt of it just above my head.

I could feel the thing in Gary, soft and small and pliable, like a tiny plush toy. My hand was finally around it. But I doubted that anything Gary gave me was going to save me now, and if they knocked me out, I wouldn't be able to wait for Marcus.

I let go of Gary's burden and withdrew my ghost hand from him.

The butt of the gun came crashing down on my head, and everything went dark.

I came to. Barely. I was drooling down some guy's back as he carried me through the woods, the feet of other captives shuffling along behind us.

I didn't even hesitate. I sank my hand into his back, and we went crashing forward into the guy in front of us, knocking men down like dominoes.

This time I came away with a knife, small but sharp.

I cut three of them while simultaneously begging them to take me back to the river and the pool.

I tried to run away. Well, more like crawl away. On one leg.

Until they hit me again. And kicked me. Multiple boots banging into my ribs, until I heard something crack, and the pain was too much, and the world went dark again.

I woke up in the back seat of a plush car, awash in pain.

I didn't even try to move.

Mike Palmer was sitting next to me with a gun in my side, which I thought was funny. They'd already proven they weren't going to shoot me.

He looked amazingly well, with only faint scarring

left from the horrible beating Jason had given him a month ago in the woods outside of Greenfield. Apparently, he was a quick healer.

"She's awake, sir," Mike said, and the man in the front passenger seat turned around and looked at me.

"It is so nice to be awake," Dr. Fineman said, grinning at me, looking hale and full of health as well. He did not look like a guy who'd been in a coma for a month.

I had imagined him, in my pleasant daydreams, skinny and jaundiced, his skin stretching tautly over his skull, but here he was looking like he'd just stepped off the golf course.

"What the fuck do you want?" I whispered, and even that hurt. It hurt to breathe.

"Never one to beat around the bush, were you?" he said, shaking his head. "Very well. I can be just as forthcoming. What I want is for you to put this back in me." He held up the cube I'd pulled out of him back in Mike Palmer's basement. Shit. How had he gotten it? We'd left it back at the McMansion. Which meant they'd been in the McMansion. "And then I want you to pull all the pretty little things out of people I tell you to, whenever I tell you to."

"Yeah, that's never going to happen," I said.

"We will see," he said. "It seems your time playing in The Hold has made you a little overconfident. But we can fix that."

"Fuck you," I said.

"Maybe," he said. "They do say, 'Like mother, like daughter.'"

I surged forward, tried to use my ghost hand on

him, but there was some kind of metal cuff around my wrist and the moment I reached for him, my whole arm went cold, flopping down into my lap.

"Wonderful!" Dr. Fineman said, almost clapping as he admired my limp arm. "It works perfectly. And now I hope you understand that you'll only be using that hand at my bidding."

"And what about this hand?" I asked, curling my other hand into a fist and smashing it into his face as hard as I could, feeling the satisfying crunch of his nose breaking.

"Hey!" Mike said, yanking me back, jamming his gun into my ribs. He pushed on the broken one until I cried out in pain and the darkness began to gather at the edge of my vision again.

Dr, Fineman was bent over in his seat, clutching his bloody nose and groaning.

"Take it easy, girl," Leo said from the driver's seat, looking at me in the rearview mirror. "Honey will catch you more flies than vinegar."

Leo. Samantha's personal driver and a major member of security for The Hold. Fuck. He was the CAMFer spy, the double agent.

I stared at him, seething with disdain, and he looked away, back to the headlights on the dark highway in front of us.

For a few minutes we were all silent as Dr. Fineman dug some wrinkled fast food napkins out of the glove box and stuffed them up his nose, staunching his bleeding.

"So, where are we going?" I asked, leaning back against the seat, willing myself not to pass out again.

"To my research compound," Dr. Fineman said, his voice muffled as he glanced sidelong at me. "I'm sure your friend David told you all about it."

"The one in Oregon?" I felt myself begin to panic. "We're driving to Oregon?" That was too far. Too far from Marcus. Too far from my mom, and Samantha, and Jason and Passion, and Alexander James. Too far from everything and everyone I knew who might help me. I couldn't go there. I couldn't.

I reached out with my left hand and grabbed the door handle, pulling on it, but it wouldn't open.

I felt a sting in my right arm, and turned to see Mike Palmer sinking a syringe into it straight through my shirt.

I looked up at him, his face and the interior of the car already beginning to grow fuzzy in my vision.

"I warned you not to come," he whispered when my face slumped onto his shoulder. "But you marked brats never listen."

36

THE COMPOUND

How long have I been in this cell? I don't know. I don't know how many days I've sat trying to keep track of the minutes and the hours, and I don't know how many nights I've lain on a cold stone slab, my body and arm numb, trying to make my ghost hand obey me.

They kept me drugged after I busted Dr. Fineman's nose, but the drive to Oregon must have taken four or five days. Unless we flew. Maybe we flew. I have no idea.

When I woke up the first time, I was wearing different clothes than I'd had on at the Eidolon and my dog tags were gone. So were Mike Palmer's matchbook and the paper with my father's inscription to Kaylee on it. But I still had on the weird cuff that kept my ghost hand from doing anything useful.

As soon as I moved I could tell I'd been tended by a nurse or a medic. My knee was taped and bound, and so were my ribs. Later, they brought me pain meds with my meals and watched me until I took them. There is an extra blue pill at night that I think is supposed to make me sleep, but it doesn't work anymore. I do not sleep. I refuse to sleep. Because, when I do, the dream comes. I have it every time I close my eyes, without fail, as if my subconscious only has one source, one pool of memory and regret, one place it must always return to.

In the dream, I'm lying at the bottom of the river in the pool beneath The Devil's Drop. Water is rushing and swirling far above me, but I'm hidden in the stillness beyond the world.

At first I always feel a swell of hope. Hope to see Marcus again. Hope that I didn't leave him after all. Hope that if I swim long enough and search hard enough, I will find him and pull him back up with me.

But then I realize I can't swim. I can't even move. I'm lying on my back, looking upward, arms floating next to me, fish swimming lazily past me that I can't even turn my head to watch.

And that is when I look down at myself, at my strange body, and realize that I'm not me. I'm Marcus. I am Marcus at the bottom of the river, looking down at the hole in my chest and the piece of water-logged tree branch jutting through it, poking up through one of the bullet holes in my shirt, disrupting my ability to reboot and come back to life forever. And, as I watch, my Marcus body begins to rot, like one of those time-capture videos sped up, first my clothes rotting off, then my skin, shriveling to black wet nothingness. When the fish come to nibble on my exposed flesh, the tug of it always wakes me up, gasping and sweating in my cold cell.

I have begun to believe that it is not just a dream, but a vision.

I left the man I love sunk to the bottom of a river, helpless, defenseless.

Anything could have happened; the stick I see in my dream, or a jutting rock. All it would take was something to break the plane of his PSS, and he would not reboot. And even if he did, would he inhale that murky water as he came back to life? Would he be so disoriented that he couldn't find his way to the surface in time?

If he is dead, I want to be dead.

That's why I stopped eating what they bring me.

I have no hunger. I have no desire to be their guinea pig or puppet or weapon of torture. I have no reason to go on.

My mother always said I was obsessed with death. And now I am.

Today, I think it was today, someone came to the door of my cell, keys jingling in the lock.

Dr. Fineman entered alone, not with Gary or Paulie this time, and I hoped maybe the interrogations about what I had done to them with my ghost hand were over. Maybe he'd finally given up trying to get me to reach into Gary and pull something out.

The armed guard who stands outside my cell brought in a chair, and Dr. Fineman sat down in it, leaning forward like he cared about me and frowning at my full lunch tray. His nose looked fully recovered, which meant I hadn't broken it, and that made me sad.

"Are you giving up so soon?" he asked, sounding disappointed. "I thought you had more fight in you than this."

I didn't say anything.

"We've been filming you, you know?" he said, gesturing at the camera mounted in the corner of the cell. "I know about the nightmares."

I looked at him, wishing looks could kill, imagining myself reaching my ghost hand into his head and scrambling his brains like eggs.

"You call out for him in your sleep," he said, snickering a little. "You moan, 'Marcus', and that isn't even his name. He lied to you about his name." Dr. Fineman leaned back. "How many other things do you think he lied to you about?"

I looked away, tried to focus on something else, something inside of me so he couldn't get to me. Because he was getting to me.

"Did he lie to you about the list we gave him?" Dr. Fineman asked. "Did he make himself the hero and say he was rescuing all those poor PSS kids from our evil clutches?"

I looked up, my neck practically snapping aloud.

"Oh yes," Dr. Fineman said. "That lie was my idea. After all, what better way to gather a group of teenagers than to give them a heroic peer to follow? Of course, we had to make it seem realistic along the way. We had to chase you, we had to harass you, had to prove to you all that what he was saying was true with that little performance in Greenfield. Otherwise, you wouldn't have followed him and gotten him a free pass to upset The Hold and get rid of so many troublesome youth all in one fell swoop."

"You're lying," I said, unable to hold my tongue any longer. "You botched Greenfield and got your soul handed to you in a box, and now you're trying to say that was your plan all along? You've got to be kidding me. I was there. I know what happened."

"Do you?" he asked, raising an eyebrow. "Do you really believe it would be that easy to get past three armed, experienced men, if they hadn't been told to let you by? And how did your Marcus know exactly where I was? Oh yes, I told him in one of our many communications. I asked him to draw you down into the lab so I could get a sample of that wonderful PSS of yours while it was exhibiting its power. And, of course, the giant minus meter—a fake, by the way— was to scare you away again, off to Samantha and The Hold. It was a considerable added bonus that we got to see what the items you'd extracted could really do in a pinch. Amazing that. Truly amazing. Jumping forward in time three days. Of course, now we do have the awkward problem of that other boy's artifact stuck in mine, but I'm sure we can sort that out together."

Fuck. How did he know about Jason's bullet in his box and the missing days? How could he possibly know? No one knew any of that except those of us in PSS camp. Yale and Nose were dead. They hadn't told him. Jason and Passion had gotten away. They hadn't told him. I certainly hadn't told him, unless I'd mumbled it all in my sleep, which I highly doubted. Which left Marcus, but I couldn't believe it. This whole thing could not have been an elaborate set-up with Marcus as an agent of the CAMFers. Marcus hated the CAMFers with every cell of his being. They'd killed his sister in front of him. He could not have faked the way he felt about them. I'd seen it in the line of his body, in the depths of his eyes, in his very soul.

"I see you don't believe me," Dr. Fineman said. "That is understandable. David is a very reluctant but convincing agent, but he is our agent all the same."

"I will never believe that," I said. "He hates you. He would never work for you or the CAMFers for any reason."

"You are mostly correct," Dr. Fineman said. "He does hate us, me particularly. But there is one reason he would do anything we ask. One very compelling reason that lives right here in this compound in a cell very much like yours—though she's been here much longer than you."

Danielle. The name echoed in my head. He was saying they had Danielle, that they hadn't killed her like Marcus had told us, but kept her to control him, to use him. And if that were true, yes, Marcus would do anything they said. I knew what Danielle meant to him. The guilt he was wracked with over her. There was no doubt in my mind that Marcus would lie, kill, steal, and lead a group of strangers to the slaughter to keep her safe. And yes, he'd even play my heart like a fiddle if it served that purpose—that all-consuming purpose. But I was pretty sure Danielle was dead, and Dr. Fineman was the one playing me.

"Danielle is dead," I said. "You told me she died of leukemia. Marcus told me you killed her. Either way, I'm pretty sure you don't have her."

"Do you really believe I would eliminate such a valuable resource as that?" he asked. "How do you think I recovered instantly from my coma? And what about Mike Palmer? He certainly made a speedy recovery. And my nose," he said, pointing to his face. "You broke it rather thoroughly, but it was nothing a little touch from Danielle couldn't fix."

Shit. Had she healed them? Was she here? Had Marcus been working for the CAMFers all along? We had known there was a double agent among us at the McMansion—someone who'd switched out the feed of Mike Palmer. Mike Palmer who had left a message for someone about Shades. But why would he warn Marcus not to go if the plan was for the CAMFers to attack there? Unless it had been some kind of reverse code to confuse anyone else who saw it. And it had done just that. It had confused me.

"Would you like some proof?" Dr. Fineman interrupted my agonizing labyrinth of logic.

"Sure," I said. "Why don't you bring Danielle in here right now and introduce us."

"I'm afraid I can't do that," he said, "but how about something almost as good." He gestured to the guard outside the cell who wheeled in a television monitor on a stand, its chords trailing out the door and down the long hallway. Dr. Fineman reached up and turned it on, and there was a cell on the screen, very similar to mine, with a girl sitting in one corner in a chair. She could have been a grown-up version of the Danielle I'd seen in Marcus's picture. Or not. It was hard to tell.

She got up, pacing the room, her PSS arm glowing up to the elbow and swinging gently at her side. I found myself knowing exactly when she would turn, and which way, because she paced just like Marcus.

"This could be footage from before you killed her," I said, trying to keep the doubt out of my voice. "It doesn't prove anything."

"Olivia," Dr. Fineman said, shaking his head. "You're going to have to face reality eventually. He betrayed you. He works for us. He has always worked for us."

"Why not have him tell me then, right to my face?" I asked. "I'd believe that."

"Ah well, he's on another mission," Dr. Fineman said, waving his hand dismissively and glancing away from me. I wasn't sure if he'd been lying to me before, but he was definitely lying to me now. I could see it on his face. If Marcus was his agent, the man had no idea where he was.

"And after all he did for you, he didn't come back and demand his sister's freedom? He didn't earn some precious time with her, or a chance to see her? He ran off immediately on another job?"

"It is what we required of him," Dr. Fineman said.

"Bullshit!" I said. "If you were using Danielle as a hostage, he'd want payoff before he did anything else." Unless he couldn't come back to collect because he was at the bottom of a river.

"Fine," Dr. Fineman said, getting up and turning the monitor off. "You will see that what I've said is true. How else would I know the intimate details of your time together? Such a naive girl, to believe he cared for you after each new lie. And that moment at the side of the road when he confessed his love for you? Truly an amazing performance. But then, he had to do that so you wouldn't ruin our plans and keep him from the Eidolon for the sake of a few dismal paintings by a dead man." He turned his back on me, ushering the monitor toward the guard. He never should have done that. It left him completely open to attack.

I was on his back, my arm around his throat, squeezing, while the guard still had his hands occupied with the rolling monitor cart.

Dr. Fineman whirled around, gasping like a fish, and charged backwards, slamming me into the stone wall of the cell and knocking the wind out of me, my ribs flaring pain again like they were on fire.

My arms came away from him, refusing to listen to me, and I slid to the floor, the rough wall scraping my back through my thin shirt on the way down.

He was standing over me, his fists clenched, his face red, his eyes as wild and crazy as my own.

Behind us, the guard finally drew his gun, much too late.

"You won't kill me," I said when I got my breath back, laughing. "Not if you want your little box back inside of you. Not if you want to understand what I do and the power I have. But, you're going to have to take off this cuff to find that out, and when you do

I'm going to strip your soul clean out of you."

"No, you won't," he said, shaking his head. "Not after we break you." He whirled and left the cell, the door clanging shut behind him, but not before he gave the guard explicit instructions on how to begin breaking me. And his words, as horrible and terrifying as they were, were nothing compared to what one human being can do to another alone in a cell with no eyes watching.

How long have I been here? I don't know anymore. I don't know how many days I've sat trying to keep track of the minutes and the hours, and I don't know how many nights I've lain on a cold stone slab, my body and arm numb, trying to make my ghost hand obey me. But I do not sleep, because when I do, the dream comes. I have it every time I close my eyes, without fail, as if my subconscious only has one source, one pool of memory and regret, one place it must always return to.

Marcus, even in this darkness, I try to swim back to you.

I swear, I do.

THE END

Coming in 2014:
Book Three of The PSS Chronicles.
Go to www.ripleypatton.com
for more details.

BONUS SHORT STORY

Before I started The PSS Chronicles, I wrote short stories. That was the writing form I frolicked in for years, winning awards, contests, and publication, before I braved the more extensive world of novel writing. I love writing short stories and reading them. For that reason, in September 2012, to celebrate the upcoming release of my debut novel, *Ghost Hand*, I sponsored a young adult short story contest for writers age 12-19. The lovely story featured next, inspired by the cover blurb and first chapters of *Ghost Hand*, won that contest earning a cash prize and publication in *Ghost Hold*. And so I present to you, with much pleasure, "Blue, Blue Eyes" by Emma Shi.

BLUE, BLUE EYES

BY EMMA SHI

When I see it, the first thing I think of is the blue poster that hangs across from me on the wall of Ms. Kingston's English class, listing an array of literary techniques. The next thing I think of is you—sitting at the drab desk next to mine—and your blue, blue eyes. The third thing I think of is that you're back. But that would be impossible.

I burst into the girls' bathroom as another memory of you fades away. Shaking, I open the tap and put my hands under the water, bringing it up to my face. It gets into my eyes, but I continue doing it; the breath of cold against my hot skin makes me feel more alive. After three more splashes, I turn off the tap and wipe the sleeve of my shirt across my face.

And then I look up at the mirror and see you standing behind me.

I jump back, heart pounding, but you're gone. All I can see in the mirror now is myself, and my muscles slacken in relief. Panting softly, I stare at my own wide eyes, a droplet of water poised just at my right temple. It was just my imagination. You're not here. You can't be here.

A flash of blue cuts through my mind and I breathe in and out slowly, willing the images to disappear and fold themselves back into my brain. But they never do. I thought I'd tucked them away safely, but now here they come again, desaturating every color I see. They bleed into reality, bringing the image of you to life. But you're not here anymore. I made sure of that, didn't I?

I dig into the pocket of my jacket, with shaking hands, and take out a neatly folded piece of paper. It flutters as I unfold it, and I read words that have been written neatly in blue ink.

Alliteration. The repetition of the same sounds or the same kinds of sounds at the beginning of words or in stressed syllables. Can be the most beautiful thing ever if the alliteration is Mia Morgan.

A girl's handwriting. That's the first thing I thought when I saw those evenly spaced words. It looked too neat, too precise to be a boy's. But it turned out to be yours. I never knew that a boy could write so elegantly. I remember you shouting "Sexist!" at me from across the room when you heard me tell that to one of my friends.

I stare at the paper for longer than I should, the silence of the empty bathroom floating around me. I'm supposed to be in class, which is why there's no one else here. But once I saw this piece of paper tucked inside my English book, I knew I couldn't sit there, half-listening to the teacher, the blue poster haunting my peripheral vision.

You and I, we had a thing for passing notes. We did it in every class we were in together, and we never got caught. Once, we were reviewing literary techniques and Ms. Kingston was going through every one of them on that blue poster. It was the day after you'd taken me on our first date. My heart flipped every time you talked to me. It was beautiful to hear the person I loved—you—say my name, Mia. And on that day, you passed me a note, a note that made me smile, a note like the one in my hand about my own alliteration.

The original was written on lined paper, I remember that. But this note is on blank white paper. It looks like your handwriting, but how could it be? Did someone else write it, pretending to be you? Does someone know what I did?

Or did you actually write this? Are you still here, watching me, taunting me?

I put the note back into my pocket and turn away from the mirror. I don't want to look at myself, but I also don't want to go back to class, so I lock myself in a cubicle and sit on the closed seat of the toilet, still shaking.

I remember how I answered your note. I looked up at the teacher to check that she wasn't watching, then scribbled down a response on a different slip of paper. I passed it to you and watched your blue eyes light up as you read my response.

Allusion. An indirect reference to a place, a person, or an event. Most effectively used when referring to an amazing boy with beautiful blue eyes called Asher Edwards.

The thing I loved most about you was how you did your best to listen to me. Even if I wasn't making sense, and even if you disagreed with me, you listened first.

The second thing I loved were your blue eyes. My eyes are achingly average: a simple shade of dark brown. But your eyes, they were a color I wanted to swim in, a blue I wanted to breathe in. I wanted to inhale that blue and feel it fill up my empty lungs, let it be the oxygen that brought life to my red, red heart. I loved your eyes most when you smiled, and I remember how they looked so pure and happy when accompanied by the curve of your lips.

I also remember how your eyes looked the day you left. Except I made you leave, didn't I? But it was an accident. An accident, an accident.

I had only reached out to touch you like I had so many times before, but this time was different. This time, the need to do so was powered by some external influence I couldn't control. It felt like my hand was a part of someone else's body. And instead of touching you, I reached further, deep into you, and your eyes went so wide as the blue drained away, leaving only a lifeless grey. When I saw that happen, I finally had the will to jerk my hand away, but you were already slumping to the ground, nothing left in you. I rushed to your side, my hand still glowing slightly, calling me to do it again. But there was nothing left in you to keep going on, even if I succumbed to the energy inside me. I felt a wave of enigmatic emotions crest in my mind, and all I could do was stare in utter disbelief for a few seconds before a broken voice—my own broken voice—cried out your name.

I crouched there next to you for a while, just shaking. I couldn't think at first and had no idea what to do. My mind was the mist at the bottom of a waterfall; every thought a droplet of water that tumbled downwards before spraying and scattering into nothing. With this fall came a rush of strange memories, pounding me. I realized later, days later, that they weren't mine, but yours. After a while, the memories slowed down enough that I could catch a glimpse of them. Sometimes it was something trivial, like walking to school. Other times I saw myself, through your point of view. It was strange and—interesting. But I didn't want it, I didn't want it. I knew that I didn't want it.

Finally, the mist in my head began to clear, and I saw you lying in front of me. Then I cracked, grabbing you by the arms. I shook you, but you didn't answer. I shouted your name, Asher, Asher, over and over again, but all I heard was my voice echoing off the empty walls. And then I staggered away and left you.

That is my greatest regret: leaving you. But I was scared, and I didn't know what I'd tell anyone if I asked for help. Your eyes looked so empty without their blue. So I ran, like the coward I've always been.

I know that you wouldn't have left me, and that thought makes my heart sting with regret. I killed you and then I left you. But I swear it was an accident. I loved you, and I couldn't control it.

When I got home, my mother looked at me strangely.

"What happened to your eyes?" she asked.

"What do you mean?" I said.

My mother frowned. "Did you get some of those colored contacts?"

Then my heart sank as I thought of your blue eyes, a blue I'd turned to grey. I didn't answer my mother. Instead, I ran to the bathroom, realization settling to the bottom of my stomach, making me feel sick.

And there, in the mirror, I saw that my eyes were no longer brown. They were blue. Your blue. I took them from you somehow, when I killed you. And now, every time I look in the mirror, I see what I did.

A bang—the sound of the bathroom door opening and closing—brings me back to the present and the memories of that day drift away. At the sound, I stiffen, even though I'm hidden away. I tell myself that whoever has come will use the bathroom and leave, and then I can too, but then they speak to me.

"Mia Morgan," a male voice says, and my heart almost stops.

That voice—it's you.

"I know you're here," you say, and a folded slip of paper slides under the space at the bottom of the cubicle door towards me.

I pick it up, hands shaking as I unfold it.

Writer's Voice. The unique features and personality of an author's writing style. The most amazing of voices belonging to a girl named Mia Morgan.

This is the last note you ever gave me, but it's not the original. The original is at the bottom of my desk drawer at home, amidst long-forgotten study notes.

Another folded slip of paper slides under the door, and I open it just as another piece follows it.

Hyperbole. An exaggeratio—

I stuff the note into my pocket before I can read any further. I already know what it says, but still, I want to read more. I grab the other bits of paper as they come and fervently read each piece, my eyes scanning words that I don't want to see, but also words that I'm yearning to see at the same time. A part of me wants to remember you again, even if it hurts.

Caesura. The—

Again and again, I unfold those bits of paper, reading only enough to remember, my throat dry.

Foreshadowing. Oxymoron. Irony. Symbolism.

Suddenly, the stream of paper stops. I stare at the one still in my hand before letting it drop to the floor.

Plot Twist.

"Mia," you say again. And this time, I respond. "Asher," I choke out. "How can you be here? I—"

I saw you die. I took the color of your eyes. I killed you. And now your memories are bouncing around in my head and it hurts so much.

"I'm here now," you reply. "Come out. I want to see you. I've missed you, Mia."

I sit there on the closed toilet seat, staring at the door, surrounded by slips of paper that carry the most precious memories I have. You can't be alive. You can't, you can't.

But what if you are? What if you're here, and you've forgiven me?

I unclench my right fist and stare at my hand, the hand that ripped away your life.

And then I open the door.

I almost cry out in happiness when I see you. That same head of black hair, that same smile, those same blue eyes. We embrace and tears are running down my cheeks, and all I can think is Asher, Asher, you're back. I thought I lost you, but you're back.

And that's when I feel your hand encircle my neck, not in a gesture of love, but tightly with the intent to kill.

Before I know it, I can't breathe and no, you're not smiling anymore. Your eyes are frigid and impassive as you take my life away and slowly do what I did to you. A bittersweet ending.

"You've got incredible power in that hand, Mia," you growl, your voice not soft anymore. "But you don't know how to control it, do you?"

I splutter as your grip tightens. You know what I did is the thought that comes to me. You know what

I can do. But it feels wrong to call this boy who's choking me you. You wouldn't do this. Your voice doesn't sound like rough ocean waves against the harsh rock of a cliff face. But maybe this is you, and this is your revenge. Maybe I deserve this.

All of a sudden, you release your grip and I fall to the floor, gasping for breath. I scramble to my feet, but you grab my arm before I can escape.

And when I turn to see you, your eyes surprise me again.

They're not cold anymore. I can see you again in those eyes, the boy who wrote me all those slips of paper. I see the boy I fell in love with, and I see that the person choking me wasn't you. Here is the real you, and like the real you would, despite all I've done, you try to help me.

"Run," you whisper, and let go of my arm, as your eyes turn raw and icy again.

And I run. I stumble to the bathroom door, closing it with a bang, and run. I can hear your footsteps behind me, and my pulse races as I run out of school to who-knows-where. I'll run anywhere to get away from your grey, grey eyes.

I've been running ever since, slowing down to a walk when I need to catch my breath, or stopping when I need to rest. You told me to run. You saved me despite what I did to you, and it would be stupid of me to forsake that. Maybe I'll find you again one day, when I've learned to love my old brown eyes the same way I love your blue ones.

But until that day, I will run. I need time to try to understand why you came back, even if it was just for a moment. I thought that was impossible, but maybe it will happen again someday. Nothing feels impossible anymore.

THE END

AUTHOR BIO

Emma Shi was born in Auckland, New Zealand. She is currently 17 years old and in her last year of high school. In her spare time, she likes writing in a range of forms, from poetry to novels, and has an interest for Ancient Greece and Rome. She also writes for the New Zealand youth magazine, *Tearaway*.

ACKNOWLEDGEMENTS

There is truly nothing I love to do more than write books. It is my bliss. But I am very aware that I could never have dedicated my life to this strange, rather self-indulgent pursuit without the support of those who love me and my stories. I cannot thank the following people enough for their support, but that doesn't mean I'll ever stop trying.

I would like to thank my husband, the love of my life, for supporting me financially, creatively, and emotionally, and for believing in me even when I don't.

Thanks to my children, Soren and Valerie, for being amazing beta readers and for putting up with a mom who lives mostly in her own head.

To my brothers and my parents, who hosted me in Indianapolis and took me to research many of the locations in *Ghost Hold*, including Shades of Death State Park.

Thanks to all the amazing book bloggers and reviewers I've met this last year who loved *Ghost Hand* and never stopped talking about it. Special thanks to my Street Team, The Paranormal Street Squad, some of the most generous women I've ever had the pleasure to meet.

To all those who supported the *Ghost Hold* Kickstarter, both familiar and strangers. Thank you for backing book two. I don't think you'll be disappointed.

To Leo, my favorite postman. Yes, he is named after you.

Finally, to the amazing team I've found that wields the magic to turn a story into a book: Scarlett Rugers for her awesome cover design, Lauren McKellar, my new forever editor, and Simon Petrie, the most efficient formatter I know.

There simply wouldn't be a *Ghost Hold* without you.

ABOUT THE AUTHOR

Ripley Patton is an award-winning author who lives in Portland, Oregon with one cat, two teenagers, and a man who wants to live on a boat. She has also lived in Illinois, Colorado, Georgia, Indiana, and New Zealand.

Ripley doesn't smoke, or drink, or cuss as much as her characters. Her only real vices are eating M&Ms, writing, and watching reality television.

To learn more about Ripley and read some of her short fiction, be sure to check out her website at www.ripleypatton.com. You can also sign up for her monthly e-newsletter there to keep up-to-date on The PSS Chronicles and win cool prizes.

Made in the USA
San Bernardino, CA
20 October 2013